FAMISHED HEART

FAMISHED HEART

a fact-based novel of discovery and loss...

Marcia K. Feese

Writers Club Press
New York Lincoln Shanghai

Famished Heart
a fact-based novel of discovery and loss...

Writers Club Press
an imprint of iUniverse, Inc.

For information address:
iUniverse, Inc.
2021 Pine Lake Road, Suite 100
Lincoln, NE 68512
www.iuniverse.com

ISBN: 0-595-26822-6

Printed in the United States of America

To my daughter, Lori, my sons, Will and Wes,
and my sister, Carole~with love

For my mother and father~
With knowledge comes understanding.

Thank you all.

"Oh, sweet as the breath of morn,
To the fallen and forlorn
Are whispered words of praise;
For the famished heart believes
The falsehood that tempts and deceives,
And the promise that betrays."

—HELEN OF TYRE
By Henry Wadsworth Longfellow

Contents

ACKNOWLEDGMENTS

I would like to thank my husband, Dave, and all of my terrific family and friends for their invaluable assistance, inspiration and patience.

I am more grateful than I can say to Pat Judkins for sharing her expertise and for cheering me on.

My thanks to all the members of L.V. Writers' Ink in Lucerne Valley, California for their support, encouragement and input during the development of this book.

STEP 1:
Dredge in Flowers…

"Dredge in flowers..."

The scrawny little girl scuffed along kicking up the thirsty Oklahoma dust.

The oversized, faded bow at the back of her tow-headed mop, bobbed up and down with each dogged step. Edna was in no hurry to reach the end of the dirt road and home. Nowhere else to go but home, and nothing waiting there but a locked door. A locked door and her. Three years and Edna still didn't understand Ruby.

This morning had started out like any other. After a meager breakfast of burnt biscuits and scorched coffee, Edna's father prepared to set out for a long day. He lifted the worn leather gun belt from the hook behind his chair and strapped on his 45's. They looked like toy guns on the big man.

Edd bent down to drop a kiss on top of his 9-year old namesake's head. Edna looked up at her daddy and her chameleon eyes mirrored his this morning, sea green playing off of his worn blue work shirt.

"You be good, Edna-Modene", his deep baritone voice joining her first and middle names, an endearment only he used. It made her feel special.

She took up her post at the front room window, parting the chintz curtains to watch her daddy as long as possible. Dark clouds scudded overhead. She watched him saddle up Jezebel, swing himself up on her back and set off for his morning stint as part-time constable for the small coal mining town of Adamsville, Oklahoma, population 2387.

By three in the afternoon the promised storm had failed to materialize and Edna's father was hard at work at the mine, on the outskirts of town. Walking home from school, she heard the dynamite blasts he was setting off, to expose the pits for the next day's mining effort. Between the two jobs of town constable and "shotfirer" at the mine, her father made enough money to keep body and soul together, but it left him precious little time with his family. Edna wouldn't see him till nearly suppertime.

As Edna neared the family's small, two-story house, she could make out Ruby's diminutive form in the front window, arms folded across her chest. Looking at her now, Edna knew she could never call Ruby mama, no matter what her daddy wanted. To her, Ruby was just the woman her daddy had married. Ruby wasn't her mama. Lily was her mama. And Lily was dead and gone, buried in a dark hole in Adamsville Cemetery.

For nearly five years now, Edna had puzzled over what she could have done that was so wicked that her mama would abandon her forever. For a long time she hoped and prayed her mama would forgive her and return. And her father would smile a real smile and their family would be whole again. But at nine years old, Edna had let go of that dream. She knew better now. Now there was Ruby, but no mama. No, Edna didn't have a mama. Not anymore.

Ruby turned from the window, as if the view had been tainted, and Edna further slowed her pace. Even in winter's chill, it would be too early to expect to find the door unlocked. Edna perched on the stone wall that rimmed the curved approach to the house and scratched lazy circles in the parched earth with a stick, waiting. She didn't want to go in anyway. It didn't feel like home anymore.

The dark wood frame building had once made a perfect backdrop for Lily's colorful patchwork of flowers. Lily Gillen had lovingly cultivated vigorous hollyhocks that stood on tippy-toe to reach the eaves. Flower beds overflowed with deep purple irises, or "flags", framed with splotches of orange and gold gaillardia, Oklahoma's state wildflower, so readily available. Lily was a great believer in using what was at hand. "Use it up, wear it out, make do, or do without", she would admonish Edna, playfully.

Now the flowers were mostly gone. Only a handful of gaillardia straggled wildly near the water pump, mingling with a few "volunteer" morning glories that clamored up the handle every spring. The property was barren in comparison to years gone by. Too many hot Oklahoma summers without Lily's care. Flowers, like little girls, needed love and a nurturing hand.

The first edges of twilight began to wrap around the faded house, perched alone near the top of the hill. Supper was nearly ready and soon Jezebel would labor up the steep road, bearing her weary master home. Ruby had unlocked the door and allowed Edna inside to do her chores. It wouldn't do for Edd to come home and find the door locked against his precious daughter. The locked door was their secret. Daddy was not to be bothered with Edna's transgressions that led to her banishment whenever Edd was away.

But tonight Edd did not come riding up the dirt road. Instead, the sound the whole town feared, the long low whistle that announced a mine disaster, sounded in the distance. Whole families poured out of their homes and headed for mine number 27, the only mine still in operation. Each one dreaded the news, but they had to know. They all had loved ones who worked the mines, and they shared a common bond as close as that of any family. Their souls were inextricably linked.

All of Adamsville had heard the multiple blasts reverberating through the hills. Today, by this time, most of the men had returned home safe to their families. Even Edna knew there was only one man who would still be at the mine.

Edna fled to her room and fell across her bed. She cowered under the weight of the covers, clutching the rag doll her mama had made for her, waiting for her world to fall apart. She didn't have to wait long.

Oklahoma News Capital   December 23, 1925

SHOTFIRER AT ADAMSVILLE MINE DIES IN BLAST

AFTERDAMP AND FIRE CAUSES DEATH OF EDD GILLEN;

TRIED TO ESCAPE BY REACHING WATER; PULMOTOR USED

Edd Gillen, a popular and widely known miner, was killed Tuesday afternoon about 4:30 o'clock, by a "windy shot" encountered in his tour of duty in the Millen Snow mine, number 27 at Adamsville. The accident was discovered almost immediately, though there was no other person on the slope when the fatality occurred.

Edd Gillen was a pioneer miner in the Adamsville field. He was married and is survived by the wife and one child. Other surviving relatives are three sisters, of whom Mrs. Tim Alden of Holmes Academy is one. A brother, Jonathan lives in Kansas City. The funeral will be held in Adamsville on Thursday afternoon and burial made in that town. All arrangements for the funeral have not yet been completed, awaiting the arrival of relatives.

TRIED TO REACH WATER

Rescue workers, who battled flames and afterdamp 35 minutes before reaching Gillen, stated that they found him several feet from the place where he was supposed to have been when the "windy shot" occurred. He had tried to reach water by crawling into the lower level of the mine, but had been overcome.

Pulmotors were used for nearly three hours in an effort to revive the spark of life. He breathed faintly after being rescued, but his large body was against him and he was unable to overcome the effects of the poison he had inhaled.

Gillen fired six shots on the east side of the mine and was preparing to complete his work when one of the shots proved unsuccessful. It is supposed to have set fire to the mine, and a blast shot up the slope, cutting off rescue parties.

WAS AWARE OF DANGER

Gillen had only recently returned from Kansas City, where he had gone when the mine closed down earlier in the fall. He was one of the most experienced shotfirers in the district and his evident plans to outwit the afterdamp shows that he was conscious of the great danger which beset him, friends at the mine declared.

❀   ❀   ❀

For Edna, the next few days fluttered by in a blur, like the pages of a book turned by the wind, with no one to read them. All without meaning or understanding, rhyme or reason. Another frosty morning trip back to that awful place. Another hole. More tears shed, more flowers. Useless flowers. All the flowers that had ever bloomed in Lily's garden couldn't make this ugly place pretty.

People were coming and going, and there was more food than Edna had seen in her young life. Old ladies kept thrusting plates of food at Edna, telling her, "Have something to eat, dear. It'll make you feel better." As if food could fill the gaping hole in her soul.

"GONE FROM OUR HOME BUT NOT OUR HEARTS", the freshly carved tombstone read. Edna stood in the icy rain, reading her daddy's name and the dates on the cold marble headstone, next to Lily's. She hadn't been back to Adamsville Cemetery to visit Lily in a long time. She hadn't wanted to come here. Now, she clutched in her hand a small bouquet for Lily, too. A few of her mother's favorites; gaillardia gathered from the hill below the house and a sprig of dried Queen Anne's Lace. The gaillardia were closing up already, dying. They had no smell. Edna tried to call up the memory of her mama's scent, but a blending of heavy, sickly sweet perfume and the smell of rain hung heavy in the damp air, overpowering everything else.

Edna's eyes strayed over to Lily's headstone. **"COME UNTO ME AND I WILL GIVE THEE REST…LILY GILLEN nee TOWNS-LEY…BORN OCT. 31, 1891…DIED NOV. 23, 1918…GONE BUT NOT FORGOTTEN…"**. Edna read the initials on her mother's small foot stone. **"EGT"**. No mention of the baby. Where was her lost new-born baby brother, she suddenly wondered. Was he with mama?

"May he rest in peace", the service concluded. Sniffles; Bobbing umbrellas as people embraced awkwardly on soggy ground. It was like a colorless dream, playing out in slow motion. It couldn't be real. Through welling tears Edna saw each face, tears mingling with rain drops until you couldn't tell which was which. One thing she knew, the pain was real.

Later Edna couldn't remember how they all got home, but here they were, back at the house, milling around. Nibbling or gorging, talking or not, crying or laughing. What was it all about? People's voices. Her name spoken in whispers.

"What's gonna happen to Edna?"; "Edna losin' her pa like that. First her ma and now this." More whispers; "Hard to figure some-thin' like this"; "This *here 'Funeral Pie'* sure is tasty. You have the rec-ipe?"; "The recipe was my granny's. They were Pennsylvania Dutch, don't 'cha know…"; "No, don't know who'll be constable now…"; "Now, here's the problem. It isn't easy, with some of these hooligans in town. Edd was prob'ly the only one the kids respected enough to tow the mark…" ; "Mark my words. This storm's gonna be a bad one."; "One more cup of that Ruby's coffee and we're gonna light out 'fore the rain hits. Been a long time comin'…"; "…comin' on hard times with the mines playin' out. If…"; "If ever there was a patient man, that was Edd. Yes sir."

On and on, the conversation droned. Edna wanted to escape. She wanted this painful day to end. She wanted her daddy. And mama. How she needed her now.

Mama. Just thinking of the sound of her name almost made Edna smile. It was easy at that moment, to remember back. She chose to go back there now, however briefly, to a time when she could hear her mama laugh. When Lily laughed, it was hard to believe anything bad could ever happen.

Edna recalled a time shortly after her fourth birthday when a sudden rain shower kept her indoors. Lily had the most wonderful idea for a tea party on the sleeping porch. Just the two of them. Well, they'd let "Baby", Edna's rag doll play as well, if she could mind her manners for a change. She was such an impudent one, always thinking and saying things not allowed of good little girls.

Lily made a great show of setting the perfect table, using matching tablecloth and napkins embellished with crocheted edging the color of pippin apples. She moved the pot of fragrant Rosemary to the table from the windowsill, where it flourished. Lily put on her Sunday hat and Edna donned a froth of mint green dotted Swiss, left over from one of Lily's sewing projects. Lily tied it just so, under Edna's chin. Following suit, Edna tied a scrap of satin ribbon around the top of Baby's head and tucked a sprig of the Rosemary under the ribbon edge.

"Isn't she pretty mama?"

"Not as pretty as you, Sweet pea."

The recollection was so perfect, so real, Edna could almost feel the soft touch of Lily's hand brushing her cheek, and caught again the familiar fragrance. As though Lily was with her, right here, today. Her mama's scent, remembered easily now. Lilacs from the pretty lavender bottle on mama's vanity. And vanilla. Like warm-from-the-oven cookies. Sweet. Soft and sweet…

"Lemon, or cream?" Lily intoned elegantly.

Edna had weighed her choices, and being a child who always took hold of all she could get with both hands, replied coolly, "Both, please."

Through soft laughter, Lily informed Edna that she didn't really want both, that she should choose one or the other. Edna being Edna, insisted.

"Oh, no, I really do want both. Pleeease, mama."

Lily tried again but there was no dissuading Edna.

"Very well." Lily calmly poured cream into Edna's tea, then deftly squeezed a slice of fresh lemon into the lightened brew. Edna's face reflected the result. The tea began to streak with cream, curdled by the lemon. A straight-faced Lily urged Edna to take a sip, telling her "Mmm. This is delicious, Sweet pea. Drink it up, before it gets cold."

Edna lifted her cup to her lips and sipped gingerly. Her face screwed up into an awful knot!

Lily loved Edna's expressive face and her absolute innocence about letting it display whatever crossed her busy mind. She was struck by the beauty inside her daughter. She hoped Edna would never lose that pure honesty that comes so naturally to the young. *Children and old people are so beautiful! It's what happens in the in between that can make a person ugly. Bitter and ugly. If you let it.*

Letting Edna suffer a bit, Lily had debated whether to make her drink the nasty concoction, to teach her a lesson. Regretting the waste, she'd relented and allowed her daughter to start over with a fresh cup of tea, and hopefully, a lesson learned. Even more than the waste, Lily regretted that Edna seemed to be one of those children who had to learn every single thing the hard way.

Idly, Lily's hand wandered over her expanding belly as she savored this time with Edna. Soon the new baby would be here and she'd have less time to spend this way, with her daughter. Sure as stars came out at night, Edd wanted a son, but at this moment, she truly wanted another girl. One who looked just like her own little Sweet pea.

If Edna had been older, Lily might have shared her own thoughts that day, thoughts to be tucked away for Edna to draw on in later life.

Someday she'd explain to her daughter about real beauty, inner beauty. The kind that comes from knowing who you are. The kind that comes from being close to nature and appreciating every beautiful thing God created and put here for us to enjoy. The kind that comes from loving and knowing you are loved. But there was plenty of time for that, another day.

For now, Lily was content to enjoy watching her young daughter talk animatedly to Baby, scolding her from time to time for not listening to her mother. The afternoon lazed by with mother, daughter and "Baby" sipping tea and laughing together on the cozy porch, watching the welcome rain slip through the bare branches of the redbud tree and pelt the bone dry sod.

As it turned out, Lily's thoughts would remain captive, and now in Edna's memories of that day, she only recalled that her mama looked happy. And smelled of lilacs and vanilla.

Not a month after their lovely tea party, mama had suddenly gotten "sick".

"It's too soon", Edd breathed, a worried look clouding his ashen face.

Ol' Doc Raines, the pharmacist, had rushed to the house that moonless, coal black night, a night as dark as the inside of a black cat. He reeked of whiskey and Edd wanted to send him away. But Lily was trying not to cry, trying to be brave, and told him not to worry. There was no one else to help.

They sent Edna to bed. Mama had kissed her goodnight, her trembling lips forming an odd, not-quite-smile.

"When you wake up, you'll get to meet your new baby brother or sister. It'll be all right, Edna. I promise."

It was the first and last promise Lily ever broke.

Doc Raines left just before sunup. Dawn was painting wispy cotton candy clouds with a rosy glow and false hope, when Edna woke up. She remembered about mama and her promise of the new baby.

She rushed out of her room in excited anticipation. She stopped short when she saw her daddy slumped at the small wooden table, his head on his arms, his broad shoulders shaking. Edna didn't know of the drama and ugliness that had filled the night. She didn't know people you trusted could make mistakes. Big mistakes. She listened but didn't hear the cry of the new baby.

Then everyone was so sad, and they went to that ugly place and put Lily in that awful hole. How would she ever get out, Edna's four-year-old mind pondered, with all that dirt. How could she come back? That was the bad part.

The only good part was that aunt Babe came and stayed with daddy and her, and doted on Edna. Though Edna still waited for her mama to come back, eventually she came to spend less time actively thinking about it.

The picture was fading now and want to or not, Edna was losing the dream. Back to the present, a bleak winter day in 1925. Back to reality. No more tea parties. No more of mama's laughter. No more mama. No more walking hand in hand with her daddy or riding to town with him on his big ol' sorrel mare, "Jezebel", to buy horehound candy at ol' Doc Raines' store. Edna knew deep down in the darkest corners of her soul that things had changed forever.

Edna's eyes swept the room and she caught sight of Ruby dabbing dramatically at cold, dry eyes. The lace embellished hanky she was using had the initial L on it—L for Lily. Edna wanted to run and snatch it from her stepmother's hand. But 'good little girls' didn't do things like that. She'd surely pay for it. It might be worth it.

Just when she felt like there wasn't a soul in the world who loved her or cared what happened to her, she saw them. Her heart lifted seeing the familiar faces of her aunt and uncle. She ran to aunt Babe and buried her face in her aunt's ample bosom, feeling somehow safe in the sheltering embrace.

Emmy Belle Gillen, was the youngest of the Gillen children. Early on she had been dubbed Babe, in keeping with Midwest custom, for the baby in the family. When Edd and Emmy's parents died, "Babe" had been only 16 years old. Edd and his brother Jonathan were living together in Oklahoma and they had taken their baby sister into their home and taken care of her. Edd, Jonathan and Babe had always been close. Like peas in a pod, they were.

Happily, when Babe found work taking care of a family in a neighboring town, the siblings were still close enough to visit each other regularly. Then, when Edd's wife, Lily, died in child birth, it left his 4 year old daughter motherless. The family was brought full circle as Babe came home to help care for her brother's child and the house they all shared. Until Ruby entered the picture.

Ruby was several years younger than Edd. Naive and self-centered, she was somehow savvy enough to know to make a good show of caring about Edd's beloved young daughter. If you didn't look too deeply into her eyes, you might almost believe she was sincere. In truth, she had little feeling one way or the other about her. Other than thinking Edna was something of a brat. She was definitely an inconvenience. Had Edna never been told "Children are to be seen and not heard"? And Ruby found Edna's frequent hands-on-hips stance a little too sassy. Perhaps that could be corrected, with proper guidance. Maybe she'd see what she could do about that, if she got the chance. And she intended full well to get that chance.

An only child like Edna, Ruby had been more a child of privilege, raised mostly by doting, well-to-do grandparents living in an affluent neighborhood of San Antonio, Texas. As a youngster, she adopted red as her trademark color, and she always wore at least a trace of it. It was what she wanted and she was used to getting what she wanted. And Ruby had been brought up with culture, not like a weed. Not like Edna, growing wild, with her untamed ways and her untamed curls, spilling out from under those ridiculous butterfly bows.

For some reason, Ruby's Southern-bred grandmother had been unable to imbue in her petulant granddaughter, any sense of graciousness. Ruby seemed to lack any genuine empathy or sentimentality.

When Ruby first met Edd, she had been drawn to him by the shiny star on his broad chest. His size and strength made her feel safe. It didn't hurt that Edd Gillen was considered prosperous for the times, owning his own home and being employed with not one, but two jobs. Edd's home place was small but neat and clean, thanks to his sister, Babe. The house had a desirable southern exposure and a "breathtaking view", overlooking the town. And unfortunately, Adamsville Cemetery. Still, all things considered, Ruby decided that Edd and his little house on the hill had "potential".

Ruby set her cap for the strapping constable—she preferred to make light of his other work—and won him over. The lonely widower was an easy mark for a girl like Ruby. A flirty, modern girl, with rolled down stockings and rouge on her knees. In no time, she wore a plain gold band, which would do for the moment. She had a cozy place to live, and time on her hands. It suited her just fine.

Yes, everything was just about perfect, except for Edna. But that fly in the ointment was easily dealt with. Ruby's new husband left early in the morning for work and didn't return home until late. He trusted Ruby with his daughter's care and supervision, never dreaming she was in anything but loving hands.

Edd's young bride developed her own way of dealing with Edna, quickly learning that she could control the child through intimidation. She need only hint to Edna that she had the power to invoke her father's disapproval of her. That was enough to control the child. And keep her silent. As far as Ruby was concerned, that was sufficient. She didn't think beyond that. What did she know about raising a child? What did she know of loving and nurturing a small, helpless soul? She had enough to worry about taking care of herself, her husband, and his house.

All in all, Ruby had orchestrated a life for herself that was fairly comfortable. Until the day they got the news that Edd had been killed. Ruby suddenly found herself a widow. What on God's green earth was she supposed to do now?

Bits and pieces of the funeral conversation pulled Ruby back to the present.

"I sure wish it hadn't happened so close to Christmas. It's a terrible time…"

"No, Christmas'll never be the same. 'Specially for Edna. Pass me another hunk o' that pie, will ya'…"

Two spit and polished miners near Edna were eyeing Ruby, across the room.

"That Ruby sure is a looker. I 'spect she'll remarry."

"Pretty young thing like that. Why if I was a few years younger…" The men chuckled conspiratorially.

Overhearing this exchange puzzled Edna. *Pretty?* How odd. Edna had never thought of Ruby as pretty.

Edna's neck hurt from looking up into the faces mouthing the meaningless words. She retreated to the sun porch that served as her sleeping quarters and pulled her rag doll out from under the quilts that layered her bed in the cold winter months. She took Baby outside and cradled the doll as they sat on a rock under the naked redbud tree. The deep burgundy, heart-shaped leaves had long since abandoned it.

Edna decided to change her doll's name to Baby-Modene, adding her own middle name as a reminder her of the special link to her daddy. She hoped she'd never forget her daddy's face. His kind, greygreen eyes and craggy features. Serious, with the pipe she loved to smell angling down from the corner of his lips. No, she could never forget his face.

Icy rain began to fall again and forced her to seek refuge inside, clutching Baby-Modene to her damp, corduroy-clad chest like a lifeline.

When Edna came back inside, she saw that her Uncle Jonathan and his wife, Easter had arrived. The family had worried at their tardiness, but they'd had to come all the way from Kansas City, Missouri. Her father's younger brother, Jonathan and their sister Babe were the ones Edna knew the best, on her father's side of the family. Not that Edna was much aware of the distinction between maternal and paternal family members.

Edna was glad to see they had brought their little girl, Grace. Six months younger than Edna, Grace was her exact opposite. She was dark-eyed, olive-skinned, and tall, like her mother. Her round face was framed by short cropped hair with the blue-black sheen of a raven's wing, just skimming her jaw line. She was a quiet child with a perpetual pout. Edna had only once seen her smile. Not that she was unhappy really, just shy and reticent. Today, she didn't want to play with Edna. They both were bewildered by all the people and the overwhelming din of voices.

Edna wished more of her mother's family were here. Most of them had moved away in recent years and only a few came for the funeral today. She especially missed her cousin Harriet. When they were small, Edna and Harriet were always together. Everyone in town took to calling them the "Gold Dust Twins", because they were so close in age and their fair features almost mirrored one another. Of course they didn't look at all like the real Gold Dust Twins, grinning out from the picture on the can of 'Fairbank's Gold Dust Washing Powder' that Edna's mama used. They were just the opposite. The real Gold Dust Twins were two little "pick-a-ninny" babies, as her mother called them, affectionately.

Harriet had an older sister, Anise, but Edna and Harriet were closer than any sisters. Where you saw one, the other would not be far behind. It had been that way since they had learned to walk. They had no way of knowing it could change. They didn't know that nothing stays the same.

Once in the shimmering heat of the summer, Lily had patiently taught Edna and Harriet how to make hollyhock dolls, turning the big, full blossoms upside-down for the dress, or body, and using a tight bud for the head. Lily showed them how to use a small twig to connect the head to the body. They amused themselves for hours stacking the colorful, upside down flower heads into satiny layers of skirts. They danced their dolls around, swirling their petaled skirts in the sunlight.

The two cousins had giggled incessantly and recited the sing-song rhyme:

Hollyhock, hollyhock dance for me. Give me some pollen for my dolly's tea."

But that was a long time ago. Before mama broke her promise and went away. And then Harriet went away. Now only Grace was here, and Grace didn't want to talk. So the girls stood silently side by side like strangers, trying to make sense of everything. But it was too overwhelming. Both Edna and Grace had eaten as ordered, but Edna didn't feel one bit better. Distracted momentarily, but that was all.

The grandfather clock in the hall sounded the hour. Six gongs. Nearly suppertime. Edna wished it was bedtime. She wanted to crawl beneath her covers, topped with the quilt her grandmother Gillen had made, and shut out everything and everyone.

Ruby too, was growing tired, increasingly impatient for everyone to leave and go back to their own petty lives. The day had dawned cold and gray, and the threat of the continuing storm had given Ruby hope that everyone would be anxious to leave early and get home to their cozy fires and leave her to sort things out. Her mind kept returning to her plight.

She knew there would be money from the mine, her widow's pension. And money for Edd's orphan. If there was enough money, she could stay in the house, maybe. She hoped it would be enough to get by. That was one good thing about working in the mines. It was hard work and dirty, dangerous as well, but they took care of their own. Ruby again mentally counted the remaining guests, while distractedly massaging her temples. All these intrusive people! When were they going to leave? Ruby had a crashing headache and longed for some peace and quiet. She was more than ready to put this behind her and get on with her life. This crush of townsfolk and Edd's people was so wearisome. Ruby spotted Babe across the room, her arms encircling Edna's small frame and a mounting rage enveloped her.

Who did Babe think she was? Babe was only Edd's sister, not his wife. But she always acted like she had some kind of claim on Edd. And on Edna. She'd probably like to get her hands on Edna, just for her share of the money from the mine. Well, she had another think coming. Just because her husband taught at some fancy, Indian boys' school didn't make them any better than Ruby. Here she was, in Ruby's house, pretending to be so sweet, so concerned. Trying to worm her way into Edna's heart. Truth be known, if she was so crazy about the kid, she could have her. Part of her wished that Babe would take Edd's sniveling little brat with her, but she wanted—no, needed—Edna's share of the money from the mine, first. Well, she could put up with the kid for awhile but it would certainly simplify her life not to have to deal with the little ingrate.

In time the mourners began dwindling away, saying their goodbyes with gentle squeezes of hands, pats on the head for Edna and all their sympathy properly expressed to the grieving widow.

Babe and her husband were the last to leave, reluctant to desert Edna. In the end, there was nothing else they could do. They couldn't take Edna with them, even if Ruby would let her go. Times were hard. What would they say at the school? Babe and Tim hadn't even divulged that their own baby was due in late spring. Their teacher's quarters were cramped as it was. No, there really was nothing they could do.

When Aunt Babe and Edna said goodbye, their pain was almost tangible. Their eyes locked and it was Babe who pulled away. Turning toward Ruby, Babe fixed Edna's step-mother with an admonishing glare.

"Take care of her." It was more a command than a casual parting remark.

Ruby lifted her chin and narrowed cold blue eyes in Babe's direction. She rested her hand possessively on Edna's shoulder and the child winced.

"Oh, don't you fret about us. We'll be just fine." Ruby's lips curved in a thin smile and Babe felt helpless to follow her heart. She had a husband now and his recent appointment to the academy meant security and a roof over their heads. They couldn't jeopardize that now. Not with the baby coming. She could be wrong about Ruby. She hoped so, with all her heart.

Finally the house was dark and quiet. The few meager Christmas gifts, mostly from Edd to Edna and Ruby, sat unopened by the front window, clustered forlornly around a struggling rubber tree, decked out in home made ornaments of Lily's making. Completing the illusion of festivity, was an angel topper made of twigs and odds and ends of lace and calico from what was now Edna's scrap basket. Edna had been afraid Ruby would try to lay claim to Lily's sewing basket as her own. She needn't have worried. "Lord knows, I don't have any use for it", Ruby had scoffed.

Tired as she was, Edna's eyes wouldn't stay shut. She lay wide-eyed in her bed watching the moonrise through the sun porch window. A frosty halo of light rimmed the moon as the stars crept across the clearing heavens.

Edna couldn't stop thinking of her mama. How Lily had loved to watch the stars. Holding that there was magic in them, she used to tell Edna and Baby mythic tales of warriors and princesses, gods and goddesses, pointing out star pictures. Edna couldn't really see them, but she could imagine them. She could still imagine them tonight. She could almost see a faint outline of Lily's finger pointing out Orion and his hunting dogs, the Little Dipper and the Southern Cross.

Edna's fingers traced the silken paths of the fans and other crazy quilt motifs on her quilt. She loved the feel of the luxurious fabrics that her grandmother Gillen had expertly pieced into interesting shapes and patterns. Edna had lulled herself to sleep many nights tracing them with her fingers, as she did now. She knew them all by heart. Lacy spider webs and swirls, cranberry red heart-shaped flowers, with lemony French knot centers. Bleeding hearts, Lily called them and Edna thought that such a sad name for so beautiful a thing.

Edna lay awake like this for a long time, wondering. She wondered what would happen now. Would Ruby let her in at all, or would the door be locked forever? Where could she go? When she left the house in the morning, she'd take her quilt with her. Just in case. She finally drifted off to sleep watching the first soft flakes of snow falling in the moonlight.

Ruby was up bright and early. Downing a quick cup of coffee and calling it breakfast, she left Edna to her own devices, as usual. Ruby dressed herself warmly and prepared for her errand, preoccupied with her own thoughts.

It shouldn't take long. The money should be available at the bank, hopefully immediately. After all, she was entitled to it.

Ruby hustled Edna outside, deciding she'd never understand that child. Taking her quilt! Ruby settled her hat and drew the black veil. She slipped on scarlet kid gloves and looped her pocket book over one arm. After locking the front door, she pocketed the key in her long woolen coat. By the time she got outside, Edna had disappeared.

The young widow set off briskly in the new fallen snow, placing her own small feet in Edna's fading imprints and made her way toward the bank. The sun warmed her face and began to make slush of the smattering of snow. As she waited to cross the street, kitty-corner to the bank, a mud-spattered jalopy passed her, clipping the edge of a puddle and swooshing a spray of mud up onto Ruby's new red Sears & Roebuck boots.

"Inconsiderate nincompoop!" Ruby muttered under her breath. She strode on toward the bank with new fervor, fired by indignation.

Inside the bank, she withdrew her gloves and stood impatiently in line, tapping her toe. In turn she stepped up to the window for her transaction, grateful for the stroke of luck that had put this homely, fresh-scrubbed young man opposite her. *This will be easier than I thought.* She was ill-prepared for the resistance she met.

The freckle-faced bank clerk efficiently counted out her share of the money from the mine, but stubbornly held that she couldn't withdraw Edna's share, in lump sum.

Ruby batted her eyelashes. "Well, what am I supposed to do?" she drawled sweetly. "I have an orphan to provide for. How am I to do that, without money?"

A shock of red-gold hair fell forward from its slicked down part as the clerk dipped his head to cover an amused smile. He expressed his sympathy for her situation, but was undaunted. Her charm was obviously wasted on the boy.

Recovering, he straightened and offered, "I'm sorry ma'am. How the trust works is, the bank holds the orphan's money. You kin draw from it periodically, for her expenses".

The logic escaped Ruby. Her tone changed immediately, and the impatient tap-tap-tapping of her rapid-fire red boot resumed.

"Let me speak with Mr. Flowers." Ruby assumed an arrogant stance, designed to intimidate. The bank clerk was not intimidated, in spite of his youth. On the contrary, he was rather amused. Mr. Flowers, the rotund bank president, had heard the commotion and was already plowing in Ruby's direction. In his best professional manner, Mr. Flowers leaned forward, and again patiently explained the trust fund policy. The bank was accustomed to handling these trust accounts for the mine, but seldom did they have to deal with a Ruby Gillen. It was not a pleasant experience.

At first Mr. Flowers' clear blue eyes smiled benignly on Ruby, but as his patience wore thin under Ruby's persistence, they took on that glassy, fevered-child look, and his fleshy cheeks and bald pate grew flushed in direct proportion to his level of exasperation. As Ruby continued her tirade, Mr. Flowers' naturally bulging eyes began to look as though they'd jump right out of their sockets, but he continued smiling his frozen smile, through now gritted teeth

The bank manager leaned away from the pushy customer, implying conclusion of the discussion. "I'm afraid you'll have to take it up with the mine." His sugary smile was still frozen firmly in place.

"We'll just see about that!"

Ruby huffed out of the bank and stomped home, grumbling to herself all the way. It wasn't as if it was a fortune they were talking about. Paltry little, really. How does that big shot banker think anyone can get along on it, anyway? She'd have to give it some thought. Surely Ol' Mr. Fisheyes could see her point, if he just thought about it. How would he like his wife and children to have to get along on so little? Yes, she'd try again, appeal to his sympathy. Surely he could make an exception.

Had Ruby been more worldly wise, she might have recognized that it was mine policy, rather than bank policy, that dictated the rules.

Returning to the bank the next day yielded the same result. Ruby had to resign herself to the fact that she could not break down Mr. Flowers' ridiculous resolve to prevent her from getting the money she felt she was entitled to.

A week Thursday and the mortgage would be due. Ruby had never worked a day in her life. She had no skills, other than what she called her "womanly wiles", which had stood her in good stead so far, but they wouldn't pay a mortgage.

Two fears loomed on the horizon for Ruby after her husband's death—the fear of being stuck in this dumpy little coal town with Edd's orphan to raise by herself, and the fear of having to go home a failure and rely once again on her grandparents to take care of her. To run from the first she must embrace the other.

The new year would find Ruby on a train headed back to Texas and Edna on her way to stay with her paternal uncle, Harry Gillen and his wife Fannie. It was a new year and a new life, for Edna and for her stepmother. Ruby boarded the train and left town that day without a look back. Edna and Ruby would not see each other again for over 30 years.

Adamsville, Oklahoma, population 2384.

STEP 2:
Stew in Own Juices

"Stew in Own Juices…"

Edna had never thought of their house in Adamsville as luxurious or modern, until she came to stay with Harry and Fannie Gillen.

The Gillen farm, squatting halfway between Adamsville and McAllister, Oklahoma, had seen better days. As the Gillen family pulled into the drive, Edna took in the dilapidated fence and the rustic barn, listing slightly to the south. One lonely milk cow kept company in the barnyard with a few rangy chickens and a banty rooster, scratching around futilely in the dirt under a faded green tractor. Two aging hound dogs lazed on the porch by the butter churn, sleeping through the family's return home. To enter the house through the sagging screen door, everyone had to step over their dozing bodies.

Edna had only known one home in her lifetime, and though some neglect of the property was immediately apparent, she had no way of knowing how different life on a rural farm might be. Her expectation was merely that there would be more animals and probably more work. It would turn out to be easier for Edna to adjust to this extended family than to a household lighted with kerosene lamps and lacking indoor plumbing.

It was logical for Harry and Fannie to take Edna in, for a time anyway, because they were close by and it was easy to arrange quickly. They had no intention of keeping Edna for long. It was understood that this was a temporary arrangement, until Edna could be placed permanently with relatives who could afford to take on another mouth to feed. All the Gillen relatives were contacted in hopes that someone would offer to keep Edna permanently. No one had volunteered, yet.

In many ways, it was good for all concerned, for Edna to be there. Fannie was already ungainly, expecting her 4th child soon. It was becoming difficult for her to tend her little ones. An extra pair of hands was more than welcome. Edna was good help and she found some comfort for herself in being part of the family.

Fannie had always been especially close to Edna and if she hadn't been expecting another child…well, that couldn't be helped. She supposed she'd have another boy and was resigned to it. How she'd love to have a little girl. A little girl like Edna. Maybe a little more ladylike, but a little girl to dress in ribbons and lace. A daughter to share sewing and cooking skills with. Someone to teach baking and the art of pickle-making. She'd won blue ribbons for 'Best of Show' the last five years at the Oklahoma State Fair for her variation of *'Crystal Pickles'*. She needed to pass along her secret recipe, but not to just anyone. Her sons wouldn't likely take an interest in continuing the tradition.

Harry and Fannie's boys were mischievous and energetic. Six year old Harry William, called "HW", was serious like his father and grandfather. He wore the Gillen features well, below a dark widow's peak, punctuated with straight, full brows. Golden-haired three and a half year old twin boys, Jake and Jayce were like little balls of summer lightning. They chattered constantly in their own exclusive twin language that only they understood. The twins fought for Edna's attention, like the hound dogs on the porch scrambling over a bone. It was a little overwhelming for an only child. It occurred to Edna that if this was what it was like to be a mother, maybe she'd skip having children. How different little boys are! And twins present their own special challenges. Much as she adored the twins, Edna hoped that if she ever did have children of her own, she wouldn't be "blessed" with twin boys.

The Gillen boys were good company and Edna found that entertaining them was fairly good distraction. Even when it involved climbing trees or shooting marbles. Edna was something of a tomboy anyway, she supposed. Having lost her mother at age four, she and her father had grown very close. He took her fishing with him, and shared other "manly interests" with her, like he might a son.

Edna's aunt was a fabulous cook and her full figure bore the proof. It never occurred to Edna that Fannie was not a nickname, but her aunt's given name. Harry managed to remain as slim as Fannie was otherwise, and he was known to refer to his wife as "pleasingly plump". Her skill in the kitchen was legendary in the family, and in the county for that matter. Edna learned that whatever else was going on, she could usually count on pleasurable meals. The old farmhouse was always full of mouth-watering aromas, hinting at the meal to come or lingering reminders of what was last enjoyed at the big, heavy table.

Edna managed to absorb some of her aunt's cooking secrets during her stay with Harry and Fannie. Her stepmother, Ruby had never been very interested in domesticities, and It was a treat to enjoy such delicious and plentiful food. It seemed she couldn't get enough. Lily had always joked about how her daughter must have a hollow leg.

Lily believed that it was due to the fact that Edna had nearly starved to death when she was born, before they found anything she could keep on her stomach. She quietly battled guilt over not being able to nourish her baby at her breast. She longed to see Edna thrive on milk from her own mother, and was terrified they'd lose her. Once Edna was able to eat she overdid it, it seemed to Lily, though she never really gained weight in spite of her preoccupation with food. Edna seemed doomed to remain forever fragile looking, like a papery pullet's egg.

As it turned out, the last third of Fannie's pregnancy was her best. She felt absolutely wonderful. Relieved of the physical strain of caring for HW and the twins, she bloomed. Her once pallid complexion was replaced by a glow of contentment in her plump cheeks, and her previously nondescript eyes took on a sparkle. She became even closer to Edna and it was mutual. Edna came to adore the boys as well, even though their sibling rivalry and rambunctious behavior often wore her out.

In later years, Edna would look back and treasure the fond memories of her days with aunt Fannie. Their shared kitchen chores were a real joy for them both, once they understood each other. There were some rocky times, in the beginning. Edna and Fannie had to get to know each other, test the waters. The first time Edna did the dishes, she tried to put one over on her aunt by putting the silverware away without drying it as instructed. *What a waste of time and effort. Who'd ever know, anyway?*

Fannie wasn't checking up on Edna. She had no reason to suspect her niece would do anything but what she was told. But shortly after Edna completed her task, Fannie decided to have a cup of mint tea to take quell her queasiness. Taking a teaspoon out of the drawer to ladle in some honey, she found it had water puddled in the spoon's bowl. Checking further she found water spotted knives and forks, and each spoon held a telltale droplet of water in its bowl.

The first flush of anger was quickly replaced with tender amusement. She straightened her back and kneaded the dull ache with her fist. Best to correct her niece immediately, set her straight.

"Edna, come here, please."

Edna appeared in the doorway and her smile fled as she saw what Fannie held in her hand. The questioning look in her aunt's eyes said it all. Edna couldn't bear to look Fannie in the eyes and lowered her own to the floor.

"We dry the silverware thoroughly, before putting it away so it doesn't water spot, dear. Can I count on you to follow my instructions next time?"

Edna nodded without a word and Fannie held out a red embroidered dish towel. "Tuesday's child is full of grace", carefully lettered in red stitches on muslin.

I guess I wasn't born on Tuesday. Edna took the towel and resolutely began retrieving the silverware, drying it properly. It was the last time she tried to fool her aunt Fannie.

When baby Sarilda Rose arrived 3 weeks early, she caught everyone by surprise, not only by her early appearance, but by her gender. No one had anticipated the delicate baby girl, and she thoroughly captured everyone's heart. Sarilda's big brothers were enthralled with her and her father became absolutely giddy with pride. Edna had mixed emotions. She had difficulty overcoming her jealousy of Fannie's successful pregnancy when her own mother had been lost. Why her? But Sarilda Rose was so perfect, Edna couldn't help but be pleased, too. No one was more thrilled than Fannie. This truly completed their family.

Having a baby girl of her own made it easier to think of saying goodbye to Edna. When Sari, as she came to be called, was 2 months old and Fannie was back on her feet, she began to give it serious thought. It had taken her longer to recover than when she'd had the boys, but she was much better now, and Sari was certainly worth it. She had her daughter. Her own baby girl, the essence of pure sweetness and joy, smelling like heaven itself. She would talk to Harry about Edna. Surely someone else in the family would be glad to have her for awhile. She was excellent help around the house and was very capable with children.

Harry was studying his baby girl as she slept in her cradle when his wife came into the room and stood beside him.

"Isn't she the spittin' image of mother? I wish she could have seen her."

"I think she looks just like her father", Fannie countered. "That widow's peak is pure Gillen. But yes, she would have been charmed just like the rest of us."

"At least she carries her name." Harry slipped an arm around his wife's diminishing waist.

Harry's mother, Sarilda Gillen had been a glove maker in England and her husband a tailor. Nimble needles on both sides of his family. Harry savored the sight of his baby daughter slumbering sweetly in a cream batiste dress, hand crafted by his mother. Even he appreciated the care with which the yoke had been smocked with pale, pastel green thread and adorned with buttery yellow roses. Harry remembered watching his mother working on the long-sleeved gown, laboriously trimming it in fine lace, while awaiting the birth of his sister, Babe.

Lost in this reverie, Fannie's next remark was jarring.

"I was thinking, now that Sari's doing so well and I'm recovered, maybe Edna could go and stay with Corrine and Allen for awhile."

"You can't be serious, Fannie. Corrine is almost fifty. They'd be the last ones to be interested in caring for a child, at this point."

"Well, being they have no children of their own…You don't know, maybe they'd love to have a little girl to dote on for awhile."

"I know Corrine would have loved to have children when she was younger, but now…" Harry's ruddy complexion deepened.

"Now is the perfect time", Fannie pressed. "I think they'd really enjoy her."

"I'm not so sure. Look how busy Corrine is. She's president of half the organizations in town and busy with her church. She just got on the cemetery board. You know how much that means to her. Kickapoo Cemetery has been so neglected and she can't bear to see the family plot in such disrepair. And her house is definitely not set up for children. It's full of antiques and fragile bric-a-brac.

He was pacing, now. "No, I can't imagine my sister wanting to take on a child at this time in her life. Not even Edd's daughter. Besides when we asked who could take Edna, they let it be known not to count on them."

"Well, there must be someone else…"

Fannie realized the conversation was threatening to turn into an argument and guided her husband away from the slumbering Sari.

Eventually, Harry resigned himself to the reality that it no longer suited his wife to have Edna in their home. It went without saying that if Fannie wasn't happy, nobody was happy. She didn't intend it to be that way, it just was. They had been married too long for Harry to disregard her wishes. Feeling like a traitor to his brother, Harry assured her that he would talk to everyone, see who might be persuaded to take Edna in.

Edna had grown fairly comfortable at the farm and attached to everyone. She hoped against hope that Fannie would find need to keep her, even after Sari's arrival. Maybe especially with the new baby. She tried to make herself useful at every opportunity. Indispensable, even.

The twins' fourth birthday was approaching and Edna was beside herself with anticipation. Many of the relatives would be coming for dinner and she prayed aunt Babe would be among them. She was dying to hold Gavin and she wanted to see him playing with Jake and Jayce. Maybe he was old enough. Not to shoot marbles maybe, but they could get to know each other. Cousins should be close. Like Edna and Harriet. Like the Gold Dust Twins.

Maybe even her cousin, Harriet would be there. But when Edna had asked about Harriet, she didn't understand Fannie's curt "No, of course not." The intricacies of in-laws and out-laws still befuddled her. They were all family, weren't they? Whether this one was on her father's side or that one, on her mother's. What was the difference?

That warm summer day found the whole family excitedly preparing for company for the twins' birthday celebration. They were expecting uncle Jonathan and aunt Easter for dinner, as well as miscellaneous aunts, uncles and cousins. Sadly, for Edna, aunt Babe had written with apologies that they wouldn't be able to make the trip. They would be unable to get away from the academy.

Still, Edna was looking forward to the family gathering. She never suspected her world was about to take another somersault. Aunt

Fannie had been somewhat distant all day, as though she were distracted. Edna couldn't seem to do anything to please her. It was like she was on edge, like in the last few days before she gave birth to Sari. Edna felt an ominous gulf growing between them, though she couldn't have named it.

After dinner, presents were opened, and birthday cake was served, garnering the usual praise. Edna had never even heard of poppy seed cake before. She thought it the most delicious thing she'd ever eaten. The men went out to the yard to talk while their wives set about putting the kitchen back in order. Everyone seeing Sari for the first time promptly fell in love with the elfin girl.

Aunt Fannie asked Edna to take the twins into the other room and get them out from underfoot so the women could work. Edna was content to keep the boys busy in the other room and listen in on the women's conversation, which ran along the lines of babies and cooking and the upcoming marriage of a cousin, Shannon Kay to a boy from Wichita. Their families were close and everyone on both sides had pronounced it a perfect match.

A wedding shower was taking shape and Edna thought it sounded like such fun. She couldn't wait. She'd never been to a shower before. Aunt Fannie was planning to go and she would surely take Edna with her. They could take Sari and show her off.

Edna heard her name mentioned but missed the context as voices became hushed. She moved closer to the door, hoping to hear her aunt saying nice things about her and how much help she'd been. It took a moment for her to realize that, where there was an element of praise in Fannie's words, there was a thinly veiled question, as well. The question was "Whose turn is it now?"

"Well, we've had her for over five months. It's time for someone else to take her for awhile", were Fannie's unfathomable words.

"But Fannie, she's been such a help to you, I'd think you'd want to keep her a little longer." Nameless whispers faint as shadows, beyond the closed door.

"Yes, she has been and I'll miss her but I have Sari now and I want to get back to my routine. The state fair is coming up and I have all these pickles and tomatoes to put up. I really don't need anyone else underfoot".

Underfoot? Is that what I've been?

"Well, we can't possibly take her. We've had to take a smaller place and…"

Edna's attention went back to the knot of boys at play on the floor, her head in a fog. How could this be? Maybe it wouldn't come to that. Maybe Fannie would relent and let her stay. But did she want to stay where she wasn't wanted? If she left, who would take her? What would life be like, somewhere else? The boys would miss her terribly if she went away and vice versa. Surely Sari would too. Yes, she wanted to stay—at any cost.

She sat there amid the blocks and marbles and looked at each intense little face. She tried to imagine life without them. Closing her eyes, she lost herself in a silent plea. *Please, please don't let things change again. Please.*

Laughter in the kitchen startled her. Good. If they were laughing, maybe the troubling thoughts had gone away and the threat was over. As it turned out, late guests had come in the back door and the laughter and hugs were in welcome of uncle Jonathan Gillen and his wife, with their daughter, Grace. Soon, cousin Grace came through the door and joined Edna and the children, having been shooed out of the kitchen. The new arrivals had already eaten and settled for coffee and cake. Grace turned up her little pug nose at cake with poppy seeds, of all things.

The men eventually drifted back into the house joining their wives who'd moved to the living room to visit over coffee. Aunt Fannie asked her nieces to bathe HW and the twins and put them to bed. An only child, Grace was virtually useless and Edna, being accustomed to the routine handled it herself. Grace watched in sullen silence.

"Now I lay me down to sleep, I pray the Lord my soul to keep. If I should die before I wake, I pray the Lord my soul to take." "Tuck, tuck", Edna crooned, tucking cozy covers around each little tyke. "Kiss, kiss", smooching each forehead and the bedtime ritual was complete. All three boys closed their eyes and trundled off to dreamland.

"If I should die before I wake?" Grace whispered, wrinkling her nose. Don't you think that's kind of scary to tell little kids?"

"I don't know," Edna responded as they slipped out, closing the door softly behind them. "I never thought about it. I guess not, if you believe in God. Besides, why would they die?" It seemed a silly question. This had been Edna's bedtime prayer all her life. Her mama taught it to her and always said it with such sweetness and reverence, she never thought to question the wisdom.

When Edna and Grace came downstairs to join the adults, aunt Fannie stopped them in their tracks by announcing that Edna would be going for a visit with uncle Jonathan and aunt Easter. The two cousins looked blankly at each other. Grace shrugged and went over to sit on the arm of the sofa, by her papa. Edna was rooted to a braided rug at the foot of the stairs.

Aunt Fannie rose from her rocker still cradling little Sari. She settled the sleeping baby into her father's arms and took Edna by the hand.

"Come with me, Edna, I'll help you pack. They'll be leaving shortly."

So that was it. Uncle Jonathan must have lost the toss of the dice. Edna assumed her soft spoken aunt must have kept silent as usual. That was not the case. Easter had said "No", but no one heard her.

If someone had to take Edna away today, she guessed it might as well be them. Maybe when she and Grace got to know each other better, it would be more fun than she thought. Edna loved her uncle Jonathan, had always been close to him, but there was something about his wife that she couldn't put her finger on. She had never been mean to anyone, that Edna knew of, but she couldn't recall ever hearing her talk. About anything. Maybe that was why Grace was always so quiet. She must take after her mother. It didn't mean anything. She liked her cousin well enough, and she would get to know aunt Easter. She was sure she'd come to like her too.

Later, as Edna handed her small suitcase over to uncle Harry to carry out for her, she kept her quilt folded over her arm. She might need it on the trip. Besides, it was her anchor.

It was a long drive back to Kansas City, Missouri. Edna sat behind her aunt Easter and filled the time wondering what it was like to live in a big city. Grace dozed off and fell against Edna's shoulder. There was no conversation in the front seat. Edna could just make out Jonathan's silhouette, facing straight ahead, looking only at the road. Aunt Easter gazed out the side window, her head turned away from uncle Jonathan. Inside that small space, stone cold darkness enveloped them all.

They reached home and settled into bed late. Everyone but Jonathan slept in the next morning. When Edna awoke in the strange bed, she reached out for the comfort of her familiar quilt. Trying to orient herself, she turned over and her arm fell across a warm little body with a tousled dark head.

"Aaaaghhh!" Grace protested.

"Shhhh. I'm sorry", Edna stammered. "I didn't know you were there."

Grace's screeching stopped abruptly and she stared at her cousin.

"I'm hot!" Grace flung Edna's precious quilt off of her side of the bed with an impassioned flourish!

"Whatever is going on in here? You tryin' to wake the dead?" Spoken softly and without mirth. Aunt Easter stood in the doorway, silhouetted by late morning sunlight, filtering in through gingham curtains. For a moment Edna was reminded of Ruby. Only aunt Easter was taller than Ruby, and so pretty. She looked almost regal. *She should be happy. If she'd just smile...*

Edna was curious about what made Easter so unhappy. She could see that her uncle Jonathan adored Easter, and they obviously thought Grace hung the stars. Their home was small by some standards, but it had a generous wrap-around porch in front, bracketed by gorgeous hydrangea bushes and overlooking a pleasant, tree-lined street. With just the three of them to take care of, and now Edna, Easter had plenty of time to do whatever pleased her. It pleased her to read a lot. She spent most of her time in front of the bay window that overlooked their well tended garden, her feet propped on an ottoman and a knitted throw over her lap, reading a book or the latest issue of Harper's Bazaar. Tiny gold-rimmed reading glasses perched low on her narrow nose.

Though she seemed to enjoy this pastime, even that failed to bring a smile to her lovely face. Edna gradually took on more and more of the household chores and cooking responsibility, as Easter withdrew into herself.

Fortunately, Grace was rather self-sufficient, requiring very little tending. Or company, for that matter. It felt to Edna as though they all lived in the same house, but separately. She would catch Easter gazing affectionately at Grace, but she didn't seem to know how to reach out to her. They didn't hug as Edna and mama had. Maybe that was why aunt Easter was so sad. Edna hugged her once, after they had all enjoyed a treat of homemade peach ice cream on the front porch. It seemed the most natural thing in the world to Edna. Her hug was met with a stiff response, Easter leaning noticeably back, away from the embrace. Edna silently vowed not to do that again. She wanted to please aunt Easter, not make her uncomfortable.

Edna was making a concerted effort to learn to be sensitive to the moods and needs of others. How else could she be sure of not making waves? She didn't want to have to leave again and start over somewhere else. Her uncle Jonathan was kind and loving to her. If Easter was less than warm, at least she didn't lock Edna out of the house. She fed her and was not demanding of her in terms of "earning her keep". She figured she could be much worse off.

If only Grace hadn't been so resentful of sharing her room. She complained every single day about Edna's "stuff" being everywhere, crowding all of Grace's toys. In truth, Edna had very little to store, but she tried to keep her things out of the way. She couldn't do much about having to share Grace's bed, however. She tried to make herself as tiny and inconspicuous as possible; unlike Grace who sprawled out as far as her arms and legs could reach to cover the small bed, daring Edna to make contact and give her reason to explode.

For some reason, Grace didn't want Edna's "ugly old quilt" on her bed. Not even as humid summer evenings turned into brisk fall nights. Even in winter, it seemed Grace would rather freeze than allow Edna's quilt on her bed. Edna went along with Grace, after all it was her room and her bed. But she missed the comfort of her quilt terribly.

It never occurred to Edna that her cousin could be jealous of her. Jealous of a homeless orphan with no treasure to her name but a rag doll and a homemade quilt, beginning to fray at the seams. Grace had Jonathan and Easter. And porcelain dolls and soft teddy bears to play with, any time she wanted. Since Christmas, she had a new soft down comforter in her favorite shade of lilac. But Grace didn't have a quilt, lovingly made by Grandmother Gillen. Grandmother Gillen had died before she could finish Grace's quilt, and it was folded away in a chest somewhere, forgotten and unfinished.

Along with hating Edna's ugly quilt, Grace hated that ridiculous rag doll, with silly embroidered words framing her face, and one eye now missing. One Indian Summer evening, Grace saw Edna sitting with Jonathan on the porch swing. They were watching fireflies flit around the yard, in the deepening twilight. Edna was talking and laughing with Grace's papa. Grace went straight to her room and threw the doll away, unable to bear that loathsome creature giving her its one-eyed stare.

It was Jonathan who found the doll in the trash, with one bird-house-embroidered arm protruding. He asked Edna about it.

"You don't want your doll anymore, Edna?"

How did Baby-Modene find her way into the trash? Edna reclaimed her doll and from then on kept her in her valise, under the bed. *I'm too old for dolls, anyway.*

In the end, it wasn't possible to be invisible enough. Easter was clearly unhappy this past year with Edna, and it seemed Miss Grace Evangelina Gillen didn't have the grace her name implied to adjust to sharing her room, her things and her parents with another child. Easter sadly reflected that it was just as well the Lord had not seen fit to bless them with other children, after Grace. On the other hand, if He had, perhaps Grace might have been happier, better adjusted. Well, there was no use crying over spilled milk. What was, simply was.

Jonathan had to admit that it wasn't working out, having Edna here. He hadn't truly believed it would, but he'd had to try. He would be seeing his sister, Corrine next week and he'd see what she could suggest.

Corrine was the oldest of the Gillen children and she and her husband, Allen had lost their only babies, twins born too early and too tiny, the winter after the couple was married. No other children came along and it was understood that discussion of the subject was taboo. Corrine's own twin sister, Noreen, had died at birth. Though twins ran in the family, it wasn't always a lucky happenstance.

Jonathan didn't figure Corrine would be apt to take Edna because they were getting too old, and Corrine's house would not lend itself well to children. She had pointedly declined to offer to take Edna in the past but, maybe she'd have another idea.

When Jonathan posed the problem to his sister over tea, she was surprisingly sympathetic. On impulse, she offered to take Edna in.

She had no idea how she would manage caring for a child and still keep up with her civic duties, but then she really had no idea of what would be involved in having a child in her home, full-time.

She'd had neighbor children in from time to time and had dealt with nieces and nephews at family gatherings and of course, her students, but rarely in her own home. She avoided playing hostess whenever possible unless it was for an occasion when she could reasonably exclude children. Not because she didn't like them, but she worried about her belongings. After all, many of her furnishings and household adornments were family heirlooms. Most of them had been brought over from England by her family, and they couldn't be replaced.

The Cookson's spotless Victorian home, just south of Springfield, reflected the old English proverb: "Elbow grease is the best polish", handed down to Corrine by her mother along with the family heirlooms. The watchwords were emblazoned on a sampler in the parlor, as well as on her soul.

The décor was centered around fragile knickknacks and frilly crocheted doilies. Priscilla curtained windows looked out on a wide veranda, skirted by lilac bushes. A small parson's table in front of the bay window overlooking the side yard was decked out in a "cigar ribbon table cover", painstakingly pieced and quilted by Corrine. Her mother had taught her the technique of using narrow cigar ribbons to create the stylish accessory, being careful to incorporate only parts of the ribbons with brand names, into perfectly even silken rows. Each edge had fluttery ribbon tails falling exactly two inches, Corrine's own creative touch. This piece was her pride and joy. A fitting spot for the Cookson's newfangled radio.

When Corrine and Allen Cookson were married, Corrine gave up teaching and looked forward to making a home for her husband and starting a family. Not having children of her own was a great loss to Corinne. Had she continued teaching it would have helped fill the gap. Now she'd been away from her career long enough that she really missed her students. She'd been an excellent teacher, but remembered mostly the fun, the challenges and rewards.

After retiring, she had compensated by filling her time with quilting and other handwork, spending hours each day on one project or another, often made as gifts for her family. Her mother had tried to teach her glove-making but Corrine never achieved her mother's degree of perfection. The skills learned at her mother's knee caught on though, and took a path of their own. She would all her life devote much of her time to needlework of some sort or another, and find reward and relaxation in her crafting.

Corrine had resisted taking Edna in the beginning for two reasons. For one thing, she felt she and her husband Allen were too old to take on a child to raise, her brother's or anyone else's. Secondly, she was afraid she would become too attached to her and they weren't really in a position, financially, to assume responsibility for a child. Having long ago given up the thought of having their own children, she and Allen had built their lives around their own comforts and interests.

Corrine wouldn't have admitted to anyone that she might have fancied that she and Edna, her brother's orphaned daughter, would hit it off and come to enjoy a special relationship. Edna couldn't replace Corrine's lost twins, of course, but maybe she could enjoy a kind of vicarious motherhood through helping to raise her brother's child. This was an opportunity. Maybe for both of them.

Corinne began to look forward to having Edna for awhile to fuss over and share woman things with. Perhaps they could quilt and crochet together. Yes, that might be fun. She anticipated enjoying their afternoon tea and delicate tea sandwiches. She never failed to get compliments on her own special recipe treats. Perhaps some '*Vanilla Milk Tea*, or *Cambric Tea*', as some called it. Corrine had maintained her parents' habit of serving afternoon tea in her "parlor", always using the formal sterling silver tea service, from England of course. Many years before they met, her parents had both immigrated from

England, and their families settled near each other, in Deer Creek, Missouri, near Lewis Station. The neighboring families became acquainted and eventually intertwined.

Even as a young girl, Corrine had ensconced herself at the center of social life in Lewis Station. Her name appeared in the social column nearly every week for a number of events or causes. She was president of her church's Ladies Aid Society, and a founding member of the newly formed Kickapoo Cemetery Committee. She had held office on the board of the Lewis Station Historical Society since its inception, and was dedicated to identifying and preserving all the local historical sites in and around Lewis Station, a daunting task. Her large parlor was the regular meeting place for the Lewis Station Quilting Guild.

Corrine was a pillar of society and entertained grand notions of introducing Edna to Lewis Station society and involving her in her many community activities. *You're never too young to develop an interest in community service. It's the kind of thing that stays with you and gives you purpose, all your life.*

Jonathan and Easter knew better than to descend on Corrine with both Grace and Edna in tow. They left Grace with a neighbor for the day and took only Edna when they went to Lewis Station to deliver her and her meager belongings to Corrine and Allen.

Corrine had invited them to come early and stay for lunch. She had prepared tea and sandwiches, and for dessert, small wedges of scrumptious Southern pecan pie. Corrine's simple luncheon had taken her all morning to prepare. She wanted everything to be perfect. She must make the proper impression on Edna, set the tone for their relationship. Allen had agreed to come home from the mercantile precisely at noon and join them for lunch. That was when things began to go wrong.

Allen arrived home at exactly noon and immediately noted there was no evidence of the arrival of his in-laws. He knew it was of less concern to him than it would be to Corrine. Failure to be punctual was a major issue for Corrine. All of her students learned the value of punctuality, early on. Allen was met at the front door by his agitated wife, wringing blue-veined hands in frustration and worry.

Corrine tilted the face on her pendant watch to read the hands, and her furrowed brow knit in increasing rows.

"Something terrible must have happened!" She absently offered her cheek for her husband's kiss, and began pacing the floor.

"Now Angel, don't get your panties in a bunch. They'll be here any minute. What say we have a soothing cup of chamomile tea? By the time we get settled, I'm sure they'll be at the door. You know your brother is dependable."

Allen took his wife's elbow and guided her into the cheery kitchen, past a raucous canary with the unlikely name of Romeo, pining noisily for his Juliet.

"Hush, Romeo. We'll keep you company."

A half hour later their tea cups were drained, and their small talk had died a natural death. Romeo dozed on his perch. A well-trained Allen rose and carried their tea cups to the sink to rinse them out. They were both startled when they heard a knock at the door.

"There they are now", Allen said lightly, with a pat on Corrine's shoulder.

Corrine rushed to the door and recognized the lace shrouded faces beyond the curtained oval window in the door. She took a quick peek in an ornate mirror on the entryway wall, assessing her appearance. It wouldn't do to answer the door without making sure her salt and pepper finger waves were neatly in place. She was appalled at the lined face gazing back at her, pale with worry. She pinched her cheeks for color and tried to call up a jollity she didn't feel.

When she opened the door, Romeo trilled a welcome as if on cue and Corrine gave herself away with too hearty hugs for her brother and his wife, ignoring Easter's dislike of such displays. She ushered her guests inside, with exclamations of concern over possible difficulties. If she'd hoped to conceal her worry, she didn't succeed.

Seeing her somewhat gangly niece, dressed as she was in a clean but shabby, faded chemise dress, Corrine's hopefulness wavered slightly. "Hello, Edna. We haven't seen you in quite some time. You've certainly grown, since…"

Her unfinished sentence hung in the air between them. *How could I be so stupid!* It would have been an unforgivable social indiscretion to bring up Edna's father's funeral! Corrine's cheeks flushed with embarrassment and she hurried on, vowing to herself to get her emotions under control. "Come in, come in."

"Hello aunt Corrine, uncle Allen."

Corrine couldn't take her eyes off of her niece as Easter and Jonathan began removing their coats. If Allen hadn't taken their things for them, they might have held them all afternoon.

"I'm sorry we're late", Jonathan rushed to explain, knowing his sister's intolerance of tardiness. "Had trouble getting the darn car started, then Grace didn't want to stay with Mrs. Devine. She forgot some of her things and we had to double back for them."

"Well, you're here now, that's the important thing. Did you have a good trip otherwise?" Corrine was smiling, though it was obvious she was unnerved.

They exchanged pleasantries and took seats in the parlor as Allen headed for the kitchen. He returned with the tea service and a plate of sandwiches, offering apologies for having to leave right away and get back to the store.

"Thank you, dear. Are you sure you can't stay just a bit?"

"No, I must get back. We're short-handed today."

He chucked Edna under the chin. "I'll see you later, little one."

"Well, good to see you Jonathan, Easter." The men shook hands and Allen waved a goodbye to his sister-in-law. He kissed Corrine on the cheek and wished them all a pleasant visit. Nothing in his manner betrayed his concerns. *Lord knows, Corrine's heart's in the right place*. He hoped it would work out. He didn't want to see either Corrine or Edna hurt. They'd both had enough pain in their lives. If it didn't work, he had no idea what would happen to Edna, but he wasn't at all sure that Corrine could handle it. He didn't know what to expect when he returned home from work.

The afternoon visit turned out to be short. Easter was anxious to get home to Grace and she felt more than a little guilty to be passing Edna off onto her elderly in-laws. Certainly Corrine was too set in her ways and too busy to fit a child into her life. In spite of the difficulties it had caused for her personally to have Edna, it tore at her heart to say goodbye to her.

Edna's little valise sat next to her by the Queen Anne chair, with her quilt folded beside it. Edna listened quietly as the adults talked. She sipped her sweet tea from the bone china cup, absorbed with the hand painted mauve roses and cornflower blue forget-me-nots. Her tea was laced with a tasty combination of milk and vanilla, and the aroma of the vanilla called up sweet memories of her mama.

Edna was so caught up in her dreams, it didn't register when she heard the clatter of breaking china. Until she felt a burning on her legs as the spilled tea soaked through her thin chemise. She jumped to her feet, feeling terrible to realize that the shattered cup and saucer were hers and she was responsible for the tea stain spreading out, discoloring the beautiful heirloom chair that had belonged to Grandmother Gillen, and her mother's mother, before her. Her eyes went wide with shock and disbelief.

"Oh dear!" Corrine was unaware the thought had escaped her lips.

"Oh, I'm so sorry aunt Corrine."

Tears began to well up in Edna's eyes. She feared her future was suddenly in doubt. In an instant, things could change. She'd been trying so hard to make the right decisions, do everything right, act like a lady.

Through tears of her own, Corrine found herself saying, "It's…alright, Edna dear…" Corrine smiled weakly and dashed to the kitchen, as fast as Corrine could dash, returning with a damp cloth. She began to dab at her treasured chair. Gradually the tea stain faded and became just a damp spot on the tan petit point fabric, and Corrine was able to relax and let her pounding heart return to normal rhythm.

It didn't occur to anyone that the frightened child, now standing next to the chair, might need attention for her scalded legs.

Edna began gingerly gathering up the pieces of china into the palm of her hand. She didn't know what else she could do. Careful as she was, one tiny, jagged sliver sliced into her thumb. A drop of blood rushed over the edge of her thumb and with horror, Edna realized it was going to fall on her treasured quilt. She closed her hand and squeezed off the flow of blood, staring at the telltale crimson stain seeping into the satin rose. No one else had noticed and she wasn't going to bring it to anyone's attention. She even managed not to react to the throbbing in her thumb. Things were bad enough already.

With the crisis of the tea stain resolved, it seemed a good time for Jonathan and Easter to make their exit. Before Corrine could change her mind. After their departure, Corrine and Edna were both uncomfortably quiet, neither one sure of what to do next. Edna still clenched her fist, lest any blood escape and call attention to yet another social blunder.

Corrine broke the silence with a cheerful invitation. "Well, Edna, you must be tired. I'll show you to your room. The bathroom is next to your room and you may freshen up before your uncle gets home"

Edna was wide-eyed with wonder at the fairy tale room that was to be hers during her stay. Her eyes slowly swept the room in amazement. Never had she seen or imagined anything like it. Corrine's pleasure lit her face.

The upper walls were papered in soft pink rosebuds, and a pale green chair rail topped whitewashed wainscoting. Sheer white curtains veiled a large bay window above a cozy window seat. The open window overlooked a small garden and a rose scented breeze wafted into the room, billowing the curtains. Massive dark oak furniture filled the room. An antique sleigh bed was made up with a cotton candy pink, biscuit quilted comforter, edged in white eyelet. Elegant ruby glass hobnail lamps flanked the bed and deep ruffles on crocheted doilies stood at starched attention, circling beneath them.

Variegated pink pansy-patterned doilies adorned the dressers and a vanity table, very much like Lily's. Precious, glittering glass bottles of various sizes and shapes mingled with old photos and tintypes in heavy frames, on every surface.

The drawers of the lace-skirted vanity had been emptied. It was more than ample. One small drawer was a perfect fit for mama's Bible. Between its pages, like a secret, hid real treasures. Mama's pressed wildflowers, like fragile memories. They would be safe and readily available in this perfect space.

"Bring a change of clothing Edna, and I'll show you to the powder room. Oh, and maybe you needn't bother with a hair bow anymore. They make you look like you're about to take wing and fly away. You're a young lady now, and you must act like one. You'll find that the young ladies in town are more apt to wear a narrow satin ribbon. It's much more ladylike. We'll go shopping for some suitable clothes tomorrow. I want to be proud to introduce my pretty young niece."

Silently, Edna hastily pulled a set of underwear and stockings from her bag, along with a clean eyelet pinafore. She followed Corrine down the hall to the powder room, where Corrine began to draw a bath in the big old claw-foot tub. Corrine emptied a handful of course ground, pale blue crystals, her own 'Mint Soother Bath Salts', into the free flowing water. She laid out plum colored bath linens.

"I'll leave you alone, dear. Please don't dawdle. Allen likes dinner precisely at five. I'll want your help in the kitchen."

Corrine stepped out of the sweet smelling room and closed the door behind her, smiling tentatively. She whispered her thoughts of satisfaction to herself. *"I think that went well enough. We're going to be just fine."*

Inside the large gabled bathroom, the air was filling with mint-scented steam, and Edna's senses were overwhelmed. She reluctantly stepped out of her tea stained dress and pulled off her shoes and stockings, tasting the foamy bath water with one foot. It was deliciously warm and welcoming. When she stepped into the silky water and lowered herself, the hot water slightly stung her scalded legs.

She lay back against the cool porcelain, closing her eyes, hardly daring to believe this was real. Minty froth edged up and touched her chin, startling her. She sat up abruptly to shut off the spigot and sloshed bath water onto the whitewashed wooden floor. She reached for a towel, dropping it into the puddle she'd made, then leaned back again, intoxicated with the luxury of this new experience.

Everything she needed was in easy reach, waiting on a wooden corner shelf, near the spigot. Every single thing smelled so wonderful. Edna luxuriated in the heavenly aroma of the soap and shampoo. She decided she agreed with Corrine. She felt very much the young lady and suddenly wished this fragrant bath, this heavenly, pampered feeling, would last forever. This was far and away the most feminine luxury Edna had ever experienced.

After a time, a gentle knock on the door interrupted Edna's reverie. "Edna, you need to dress and come downstairs. It's getting late."

"Yes, aunt Corrine, I'm drying off." Pulling the plug produced a loud gurgling, giving away her fib. Embarrassed, she retrieved the slightly soggy towel and did her best to oblige her aunt by drying off and dressing quickly. Magically, as she stepped out into the hall, soft strains of the Benson Orchestra's rendition of "The World is Waiting for the Sunrise" playing on the radio, wafted up the stairs and found its way to her feet, coaxing them into a natural, almost lyrical gait.

Unfortunately, the spilled tea incident of the first day foreshadowed the weeks to come. Edna seemed always on the verge of acceptance, but she never quite met Corrine's expectations. It turned out she wasn't a very apt student of needle arts, try as she might. She really wanted to please Corrine but her stitches were never quite small enough or straight enough. She couldn't seem to master the critical rhythm of "rocking" of the needle through all the layers of quilting and was less than nimble at manipulating the fabrics.

Edna was frustrated and disappointed. Corrine was more so. In all their time together, spent in instruction of needlework, the only thing Edna seemed to master was how to crochet circles. She enjoyed the success she achieved in making them and their uniformity. And so she repeated this one item, over and over. She made dozens, and then dozens more. In all the colors of the rainbow. She used up all of her aunt's yarn scraps creating a basketful of circles with no plan for their use.

Finally, aunt Corrine asked her what she planned to do with them. When Edna said she didn't know, Corrine suggested she join them into strips and showed her how to crochet them together.

"Now, if you join the strips together, you'll have a lovely afghan. Edna's Afghan of Many Colors!"

Joining the strips, Edna nested them so that the rounded edge of a circle, fit into the hollow of the two circles next to it, where they came together. This developed into a scalloped border, top and bottom. When the strips were joined together, Corrine showed Edna how to fringe the ends, and using the matching color for the edge of each circle, it gave the appearance of the color of the circle flowing down into the fringe. Edna was thrilled with her creation, and it gave Corrine some sense of satisfaction, as well. At least she'd been able to accomplish something with the girl, and her time and talent weren't totally wasted.

Other homemaking skills continued to elude Edna, to Corrine's obvious dismay. No amount of time spent working on projects met with much success. Still, they struggled on, Edna trying to fit in, and Corrine trying to fit Edna into her busy schedule and into the proper circles. Having responsibility for her niece seriously compromised Corrine's routine. Edna was living in the lap of luxury, in comparison to her previous life. She enjoyed it, but it wasn't a really comfortable fit. It was no substitute for being with people you were genuinely close to.

Things might have continued this way until Edna reached adulthood or until Corrine suffered a fatal attack of apoplexy, if fate had not intervened. Corrine's nerves were fraying and Edna was ever aware she was falling short of her aunt's expectations. The unexpected letter from aunt Babe couldn't have come at a better time.

Babe was happy to share some good news for a change. Tim had received a promotion at the academy and they had moved into larger quarters. He was now in a position of some authority and even power. Babe was hoping that she and Tim might be able to have Edna come and stay with them for awhile. That is, if Corrine wouldn't mind. An observer would be hard pressed to say who was more excited or pleased at the prospect—Edna or Corrine.

School would be letting out for the Christmas holiday, Babe's letter continued and, except for some remedial help for a few of the boys, Tim would have a breather. They could come for Edna the last weekend in December, if that met with Corrine and Allen's approval. Several letters were exchanged between the two sisters as arrangements were finalized.

Corrine was plagued with doubts. She considered withdrawing her consent but she hadn't been feeling well and she knew the stress of trying to keep up with everything was wearing her down. Still she was torn, right up until her last day with Edna. The nine months she'd mothered her niece, was akin to carrying a baby, and it was difficult to let her go.

At the last minute, as she and Edna said their goodbyes, Corrine held back her feelings, not wanting to make it any more difficult for Edna or for herself. She wished Allen had been able to stay home that morning. The house would feel so empty, once she was alone again.

"Goodbye, then, Edna. You take care now." Surely the child knew how much she loved her, she needn't draw her a picture. *Why make it more difficult?*

Edna took Corrine's reserve as a lack of feeling and so she held back as well. She really would miss Corrine and Allen, and the luxuries that staying there had afforded her, but she didn't want to impose herself any longer. It was just as well to get on with the exchange. Besides she couldn't wait to get home with Babe and Tim and see what the academy was like.

Tim and Babe stood on the front porch and Edna held Gavin awkwardly. Gavin's chubby fingers trailed in Edna's curls and he bubbled with delight. Edna was in heaven. They all waved goodbye, and piled into the Alden's dust coated Studebaker Erksine, anxious to be on the road.

Taking advantage of the unseasonably warm December weather, aunt Babe had packed a picnic basket, and just before passing through Adamsville they parked the car along a country road and found a spot by a small creek to enjoy their late lunch.

The sun dripped like warm honey onto their golden afternoon. This was the best—aunt Babe's fried chicken and biscuits, shared with family she loved. Good times. *I'm going to save this day, like a pressed flower memory. I'll tuck it away in mama's Bible with her wild flowers. When will there ever be a better one, for me?*

They wouldn't be going by the old Gillen place, but Babe planned to offer Edna the opportunity to stop by the cemetery. They all needed fortification, in case the visit to Edna's parents' graves proved difficult.

"Edna, your uncle and I would like to stop by Adamsville Cemetery, if it's all right with you. Would you like that?"

Caught off guard, mid-bite, Edna fairly choked on her fried chicken. Her mind began racing. *Like it?* She wouldn't have described her feelings that way. It would be good to go by there, but maybe they could do it another time. She wasn't ready.

Babe understood Edna's reluctance. "You know it's quite a distance from the academy. It might be awhile before we get back this way. This far north."

Put that way, it took only a moment to decide. Of course she wanted to go by. It had been a long time.

"Do I have time to gather some flowers?" Her hopeful question, directed at her uncle Tim. "I have to take mama some flowers"

Tim couldn't resist Edna's sweet gesture. "Of course, Edna, if you can find some. But make it quick. We want to try and be home by dark."

Edna put the remains of her drumstick into a paper sack and stood up, shaking crumbs from her lap. She looked around and spotted a patch of rust colored, dried buckwheat that would do for a start.

Edna disappeared over the brow of a low hill and returned a few moments later with a fistful of winterfat, their papery white blossoms creating a rather pleasing effect against the dark tones of the buckwheat. She'd found a few cattails by the stream and a tattered plume of pampas grass. Her fingers bore small razor cuts from the pampas grass, but she hardly noticed. *I wish mama could see them. I wish she knew how much I miss her and daddy.*

Their belongings were packed and ready to be loaded back into the car when Edna returned. She offered to carry Gavin to the car, enjoying breathing in his little-boyness on the way.

Soon they swung into the drive of Adamsville Cemetery, lonely and empty at this time of day. Tim followed the familiar serpentine course and located the gravestones easily. Edna found herself in the familiar muddle. It wasn't fair. It really wasn't.

She read the dates again on her mother's headstone. "BORN OCTOBER 31, 1891—DIED NOVEMBER 23, 1918". *What of the in between? What about daddy, and me? What of my baby brother? Was this all there was?* It wasn't enough.

"I brought these flowers for you mama. I love you." She laid her small bundle of winter gatherings on top of Lily's headstone. *Why did you have to leave me, Mama?*

Her gaze shifted to her father's grave next to Lily's.

"Hello, Daddy. I miss you. I didn't bring you any flowers but you can share mama's." After a long pause, "I'm being a good girl."

Well, she was trying to be good. She wouldn't want her father to be disappointed in her. Just in case he was somewhere watching her, like a guardian angel or something.

Edna couldn't think of anything else to say. She didn't know what she was supposed to feel. She stood there a moment longer, in uneasy silence.

"I'm ready to go", she announced, suddenly overwhelmed with sadness.

Walking back to the car, Edna kept her eyes on Babe's back, on Gavin's cherubic face bobbing over Babe's shoulder, anything but her surroundings in Adamsville Cemetery. Sad as she felt, she realized this was the first time since her father's death, she was able to think of them here and manage not to cry. She drew some comfort from the realization that they were together. Something she hadn't thought about before.

En route to Holmes Academy, Edna was glad to have Gavin's company in the back seat until he fell asleep, leaving her to her own thoughts and dreams. Miles of open prairie droned by, dissolving into an ever changing horizon. Edna amused herself by creating and recreating the fantasy her mind held of the "fancy, Indian boys' school" that her stepmother had scorned.

Nothing her imagination conjured up could have prepared her for conditions at what was to be her new home, or the scene that greeted them, as they arrived.

STEP 3:
Season With Bitter Roots

Season with bitter roots

To Edna, It looked like a game at first, or some sort of ceremonial dance. Two rows of Indian boys, another young boy scuffling along between the two lines his head down, arms flailing. Edna caught only glimpses of his youthful face, long trailing fingers of red, snaking down each cheek.

War paint! Like on the cigar store Indian in front of Doc Raine's store. *How primitive and exciting!* Edna was fascinated. She had never seen war paint, never seen a "real" Indian. Well, Grandmother Townsley was one-quarter Cherokee, but that was different.

Shouts of excitement rose above the participants' heads, and were lost on a swirl of fierce, Oklahoma wind. Only two adults were present, one standing at each end of the lines, cheering wildly, gleefully it seemed. It was as though they were rooting for someone but for whom?

As Tim Alden wheeled the car to a dust-enveloped stop, he growled something under his breath and launched himself from behind the wheel and out the door, leaving the engine running, and Edna bewildered.

"Be careful, Tim!", his wife cautioned. She knew how her husband felt about the "hot line", and that he'd butted heads before with the school superintendent, Mr. Thornbury, in an attempt to get the disciplinary practice outlawed. The gauntlet, as it was also called, was a cruel form of punishment whereby students were forced to beat their classmates wielding belts, sticks and hairbrushes. If the gauntlet, was ineffective, they had the "big guns"—makeshift jails where students were chained, sometimes for days. The goal of the punishment was simple. To strip the Indian boys of their culture, their language, their spirituality. The goal was to turn them into white boys, make them acceptable.

By the time Tim reached the group, the beaten boy had reached the end of the line and was on his knees in the dirt, fists clenched in raw rage. The teacher, Mr. Wolf was bent over at the waist, hands on his knees smirking openly at his target. The fingers of blood snaking down the boy's cheeks seemed to fan to life, flames of the teacher's own smoldering rage.

"What's that you were sayin' boy?" Mr. Wolf gestured to his mouth, distorted in an ugly sneer. "That gibberish supposed to mean somethin'? You know we don't allow no Indian talk here. You don't hear me talkin' like that."

The boy raised his head in defiance, staring into the distance, beyond his tormentor's shoulder, refusing to give the half-breed teacher the satisfaction of casting his eyes down, as though he were afraid. But he wouldn't look him in the eye, either.

Grey Wolf was livid that his student wouldn't yield. "You look at me when I'm talkin' to you…"

"Hold it Wolf!", Tim bellowed, intercepting the intended blow. "You know better! It wasn't that long ago that you were this boy. You've been there!"

"Yeah, I've been there an' that's how I know. I'm only tryin' to help him. If he wants to amount to anythin' in this white man's world, he's gotta learn. Where do you think I'd be today if I still went around wearin' medicine bundles and braids?"

There was nothing more to be said. Tim's eyes held Grey Wolf's and it was communication enough. Frustrated and unwilling to admit defeat, Grey Wolf broke the trance and dismissed his students with one final dig.

"This is the last time I'm warnin' you. You better learn, boy." Then, glaring at his accuser, Grey Wolf hitched up his pants and sauntered off.

Learn? Maybe it was too late for Grey Wolf, but not for the boys. Tim would write more letters. He'd invite President Coolidge himself to come and visit the school. If the politicians could see first hand how the Indian children were treated, here and across the country, they couldn't help but be ashamed.

Tim sighed in resignation and walked back to the car and his family, his sloping shoulders giving mute testimony to his own shame to be a part of this system. Wearily, he considered the unusually cruel punishment, for even Grey Wolf to mete out. Normally, the price to pay for the high crime of lapsing into one's native tongue was to force the offender to eat lye soap.

As it happened, this unpardonable crime was committed on a particularly bad day for the former boarding school resident, now teaching boys from a similar background. Early that morning, the anniversary of his brother's death, Grey Wolf had visited Holmes cemetery to pay his respects. Damn sure no one else would.

Grey Wolf and his brother, Eagle Feather had surrendered their childhoods at a government Indian boys' school not unlike Holmes. Taken from their parents in their youth, they'd been kept isolated from their family in order to protect them from "contamination" with their native culture.

After their parents died when the boys were teenagers, Grey Wolf and Eagle Feather were fortunate to be moved to Holmes Christian Indian Academy, where punishments were less severe and there was more of a sense of hope.

While living there, both boys were farmed out as hired hands during maize harvest. It was there that Eagle Feather fell from a combine and was badly injured. Later that night he died, before he could be sent "home", as was customary with seriously injured or ill residents. Masquerading as kindness, this practice served to effectively conceal tragic statistics. As with hundreds of others, only a small white cross marked his resting place. Grey Wolf was the only visitor to his forgotten brother's grave. Even Tim didn't know the heartbreak he was reliving on this painful day.

At supper that night Babe's husband was still seething and had little interest in the sumptuous pot roast she set before him. His beefy hands lay idle by his plate.

"You know brooding about it won't change a thing".

"I know, but I just don't understand how coming from the same system, Grey Wolf can turn around and…"

"But that's exactly why. Surely you can see, it's what he learned."

"Still, he's a grown man! He oughtta be able put to that aside, see these boys as human beings. Seems he'd have vowed never ever to treat a child as he was treated. It doesn't make any sense to me." An edge crept into his voice.

"But we all do that, dear. Yet we do the same things, things we knew even as children were wrong. Or we go too far in the opposite direction, like an inevitable pendulum. It's hard to find a middle ground, somewhere between what we learned at our parents hands, and what we know in our hearts. Don't you see, he feels he has no value as an Indian? He doesn't want his students to be treated poorly because, as Indians, so many people will see them as inferior. I guess his own pain has never gone away."

Tempers were starting to flare and Babe didn't want to pursue the subject during supper. She sighed gently. A knowing look and her head inclined toward the children emphasized her cautionary words. "Little pitchers have big ears, husband."

Tim looked at Edna's and Gavin's eyes, peering at him with some degree of curiosity and confusion. He smiled meekly and let the subject drop. Stuffing his anger for the moment, he redirected his energy by stabbing savagely at a helpless hunk of beef.

For Edna, any confusion stemmed from a vague awareness that she was "part Indian", herself. She'd heard it mentioned, but she knew some of her family denied it. If her Grandmother was one-quarter Cherokee, what was she? Part Cherokee? What part? She contemplated her long white arms and the white hands sprouting from them.

Maybe that's why no one wanted her. No one but this dear aunt and uncle who shared their home with her. If they were part Indian too, maybe it didn't matter to them that she was inferior. That her aunt Babe Gillen Alden was on her father's side of the family and the Cherokee blood was on her mother's, escaped her.

As Edna helped clear the table, Babe noticed, she couldn't resist finishing up the scraps from Gavin's little bowl. It seemed Edna couldn't bear to throw food scraps to the animals, as was the Alden household custom. It was too good to waste. Thus began an insidious habit that would be hard to break. Babe didn't mention it to Edna, but she shook her head, curious about what Edna had been subjected to, that she would appear so ravenous after a perfectly satisfying meal. Babe didn't hear Lily's musical voice as Edna did, ringing in her ears—*Waste not, want not.*

Edna began to settle into a routine at the academy that was mostly enjoyable, and she adjusted fairly easily, largely due to the love and acceptance of Babe and Tim and the joy of sharing everyday life in this loving family. She adored Gavin and participating in his care.

Accommodations at Holmes Academy were somewhat cramped and primitive. The Aldens were fortunate to have their own quarters, separate from the dorm, and though their small cabin wasn't equipped with a bathroom, under each bed resided a chamber pot. Having her own pot was a far cry from the pitiful excuse for a bathroom, in the classroom, essentially a row of chamber pots lined up in a coat closet with a cluster of the ever-present coat hangers dangling over the students' heads, literally as well as figuratively. No matter what, Edna made sure to defer her bathroom visits on school days, until after she got home.

School had always been relatively easy for Edna and it was even more so at Holmes Academy. Classes were structured to give students the basics, much of which was already second nature to the bright young girl, but the leisurely pace was more than welcome.

There were really only two negative aspects to school days at the academy. One was the other students. The only girls at the academy belonged to families of the director and other staff. The government had the foresight to create separate boarding schools for the girls and boys, in order to make the transition easier. It assured less distraction as well as eliminating the worry of perpetuating the Indian culture by providing potential same culture mates in the future. It was well understood by the resident boys that they were not to "socialize" with white children of either sex. The students, being mostly boys, challenged their educators at every opportunity and often fought among themselves, which Edna found distracting. The other negative was the uniforms, common grounds for objection for all students. Not that Edna had ever been a clothes horse, mind you, but the dull as dishwater uniform jumpers did nothing for any sense of fashion Edna might have wanted to develop.

For the boys fashion wasn't their concern, it was much more personal. They were forced to abandon their tribal clothing in favor of foreign feeling, stiff white shirts and knickers the color of stale gravy. Moccasins and jewelry were not allowed. With their hair cut short, they barely recognized their own empty faces. They were forced to attend Christian services, renouncing their tribal religion, and marching with military discipline, something Edna and the other girls were exempt from.

Holmes' library was a favorite place for Edna to spend her time. It had been since her first visit there. Library was actually too grand a word for the narrow cubicle that housed the academy's small store of books and reference materials. Wood paneled walls were lined with over-stuffed bookshelves. Two tables and several mismatched, wooden and cane-backed chairs, held center stage. One table served to hold newspapers and current periodicals such as "Life" and "The Old Farmer's Almanac". The other table was dedicated to studying.

The most comfortable spot in the library was a huge leather chair, angled into a corner by the only window in the dingy room. Before coming to Holmes Academy, reading had never been a preferred activity, but then Edna had never had access to so many books! She would curl up in that cozy niche and lose herself for hours in the world of books, sometimes reading and re-reading her favorites like Grimm's Fairy Tales, Arabian Nights and more.

When her lessons were completed and the library in order, if there were no students needing assistance, her time was her own and Edna made the most of it. She couldn't get enough of the library and its treasures. She loved it all—fiction, non-fiction, the maps and gazetteers, the dictionaries and encyclopedias.

Within just a few months Edna greedily consumed dozens of books. Wonderful stories like Uncle Tom's Cabin, wherein she easily identified with the little orphan slave girl, Topsy. Sometimes she felt like she was just like her. That she too, had "just growed", like Topsy.

She read everything she could get her hands on that pertained to medical practices, home remedies using herbs and other medicinals. How they worked and why. In time she developed a keen interest in the life of Florence Nightingale and her struggles. Now there was a noble calling—nursing, helping others. It was suddenly clear as well water what she wanted to do with her own life. Something where she could help others, nursing even. Maybe.

Edna quickly mastered the task of shelving books in proper order and became the right hand assistant to the official librarian, Mrs. Thornbury. Classes took up the first half of the day and students rarely had opportunities to avail themselves of the library and its resources. The balance of the residents' day, was spent at hard labor, either working on construction at the school, farming, or maintenance of academy livestock and beehives. Holmes Academy honey was the best around and served as a cash crop, though it was not made available to those who nurtured it. Many students were farmed out as hired help, as was customary in most Indian boarding schools. Holmes academy was the sole beneficiary of all wages earned.

When residents did find time for library visits, it was mostly because it was required. It often fell to Edna to help them and she found great pleasure in being of use. It made her feel special again, and needed.

Short school days, built around the duties that resident boys were required to perform, left Edna with time to herself. After her own chores were accomplished and Gavin was safely tucked into bed, she enjoyed that quiet time for reading from mama's Bible, partly as an excuse to re-examine the pressed wild flowers tucked between the pages by Lily, marking comforting passages. In touching them, she felt she could almost touch again, the memories associated with the faded blossoms.

The only really dark cloud hanging over the family was the unending conflict over treatment of the residents. Babe and Tim were constantly embroiled in a struggle to raise the quality of life at Holmes Academy. Current thinking of those in charge was still rooted in the past. Superintendent Thornbury quoted the words of those who went before him as though he were quoting Bible verses, or some Bible-thumping religious zealot.

"We deal with a primitive race, with persons who often lack appreciation of the reasons for good behavior". The gospel, according to John. John B. Brown, Phoenix Indian School Superintendent.

Indians must be forced to follow "the superior methods of the white man", preached in 1890 by Wellington Rich, first superintendent of Phoenix Indian School.

"Kill the Indian, save the man", prophesied by Gen. Richard Pratt, former commander of an Indian POW camp who, in 1879 founded the first off-reservation federal boarding school.

But Tim's all-time stupidity award would be accorded to U. S. Indian Commissioner, Thomas Morgan who said it was "cheaper to educate Indians than to kill them." His predecessor and hero, Carl Schurz, had calculated in 1882 that It cost nearly $1 million dollars to kill an Indian in battle, but for a mere $1,200, he could be maintained and educated for 8 years.

And what do you have then? Tim mused. A segment of the population of this great country who just don't like themselves. A people who think they are "bad", worthless, with no chance, no hope. A people who feel the taint of their Indian blood forces them to live in a nether world, not knowing where they truly belong.

In his heart, Tim knew that part of Grey Wolf's attitude sprang from a deep abiding resentment of his father for taking a squaw as his bride, forever branding their children as half-breeds, sealing them off from success in a white man's world. For placing him and his brother in that no man's land, not a true member of either race.

But Tim couldn't truly know what it was like to be Grey Wolf, who for most of his 47 years, had been taunted as an 'apple'—red on the outside, white on the inside. Grey Wolf, who in his darkest moments thought maybe he heard his brother calling to him from his grave behind the academy. Grey Wolf who more than once considered following in the moccasins of John Thomas, who couldn't live with not being able to decide which world he belonged in, never being accepted by either, and so, committed suicide.

There was another element to the discontent of Grey Wolf and many of the dorm workers and teachers. It was overwork. The ratio of 60 or more resident boys to one adult, was simply overwhelming. "No one here has time to do their job properly. It's sad but it's the god's truth." Babe was fond of pointing out to her husband, ever mindful that there is a reason for everything. *Or an excuse,* by Tim's book.

Not all dorm workers and teachers were abusive, some were like the Aldens, kind, trying hard to create a happy environment in the dorm. Tim counted himself among reformers like John Collier, who wrote of his beliefs in 1923, that it was a "beautiful, civilized life we are chopping to pieces."

Tim wanted change more than anything, and he wanted it yesterday. But it wasn't going to happen. Not now. Maybe not in his lifetime. Still, if he wasn't here, he couldn't do anything to help, to change the system. Deep down, he believed it would change, eventually. It had to. He might not have fought on so valiantly if he'd known how long it would take and that the government, his own government, would never apologize for the inhumane treatment.

So, more often than not, Tim felt helpless here, fighting an uphill battle. There were too many boarding school officials clinging to the old ways. In 1928 Washington officials ordered a halt to corporal punishment, but it was met with defiance and general disregard. It would be decades before significant change would come.

In the meantime, the Aldens struggled along making inroads wherever possible, living as best they could under the circumstances.

Babe usually found a way to bring some semblance of joy to mealtime. Meals weren't fancy but owing to Babe's creativity, they were satisfying and tasty. Plain food, conjured up from whatever was on hand or currently available in their small vegetable garden. Where Edna was used to her English relatives soothing tensions over tea, aunt Babe was more inclined toward sweet treats or a good, heaping serving of her specialty, 'Irelandish Potatoes', a delicious variation on mashed potatoes flavored with steamed, shredded cabbage and swimming in butter. Comfort food, she called it. "It'll fix anythin' that ails ya'", according to Chef Babe.

Holidays and birthdays also added some levity to their often humdrum existence. Edna's thirteenth birthday was just such an occasion. According to Babe, a girl's thirteenth birthday was a special one, and Edna had been allowed to Invite a friend for her birthday supper. She'd invited Susanna Thornbury, Director Thornbury's daughter. Of the few girls at Holmes, Susanna was the nearest to Edna's age, and the closest thing she had to a friend. It was the beginning of October and they hadn't yet received their allotment of flour, so birthday dessert was 'Charlotte Russe', because Babe happened to have ladyfingers on hand. It suited Edna just fine. It was her favorite anyway.

A single present from Babe and Tim was a delightful surprise. Edna was well aware that there was little money for extras, but somehow Babe had managed. The wrappings fell away as Edna excitedly tore open the package, revealing an exquisite hairbrush. Intricate patterns gleamed on the back and handle of the creamy pearl surface, inlaid with irregular pieces of mother of pearl. Pulling off her hair ribbon, the birthday girl slid the natural bristles through her curls and it fairly glided, like a hot knife through butter. She was so absorbed in the joy of it she didn't recognize the look of pure jealously it sparked in Susanna's eyes.

A perfect ending to a perfect day. She felt so grown up. Suddenly! As if it really happened at the magical moment that one day turns into another, a whole year falling away instantly, like when she fell through the ice in the pond at age three. Whack! Instantly.

It brought into focus for her how lucky she was, really. With everything that had happened, with all her losses, still she was here now, growing up with the Aldens. Many times she'd thought she'd die of a broken heart, like they all said happened with Grandpa Gillen when he'd lost Grandma. Other times she'd wished she'd just go to sleep and dream pleasant dreams and just never have to wake up. Never have to move again and start over. Maybe everything would turn out all right after all. Life was good.

Events were set in motion one unusually warm evening the following spring, that would change the course of Edna's life. It seemed like such a small thing, surely the aftermath was out of proportion. It was an accident, after all. Maybe if Edna hadn't been so tired that night, she would have remembered.

It had been a long day, for everyone, but especially for Edna. Gavin woke up early with bad dreams and Edna had gotten up to quiet him. She rocked him in the bent wood rocker, humming "You Are My Sunshine" into his downy hair. Aunt Babe had roused and come to the doorway, but Edna had put a finger to her lips and motioned her away. Babe had worked hard all day, preparing for a special Palm Sunday program with the students. Edna knew the next couple of days would be trying and busy, and she wanted to give her aunt a chance to get a little more rest.

Gavin finally nodded off in her arms and she carefully tucked him back in under his covers. Falling back onto her own bed, she lay awake too exhausted to fall asleep. Contrary to her aunt's instructions, Edna was in the habit of sleeping with the shade and window open, to watch the stars and breathe in the fresh, prairie air. She watched the sunrise play out, with the small east window in her room acting as a stage. A glorious performance with fingers of molten color reaching out across the sky like a fisherman's net, cast out to gather in errant, lingering stars.

Dragging herself out of bed and into the kitchen to start breakfast, Edna was joined by Babe and Tim, carrying Gavin on his shoulders. The small family began their busy day with strong coffee and *"Fried Corn Meal Mush"* with butter and honey. It was a step up from the thin gruel that would be portioned out to the residents. Edna counted this among her blessings, every day. She'd been too hungry, too many times and could not imagine having to eat so sparsely. But the food budget for residents was 11 cents a day. That sum provided each boy with watered-down oatmeal, moldy molasses and an anemic beverage the staff called coffee. Never mind what the boys called it.

Immediately after lunch that afternoon, Edna rushed to the library as she was to help a student research a paper on the thirteen original colonies.

Today's lesson was more challenging than most. She liked Joe. She really did, but he didn't seem to like her at all. It felt like he was resisting her every effort. She knew he was smart, smarter even than many of the older students. Sometimes she thought he was smarter than Grey Wolf, though she wasn't sure Mr. Wolf was as smart as he thought.

Joe was late and just as Edna was about to give up, he sauntered in, slouching silently into a chair by the newspaper table, rocking his chair back on its haunches, seriously stressing its wobbly back legs.

The lesson was slow. Like pulling teeth. Joe wouldn't talk to Edna, merely grunted. She looked up once to find him almost smiling, but when he realized she was looking at him his gaze turned to stone.

Edna was trying to explain to him the library system and how to find relevant information, trying to interest him in his assignment, but she couldn't be sure he was even paying attention. Something in the way he looked at her made her uncomfortable but she couldn't put her finger on it. She just couldn't read him.

"Joe, are you listening to me?"

No answer. In his shyness, when he did speak to Edna, he was either surly and uncooperative, or he played dumb. *Why should I answer her? Why should I answer to that name? She doesn't like me, why would she? Why is she pretending? Who cares, anyway?*

"Do you think ol' Mr. Thornbury would answer to Thorny? That's what we call him you know. He's like an old paint horse with a thorn under his blanket." Joe laughed, self-consciously.

"No, I didn't know that. It doesn't sound very respectful." Not knowing where else to look, Edna cast her eyes down at the encyclopedia open before them.

"What's to respect?" He studied her now, waiting. Hoping for a sweet smile, hoping she would find him amusing, at least.

Edna didn't rise to the bait, merely closed the book they'd been studying and announced it was time to go.

Even after his lesson, Joe continued to hang around the library, pretending to look for more material for his report. Edna saw him watching her and it made her nervous. Following her own homework, there would be rehearsal at chapel for the program. She didn't have time for this foolishness.

Edna didn't feel like sitting down to a late supper. She was so tired, nothing looked appetizing, least of all cold peas and cold roast pork. She didn't figure there was time to sit anyway, and settled for a slice of sweetly tart strawberry-rhubarb pie, which she one-handed while finishing her math problems.

By the time Edna had bathed Gavin, washed up the few dishes and returned to her own room, the day's hectic activities were catching up with her. She was tempted to crawl right into bed in her school uniform, but she knew she'd regret it.

A soft breeze trickling in through the open window spun the small round shade pull, in spite of the weight of an old arrowhead Edna had tied from its center. She might have pulled the shade if she hadn't been so doggoned bone weary. And if it hadn't been so all-fired hot! *People talk about "false spring". Is there such a thing as "false summer?"*

Edna hadn't been told of the previous incident, still she knew it wasn't proper to dress for bed with the shade up. She knew better but she was just too tired to care about being "proper".

Pulling off her uniform jumper and tailored shirt, she sat at her little desk in her underwear, dutifully brushing her hair 100 strokes with her glamorous new hairbrush. Over her head. To the left and then the right. Then bending at the waist to brush it up and over the back of her head until it dangled in front of her face, reaching almost to her ankles. She sat up again, tossing it back out of her face, and giggled at her image in the tiny cracked mirror, hair standing out around her face, alive with electricity. *Crowning Glory? Hardly.*

She almost thought she heard her laughter echo in the small room, but it failed to register in her tired brain. Thoughts of something her mama had said at a long ago tea party were crowding everything else out.

Not as pretty as me, mama? Am I pretty? Am I really? How do you know, mama, if you're pretty?

Edna stood up and turned at right angles to the mirror, assessing her changing profile. She smoothed her hair and flipped it up on top of her head dramatically, cocking her head to one side. She sucked in her tummy, standing tall and squaring her shoulders, coaxing the new curve to her bodice into what she imagined to be a provocative pose.

Pretty? Maybe I should ask for a sign. Like in the Bible.

As if in answer, Susanna's face appeared like a vision over Edna's shoulder in the mirror, and the thought immediately fled, because in that moment, she knew. She knew that if you're beautiful, Susanna Thornbury beautiful, you just know. You don't hunger for it. No one needs to tell you. You just know.

Disgusted, she let her hair fall and made a face at her image in the mirror. *You can't suck in hips! Why can't I have slim hips and a narrow waist like that little snip, Susanna Thornbury? No more pie for you, young lady!* She waggled a finger at her image in the mirror. *Hmph! Susanna can get away with eating pie, I've seen her!*

A half hearted pirouette and more appraisal. She shook her head at her rag doll, propped against the wall by the mirror, legs askew.

"What are you grinning at?" Then she read the words her mama had stitched up one muslin leg and then the other a thousand tears ago—"I wish I could be like the rose…who gathers beauty as she grows". She slumped back into her chair in front of the vanity.

Pretty? Why did you lie to me, mama?

Resignedly, she ducked out of her cotton undershirt to slip on her lightweight gown and was startled by a faint noise outside her window. Clutching the gown to her budding bosom, she flew to the window to draw the shade. Now snickering sounds were unmistakable, and Edna saw a flash of light colored clothing as two fast moving shadows scrambled to escape detection.

"You nasty little creeps! You better run! If I get my hands on you..!" Shrill screams hurled full force, at their backs.

Hearing the commotion, aunt Babe burst into the room and rushed to her niece's side, just in time to see two retreating boys fall ass-over-teakettle, hastily righting themselves and scampering out of sight.

Babe snapped the shade down and her arms enclosed her niece protectively. She smoothed Edna's hair across her forehead, rocking her.

"It's all right. They're gone now. You're all right, aren't you? They didn't get in? They didn't…hurt you?" Babe needed the truth but didn't want to reveal her own terror that the incident might be more serious than the previous one, a peeping into the bedroom window of Susanna Thornbury, the director's less than innocent fourteen-year-old daughter.

"I'm okay, I guess. But what's wrong with those stupid boys, anyway? They make me so mad!"

Babe's heart was breaking, not only for the innocence shattered but because she understood only too well the seriousness of a second incident and knew what the consequence would be. The peeping Toms would be long gone, with no way to identify the guilty parties. But the situation could not—would not—be tolerated at Holmes Academy. There was only one solution.

If only Edna hadn't been so careless. Maybe if she'd known about the other time. If only she'd had enough sense to lie and say she'd had a bad dream. How many times had her aunt stressed for her to be sure and pull the shade? If only she'd listened! Now it was too late. Too late for her and for the other girls. She had sealed not only her own fate, but that of all the other teachers' daughters.

Mr. Thornbury lost no time in issuing his edict. All the girls must leave the academy. They must go live "in town". Or wherever, but not at Holmes. He couldn't afford to take a chance on something serious happening. He regretted to have to include his own daughter, but he had no choice. He had a responsibility to protect her and the others. And their innocence.

It wouldn't have mattered if he'd known, and he'd never have guessed that Susanna had done it on purpose. Of course, she didn't anticipate the outcome of testing her new powers of seduction, or she might not have tempted fate. The last thing she wanted to do was to leave the academy and all the boys. Boys who were more than appreciative of Susanna. It was such fun, tormenting them. Like her daddy would ever let one of them get even close to her.

Susanna and the Lawson sisters, and even homely little Eva Winston, moved to nearby Atoka, to stay with relatives and attend school. School in Atoka would prove to be decidedly less interesting to Susanna, with fewer subjects to appreciate her charms. Those that were there were up for grabs, and Susanna had plenty of competition. At the Academy, Susanna and Edna had been the two oldest of only five girls in the running for romantic attention. At the academy, Susanna knew that without a doubt, she topped the boys' list of available temptresses. At Atoka, she'd have to work much harder to be noticed.

"It isn't fair! It really isn't. I didn't do anything wrong, why should I be punished?" Edna felt like she was fighting for her life. In a way she was.

"That's true enough. Life doesn't guarantee us 'fair'. A chance, maybe. It's time you leaned that. It's up to us to make the best of each chance, each open door." It was all Babe could offer, in hopes that Edna would find a way to understand and use it. "Sometimes we have to make our own chances. Make 'em up outta' whole cloth, if necessary."

There was no one in town for Edna. As a matter of fact, there was no one left to take her at all. Everyone who was willing, and a few who hadn't been, had already taken a turn. Edna understood that Tim couldn't leave the academy and give up his livelihood, his family's security.

Edna's moment of carelessness would cost her the most loving, comfortable home she'd known since her father died.

STEP 4:
Stuff With Sour Grapes…

Stuff with sour grapes…

With mixed emotions and heavy hearts, aunt Babe and uncle Tim set out to deliver Edna to her next caretakers. The family piled into the faded blue Studey and drove across the Sooner State to Triple Tree Children's Home under the canopy of a sprawling buttermilk sky. It was a last resort. Edna's last chance.

As Edna's legal guardian, Tim filled out the paperwork to "give her over to the Triple Tree Children's Home…to be cared for, disciplined, maintained, trained and educated, under and by the rules and regulations of said Home…and it appearing to the court: That the parents of said child are dead and that T. G. Alden, petitioner herein, is the legal guardian of said child; that he has had her care and custody for the past 18 months and is not able to keep, maintain and educate her, and that said girl has no relatives who are able to assume her custody, and no property or means of her own, and the court having fully investigated the conditions…finds that it would be to the best interest of said child that she be placed in said Triple Tree Children's Home…"

Doctor Redewill had signed the Certificate of Physician and Edna was certified to be of legitimate birth…not addicted to any vicious habit…advanced in school to 7th grade…no disease of the scalp, no defective speech or hearing, no epilepsy, tuberculosis, catarrh, or syphilitic taint…no evidence of evil results from any disease…not in the least feebleminded or idiotic…no deformity." It was further noted that "the child is smart, quick and likeable with no bad habits. A splendid child indeed."

While the adults tended to business, the thirteen-year old orphan sat bereft on a hard wooden bench by the tall bay window, her treasured quilt folded beside her. She gazed out the window, idly surveying the grounds. No children, that Edna could see. An overcast sky had drifted in, cloaking the scene in leaden gray. An elderly caretaker was alternately trimming brown spent blooms from a lone rosebush, and absently rubbing at the stubborn ache in his hip. A red bandana waved from the back pocket of the old man's overalls, the only shred of color that caught the girl's eye in the bleakness of the scene. As the old man circled the bush he was working on, Edna noticed a pipe angling down from his lips and was painfully reminded of her father.

Triple Tree Children's Home was an imposing structure, almost severe in its architecture; from tall milk-white columns flanking an expansive portico at the entrance, to intricate beveled windows in the double front doors, curtained in fresh, white lace panels. White. Everything was so white.

Sparkling cut glass doorknobs graced every door, and Edna allowed herself to be distracted by them. The one in this room was a pale lavender, the color of summer lilacs, and it made puddles of rainbow-hued light on the polished floor next to Mrs. Pennyworth's desk. Mrs. Pennyworth was the director; had been ever since she lost her husband and the orphanage had been moved last year from Arkansas, to its current location. Mrs. Pennyworth was as imposing a figure as the institution she presided over. Her cool reserve and businesslike manner felt uncomfortably foreign to her newest charge.

All the documents had been signed and duly witnessed. Mrs. Pennyworth deftly blotted the signatures with a fresh ink blotter. She rose, tamping the edges of the papers into a neat stack.

"Well, everything is in order. You realize of course, it's unlikely anyone will choose to adopt the child? Most couples are looking for infants. But we'll do our best and I think Edna will be happy here."

Maybe Edna would beat the odds. Maybe a loving family would adopt her and give her a good, stable home. Aunt Babe certainly hoped so. If not, she hoped Edna would find some measure of happiness, here. At least not be unhappy. Maybe that was all she could ask.

Babe scooped Gavin up from the sunlit spot on the floor where he was about to nod off. She settled him into the crook of her arm, needing both arms now, to support the toddler's weight and bulk.

She began unconsciously rocking him, as if he were still a baby. He nestled in and promptly fell asleep. He didn't get to tell Edna "Bye-bye". Edna was allowed to accompany her aunt and uncle, along with the director, to the front door to say a proper goodbye.

"You must write", aunt Babe murmured in a strained voice, unable to sound as cheerful as she'd wanted.

"Yes", echoed Uncle Tim, "We expect at least one letter a week. Let us know how you're getting on and if you need anything. We'll be back to visit as soon as we can get away."

Edna reluctantly leaned forward to hug her uncle, and then aunt Babe. She wanted never to let go. Babe pulled away, gently disengaging Edna's grip. She offered Gavin's sleepy presence and Edna kissed the top of his curly head, something ominous tugging at her heart.

This was it then. Edna had hoped against hope that somehow, some way, this moment could be avoided. Mrs. Pennyworth, adept at bringing to a close these awkward goodbyes, shook hands with Tim and smiled thinly at Babe as she shooed them on their way. Just as Mrs. Pennyworth grasped Edna firmly by the shoulder to steer her away from the door, Edna caught a quick movement out of the corner of her eye. A small dark-headed figure had darted across the doorway to the hall. With a flash of ruffles and a clatter of little feet, one of the residents had betrayed her presence. Edna didn't notice Mrs. Pennyworth's spine stiffen within the confines of her tailored dress and crisp white apron. A giggle issued from the somewhere beyond the same doorway.

Edna glanced over her shoulder and through the beveled glass, and glimpsed the Alden's retreating figures. She truly hoped they would come to visit. Soon.

The directress brought Edna back to reality with a simple question. "Is that all you have with you? Just your valise and your quilt?

"Yes", Edna mumbled dully. She quickly learned Mrs. Pennyworth did not like mumbling.

"Speak up child! You will say, 'Yes, ma'am' or 'Yes, Mrs. Penny-worth' when you address me. Is that clear?"

"Yes. I mean, yes ma'am, Mrs. Pennyworth", Edna blurted out, wanting to comply.

"Very well. I'll show you to your room. You'll be sharing with several other girls, all about your age. You'll meet them later, at supper. The children are all in class now, and then they have their chores. You won't see them until supper time."

When they reached the northeast corner of the second floor, Edna was surprised to be ushered into an enormous room, containing a dozen or so mismatched beds. All were neatly made with a mish-mash of linens and bed covers. One was occupied. By a well-worn stuffed bear propped up on the pillow. The stern directress, snatched the bear and stuffed him unceremoniously into a battered trunk beside his mistress' bed.

Mrs. Pennyworth indicated that the white iron bed nearest the East window would be Edna's. She set her suitcase down at the foot of the bed. A distressed but clean, pea soup green table with two shallow drawers was next to the bedstead. It's only occupant was a tiny reading lamp with a yellowed parchment shade.

"I'll leave you to put your things away and settle in."

"Yes, ma'am", Edna replied dutifully.

It wouldn't matter that the drawers were small and had little storage space. Edna had very little to put away.

When Mrs. Pennyworth left the room, she closed the door behind her. Edna opened her valise and emptied it onto the bed. She tucked her unmentionables and several pair of stockings into the top drawer and wiggled it back into place. She took off her lightweight sweater and put it in the second drawer with her hairbrush, a few toilet articles and the Bible that had been her mother's. She picked up her doll, Baby-Modene, then spread out the quilt her grandmother had made on top of the nondescript covers and fell on it, curling into a tight ball. Her fingers meandered over the familiar patterns. It was 3:00 in the afternoon and Edna fell asleep on the unfamiliar bed, on the second floor of Triple Tree Children's Home, clutching her homemade doll like a little child.

Edna woke up to the whispered chatter of unfamiliar voices, and for a moment she couldn't make sense of her surroundings. Her field of vision was ringed with six youthful faces.

"Shhhh! She's waking up".

This from Jillie, a carrot-topped imp that Edna presumed to be slightly younger than herself. Jillie's ginger-spiced eyes were alight with an odd blend of excitement and mischief, a perpetual state for her. A generous sprinkling of freckles spilled across her nose and onto radiant, chubby cheeks, camouflaging a peaches and cream complexion.

"I'm Letha", drawled a chocolate-skinned girl, next to Jillie. Coffee brown eyes formed unspoken questions but she said nothing more.

From the foot of Edna's bed, two blonde-haired, apple-cheeked cherubs chimed a greeting in unison. Edna presumed them to be twins. Deliriously happy ones, apparently. Actually, Sonja and Cecelia were sisters, ages six and seven, respectively. Their cheerful demeanor was due to their pure delight at being in the most stable home they'd ever known. Until Edna came along, they'd been the newest residents at Triple Tree, and had joined the ranks just in time. Jillie was definitely getting too old to be the 'poster child' for the orphanage, and there were often times when Mrs. Pennyworth needed to produce small, cheerful children as examples of their charges. These two filled the bill, and had been very useful for photos, and to parade before those contemplating placing children in Mrs. Pennyworth's care.

Camille was next, around the circle. Her greeting was decidedly less enthusiastic. Cool green eyes revealing nothing, peered out from under ragged bangs, reminiscent of a palomino's mane. The set of her square jaw was partially hidden by her left hand, balled into an almost-fist, with her thumb poised just below her lower lip. Whatever she mumbled past her swollen thumb was barely audible.

Camille received a sharp nudge to her ribs from Amaretta, the tallest one in this gaggle of girls. As Amaretta opened her mouth to speak, a sharp "Clap, clap!" startled them all into silence. Jillie spun around so suddenly that the pencil tucked over her ear, fairly flew onto the bed.

"Girls! What are you doing in here?" Mrs. Pennyworth scolded from the doorway. "If we're to have supper on time, you'd best get yourselves downstairs to the kitchen. I see you've met Edna. You'll have time to get acquainted at supper, before evening vespers. Tomorrow Edna will be added to the chore chart. I'll expect you all to help her learn the rules. Run along now."

Mrs. Pennyworth smoothed the front of her perfectly smooth apron, and tucked an imaginary stray hair into the perfectly formed russet bun at the nape of her neck. She absently fingered a gold filigree locket at her throat as her eyes swept the room, making sure everything was in order. Her keen eyes fixed on an errant black lisle stocking toe, barely peeking out of Edna's top drawer.

"This won't do at all, Edna. Cleanliness is next to Godliness, and neatness is on the other side". Edna scurried to stuff the offending item into the drawer. A less than perfect solution, judging by the directress' decidedly arched brow.

Edna was given a brief tour of the home. It ended in a huge dining room where two younger girls were putting the finishing touches on setting the tables. Winifred, known as Winnie, was eight years old but small for her age. Her large, luminous eyes appeared even more so through thick-lensed, wire-rimmed glasses. Winnie's sleek, dark hair was cut in a short bob that cupped her face, and she had been blessed with clear olive skin. She lisped a brief greeting through a gap-toothed smile and returned to concentrating on her assigned task.

On the other side of the table, carefully arranging the flatware, Belinda smiled tentatively at Edna. Belinda looked to be about 10, and her pale features were the exact opposite of Winnie's. Fly-away, colorless hair straggled about her thin face. She had one blue eye and one that was 3/4 brown, like a clock face at 3:00 o'clock.

"Belinda! Don't be so easily distracted. You have other tables to finish. This is Edna. The extra place you're setting is for her."

Mrs. Pennyworth's reprimand caused Belinda to draw in a sharp breath. Edna could hear a rattle, or a wheeze, from clear across the room. Belinda quickly looked away and returned to her task, before seeing Edna's smile of greeting.

Supper was a slightly noisy affair presided over by Mrs. Pennyworth and interrupted briefly by the late arrival of Francine. Had Francine arrived and been seated ahead of Mrs. Pennyworth, her shoeless feet might have been overlooked.

"Francine," Mrs. Pennyworth chided, "please go and put on your shoes and stockings, like a lady. Then you may rejoin us."

Edna watched the black girl lower her head and look down at her oversized bare feet, wiggling her toes. Then Francine raised her head dramatically and rolled her almond eyes heavenward. She mumbled something under her breath and retreated self-consciously. Her parting words, "Yes, ma'am", with the emphasis on "ma'am" were heard by all.

Grace was said at all the tables, in unison. Napkins were placed carefully on laps and great bowls of steaming vegetables and mashed potatoes were passed clockwise around the long trestle tables. Biscuits heaped high onto massive blue and white platters quickly vanished. Gravy was ladled over pot roast and potatoes, from stoneware gravy boats. The meal was washed down with large glasses of ice cold buttermilk, Edna's favorite. In her nervousness, Edna didn't realize she'd eaten three helpings of potatoes.

The girls chattered back and forth nonstop. At mealtimes, the residents had a little more freedom to speak, as long as they didn't become "too rowdy" or unladylike. Those at Edna's table fired questions at her in between snippets of conversations. Edna answered as best she could and tried to fix in her mind the names and faces of those nearest her.

She missed aunt Babe terribly. The mushy vegetables, though filling, couldn't hold a candle to aunt Babe's fresh-from-the-garden ones. But along with meat and other dishes, they succeeded in filling her tummy. Overfilled it, as it turned out. A tummy ache later would be her reward.

Looking around at the tables, Edna was puzzled. Most of the girls appeared to be happy, overall. Well, it was easy for all of them to smile and laugh. They hadn't been through what she herself had endured. She knew she would never be that happy again. Especially not in a place like this, without any family. She concluded the girls must all be very self-centered and what her aunt Babe called "shallow". Whatever their reasons for being placed in an orphan's home, their stories couldn't be half as tragic as hers. She couldn't have been more wrong.

Francine returned to the table, feet clad in stockings as ordered. And Indian moccasins. When she resumed her place at the table, Mrs. Pennyworth nodded almost imperceptibly and continued with her meal, keeping an eye on everyone at once, it seemed to Edna. Though Francine remained quiet, Edna noticed that she hungrily observed everything going on around her.

Francine maybe fit the word 'waif', which Edna kept hearing applied to all of them. To Edna, the implication of the term was a pitiful, homeless, unwanted child. An orphan, on the other hand, was a child who'd lost her parents, like she had. The words were not interchangeable.

Sharing her meal with so many new faces was a strange experience for Edna and she couldn't help but speculate on the backgrounds of the different girls. Indian moccasins. How odd. And Letha was obviously of "dubious parentage". Her lazy drawl and curious speech patterns had Edna envisioning all sorts of scenes in misty bayous and swampy, dark corners of the deep south. How long had they all been here, Edna wondered.

"Amaretta," Mrs. Pennyworth said over dessert, "I want you to take Edna under your wing. Show her around, explain the rules to her. I'll hold you responsible for any infractions for the time being. Show her where the 'chore chart' is, for tomorrow morning."

"Yes, ma'am."

Edna and Amaretta exchanged curious glances.

"And show her how to properly make her bed. Square corners. Edna, please sit up straight. You mustn't slouch."

"Yes, ma'am." Edna lengthened her spine.

I know how to make my bed! What in the heck are square corners?

At least she felt that maybe she had a friend in Amaretta. She was glad it was Amaretta who had been "assigned" to her. Well, Maybe it wouldn't be so bad. It was interesting, at least. After all, it wouldn't be forever. Things could change. It happened all the time. Nothing ever stayed the same. She decided not to get too comfortable.

As supper wore on, Edna's attention kept returning to Amaretta. There was something about her that Edna was drawn to. Her looks were "nothing to write home about", as mama would have said, but there was warmth and laughter in her hazel eyes. She was quick-witted and funny, and activity tended to naturally center around her. Of all the girls, Amaretta made her feel the most welcome. Edna hoped it wasn't just because Mrs. Pennyworth had made Edna her 'job'.

After supper, empty dishes and serving bowls were quickly cleared and dishwashing began. Girls who weren't on clean-up duty had a few minutes to themselves before evening vespers. Edna wandered back to the dorm room, for lack of anything more purposeful to do.

She found Jillie sitting on the floor in a corner, animatedly scribbling something on a wide tablet, braced on her knees. She was so absorbed in her activity that she didn't notice when Edna came into the room. Amaretta, too, was seated on the floor, at the foot of her bed. The one with the tattered stuffed bear, now defiantly back in place. Her back was braced against the footboard as she wrote in a pad of paper that served as a diary.

∾

"Dear Diary,

We got a new girl today. Her name is Edna and she's pretty quiet but I like her. I think we're *going to be great friends!*"

Amaretta looked up when Edna came into the room. Edna apologized for disturbing her. Amaretta waved the apology away in the air and motioned for her new friend to join her. Edna started to perch on the bed and was promptly scolded.

"No! Not on the bed! Here, beside me. On the floor. We aren't allowed to sit on the beds."

"I'm sorry. I didn't know. I mean, nobody told me...what difference does it make? You're going to get in it soon, anyway."

"Well it makes a big difference to Miss Pennyworth. Trust me. It's just the rules, that's all. Nobody said it had to make sense. Now you know, so don't say I didn't tell you." After a pause, she made an effort to make up for her cross words, by adding, "I'm just writing in my diary. Do you keep a diary?"

"No, I never thought about it." Edna lowered herself to the floor, and sat Indian-style by her roommate.

"You really should, you know. I couldn't go a day without writing in mine." Amaretta closed the tablet and put her pencil on top of it. "So, your bed is right next to mine. I'm glad."

Edna smiled a 'Me, too'.

A small, clear bell sounded near the door and Amaretta breathed, "Oh. Time for evening vespers. Come on, we're in the first group. You can sit next to me."

She grabbed up her tablet and an extra pencil, ripping out a sheet of paper for each of them, then tossed the tablet into her drawer with a half dozen others. She folded one piece of paper and offered it to Edna.

"For notes. We can't talk during vespers. It's against the rules." Presumably writing notes was not.

Edna took the paper and pencil and the girls set off together, joining up with the others at the top of the stairs. Jillie stamped along behind. She'd had trouble giving up her drawing, mid-sketch. Her little hands were clinched into plump fists.

"Ooooh! I just can't get it right!"

Edna hadn't even noticed the old white chapel when she had first arrived. It crouched in the shadow of the main building and was tiny by comparison. Narrow oak pews easily held the staff and residents of Triple Tree, divided into two separate meeting times. Narrow window panels made of alabaster, native to the area, lined the East and West sides of the small building. At this time of day, they were opalescent in the light from the retreating sun and radiated a warm, almost rosy glow on those present.

Edna had no idea what to expect of evening vespers. She sat with Amaretta on one side and Camille on the other. Evening vespers was much like a short church service, consisting of a few old hymns, a Bible reading, prayers and more hymns. The service ended with "In the Garden", Lily's favorite and Edna felt comforted, but it reminded her of things she'd rather not think about. As it turned out, the note passing between Edna and Amaretta was minimal. Amaretta didn't want Camille reading any of her secrets over Edna's shoulder.

After vespers the girls all returned to their respective rooms with a few minutes to themselves before lights out. Edna, Amaretta and Camille shared their room with Jillie, among others. At only eleven, Jillie was quite a bit younger than the others. Mrs. Pennyworth, tried to keep her charges grouped by age, but this couldn't be helped. Letha at 13, was much closer in age, but then she had to place her in the tiny dormer room carved out of the attic, with Francine. Again, their ages were disparate, but what else could she do? Surely Francine and Letha had much more in common anyway, given their backgrounds, despite their age difference.

Edna's first day at Triple Tree had slipped away, and as everyone prepared for bed they whispered quietly and comfortably, for the most part. Edna noticed that Camille didn't contribute much to the conversation and when she did, it was apt to be a caustic remark. When Amaretta bestowed one of her treasured notepads on Edna to use as a diary, Camille couldn't resist a jab.

"She prob'ly can't even write."

Edna ignored Camille and thanked Amaretta graciously. She knew it was a gift of love and was more thankful for the sentiment than for the notepad, itself. She neatly penned her name in the front, and beneath it wrote:

My Personal Diary
Triple Tree Children's Home
1929

Her first entry read:

> I received this diary as a gift from my new friend Amaretta on my first day at Triple Tree. Amaretta is my best friend. It's been a good day. As good a day as it could be. I miss aunt Babe and uncle Tim and mama and daddy.

Then, feeling a need for a closing she added:

> "Good night, dear diary. Sleep tight. Don't let the bedbugs bite."

Edna would learn that a diary can be a very good friend. From that time on, she managed to write in her diary almost every day. She began to treasure the opportunity to put her own words on paper. It was a new experience and welcome diversion from the drudgery.

Three sharp raps from Mrs. Pennyworth on the door announced lights out.

"No more talking! Good night."

It took concentrated effort to ignore the quiet simpering Triple Tree's newest resident heard in the dark. In the quiet moonlight of the dorm room, Edna learned not everyone was so happy. Who was crying so softly? Listening carefully she couldn't determine the direction. Must be more than one, she finally decided. A better question would be who was not crying. Sleep eluded her until early morning.

The next day was Saturday and everyone rose with the sun. Again, Edna found herself disoriented. All the clamor, all the voices. So many people taking turns in the only upstairs bathroom. Of course, if one was in too big a hurry there was always the old privy out back. Edna decided to wait, no matter how long it took. She'd had quite enough of outhouses.

When Edna went downstairs, she found her name neatly lettered in on the "chore chart". Edna—breakfast preparation, floor scrubbing—first floor, and supper clean up. Well, first things first. She certainly knew how to fry an egg, for Pete's sake. But the scale was a little larger here. She found it a horse of another color to be responsible for preparing such large amounts of food, as opposed to cooking for a small family. Mrs. Covington, the caretaker's wife was in charge of the kitchen and the chipped crockery bowl she gave Edna to mix the biscuits in was huge. Edna could scarcely get a grip on it. She nearly dropped it more than once on the first batch, alone.

Everyone else in the kitchen was busy with their own tasks and Mrs. Covington's instructions were sketchy, at best. "Whatever you do, just do the best you can", Edna recalled her daddy telling her, implying that would be good enough. She did the best she could. It wasn't necessarily good enough.

"Who made these biscuits? They're hard as road apples and taste as icky!"

Edna took another biscuit and buttered it heavily and angrily, in self defense of her creation. Noting the source of criticism, she decided to let it go and give Sonja the benefit of the doubt. After all, she was only six. Mrs. Pennyworth wasn't so generous.

"Sonja, you must apologize to Edna. It's her first time. With practice she'll be making biscuits light as mine and nearly as delicious." In truth, if Mrs. Pennyworth knew how to bake biscuits, it couldn't be proven by the girls. No one had ever seen her do a lick of work in the kitchen.

"Until you've made your own first batch of biscuits, you ought to hold your tongue. Perhaps tomorrow would be a good day for you to learn the fine art of biscuit-making."

"Yes, ma'am. Sorry, Edna."

Edna made a mental note—*Don't criticize the work of others. It may earn you an opportunity to learn a new skill...*

The exchange put a temporary damper on conversation, but soon everything was back to normal. Relatively noisy normal.

"Speaking of biscuits and gravy, Camille, you've had quite enough," Mrs. Covington chided. "You're going to have to start watching what you eat more carefully or we're going to have to let out your clothes. They can't say we don't feed our children well". A satisfied smile radiated all the way to her eyes.

Camille had been unusually quiet all morning. She claimed she was fine, but Edna thought she looked a little green around the gills. She'd mostly just poked at her food.

After breakfast, Edna picked up her plate out of habit, to take it into the kitchen, but it was whisked out of her hands. Clearing the table was not her job today. She had other work to do.

"Jillie, show Edna where we keep the bucket and scrub brushes. And don't forget the lye soap. No shirking this time, missy!"

As Edna stared alternately at the bucket of soapy water and the expansive parlor floor, she was amazed at how the room appeared to grow before her very eyes. Was it really only yesterday?

As Edna debated where to start, Jillie breezed by the doorway with a dust rag in her hand and chirped, "Better get busy if you want to finish the downstairs before lunch."

The downstairs! The whole downstairs? Before lunch? It was impossible! Edna was used to hard work and had scrubbed her share of floors in her young life, but this. This was too much. How could they possibly expect her to do all this before lunch?

Mrs. Pennyworth silently entered the room and paused just inside the doorway, observing Edna standing idly over her bucket.

"Edna! The floor won't scrub itself. On your knees girl, or you'll never finish in time. Besides I need this room cleaned and dry as soon as possible. I'm expecting another charge to arrive today."

She turned on her heel and left, amid the soft rustle of petticoats, confident that Edna would comply. Mrs. Pennyworth was rarely wrong.

Wordlessly Edna grabbed the scrub brush and splatted a soapy blob onto the hardwood floor. She'd write aunt Babe the first chance she got. Surely her aunt and uncle didn't realize what kind of people they'd entrusted with their niece. That decided, she threw herself into her work. Her mind was going a mile a minute as she mentally composed her letter. It would take a few days for the letter to reach her aunt and uncle. Then they'd have to wait for a day off to come and get her.

Well, she could do this for awhile. She learned long ago that she could do almost anything for a short period of time. If she had to. Now that she'd made friends, especially with Amaretta, it would be a little easier, but this was definitely not working out.

Edna got through the day somehow. She barely finished the downstairs mopping in time to clean up before a welcome lunch. All this scrubbing certainly worked up an appetite. Edna's afternoon was spent in more orientation in terms of what was expected of her, where things were located, and rules on top of rules, on top of more rules.

On her way to do her upstairs chores after lunch, Edna ran into Mrs. Pennyworth and her new "charge", on the stairs. Mrs. Pennyworth introduced the two orphans, and Edna repeated the unfamiliar sounding name. "Dyani?"

Lifting her chin regally, Dyani informed Edna "It means deer."

The doe-eyed girl continued on her way, and Edna was struck by the perfect suitability of her name. She moved with a grace belying her youth. Edna envied Dyani's long straight, ebony hair, just skimming her hips as she glided up the stairs, followed by Mrs. Pennyworth.

By the time the evening meal was over, Edna was ready for bed, not kitchen clean up. After that was accomplished, she decided to check the chore chart for the next day. She was not surprised to find next to her name, "scrub second floor", as well as "breakfast preparation" and "windows, first floor".

Finally Edna was able to retire to the dorm room. She was so exhausted she didn't notice Amaretta's bed was at least a foot closer to her own than it had been that morning. All the beds on the North wall had been inched closer together to make room for Dyani's bed, now wedged into the Northwest corner of the room.

Mrs. Pennyworth had been in a quandary over that one. She would have put the dark skinned girl in the attic dormer with Letha and Francine, but there simply wasn't room. It wasn't as if Dyani was full-blooded Indian. Fortunately the poor girl was half white. Maybe if she cut her hair and were properly dressed, people would hardly notice this defect.

Edna saw Amaretta engrossed in her daily diary entry, but Edna didn't have the energy to do the same, or to write the rescue letter to aunt Babe and uncle Tim. Edna fell into bed and drifted off to sleep without even saying good night to her best friend.

Early the next day, before the sun came up, Edna's little reading lamp cast a narrow shaft of light onto the back page of her tablet as she wrote:

~

"Dear Aunt Babe and Uncle Tim,

I hope this finds you and little Gavin well. I sure miss you.

Things aren't going well here. I am wondering how long I must stay. Would it be possible for you to pick me up and take me back to Holmes Academy? I know there were problems there before, but I'd be ever so good, if I could come back. I'd close my window shade carefully and I'd do anything you ask. I'd help you with Gavin again and the cooking and cleaning. You could teach me at home.

They'd hardly know I was there. Maybe we could even keep it a secret. Anything, if only I could come home. I'll be looking for you soon. Take care.

Love, your niece,

Edna

She felt better already. She knew aunt Babe and Uncle Tim wouldn't want to see her so unhappy. Surely her post script, hastily scrawled below her signature would tip the scales:

~

PS—You know we aren't allowed to have our own underwear here?

It all goes in the laundry together and you get back whatever you get back. Please come soon. I can't bear another day here thinking of someone else's unders crawling up my backside!

She hoped they'd come soon. Maybe next weekend. She'd get her things packed on Friday, just in case.

Sunday morning was spent mostly in worship of one sort or another. No chores were listed except for those required, like cooking and cleaning the kitchen. The residents had some time to visit, but no one really tried to get acquainted with Dyani. And she was content to remain aloof, keeping to herself, silent. During vespers she sat alone, straight and tall, her long dark lashes resting on perfect, tawny cheeks. Why, Edna wondered, didn't the thread of Cherokee blood flowing in her own veins, result in the enviable high cheekbones bestowed on the mysterious Dyani.

On Monday morning, Edna put her letter in the mail. She had breakfast preparation again, then work in the vegetable and flower gardens with three other girls and Mr. Covington. Edna found the caretaker to be an extremely likeable sort, and enjoyed her time in the garden immensely. She reveled in the faint scent of Mr. Covington's pipe smoke, putting her to mind of her daddy.

The work that day involved mostly separating some iris bulbs, and that too reminded Edna of home and mama's garden.

"Not too deep, "Mr. Covington instructed calmly. "Irises don't like to get their feet wet."

"Like this?" Edna was anxious to please this gentle man.

Mr. Covington's smile blessed her work. The chores sped by, hardly feeling like work at all. Until her aching body brought the point home, later that night.

Before she knew it a week had gone by. A whole week and then the weekend without word or a visit from aunt Babe and uncle Tim. Well, it would take time for them to get the letter, she reminded herself. It had better be soon. She had stretched her supply of underwear as far as she could. Now each and every piece of her own underwear was out there somewhere in Launderland, destined for who knows whose dresser drawers.

She finally heard from aunt Babe, but the letter didn't mention Edna's letter. Or when they might come for her. Edna continued to write every week, receiving one letter from them for every two of her own. Aunt Babe signed off, "We hope to see you soon. Affectionately, Aunt Babe". Another week went by and then a month, but Edna didn't give up hope.

One Saturday, as Edna was cleaning the tall windows in the parlor, she saw a trail of dust working its way up the dirt road that led to the orphanage. From time to time, she could make out a faint blue fender, but she didn't dare hope it was the familiar Studebaker coupe. She thought her heart would burst when she saw the Alden's car pull up in the dirt drive. She dropped her rag and fairly flew outside into aunt Babe's waiting arms. Uncle Tim had Gavin in tow, and Edna was overjoyed to see them all. She had unpacked her suitcase, but it would be a simple matter to throw her few belongings into it again, and she'd be ready to go.

Since it was Saturday, Mrs. Pennyworth grudgingly allowed Edna to enjoy a picnic lunch with her aunt and uncle and the beloved Gavin. Aunt Babe didn't have to come out and tell Edna they weren't there to take her home with them. As their time together wore on, aunt Babe asked her how she was adjusting and talked about the coming holiday, and it became apparent. Aunt Babe talked of how difficult things were at the school and about the friends that Edna had known there, and how they were adjusting to their new circumstances. She even brought Edna a letter from, Susanna Thornbury. Edna tucked it into her apron pocket to read later, after her company left. This precious visit with them would be all too short.

When their time was over, aunt Babe hugged Edna tightly and told her she wished she could take her home with her. That was as close as Edna would come to an answer to her unasked question. Edna's eyes were so pleading, aunt Babe had to look away and head for the open car door. Uncle Tim gave Edna a brief hug. Gavin had to be pulled away.

Edna braved a smile, waving an exaggerated goodbye to the little face peering over aunt Babe's shoulder through the oval back window, as the Studebaker pulled back out onto the road and disappeared in a cloud of dust. She watched, waving broadly until the dust cloud completely disappeared. She wiped her tears away, lifted her head and went back in to finish her window washing. Soon, it would be time for supper and she longed for lights out.

Back at her task, on a wide sweep across the window, Edna's arm brushed her pocket and the rattle of paper reminded her of the letter from Susanna. There being no one around to observe, Edna stole a moment to open the letter.

∾

Dear Edna,

Hi. I hope yer fine. Im fine to. Except its so boring here! Theres nuthing to do fer pete sake. I wish I could see you. the only intresting thing is theres this cute boy named Jefry next door and I think he likes me. But my mean ol aunt Sara lives here with us an she won't even let me sit outside on the porch with him. Mama says its cause shes an ol maid an doesn't want anyone to have any fun. Shes got eyes in the back of her head I swear! So I hafta sit in the house after school and read. Shes tryin to teach me to nit but its to dang hard!

I hope yer not bored like me. Are there any boys there? Well I gotta go. rite me a leter I cant wait to hear from you.

Yer frind Susanna Louise Thornbury

Edna smiled and tucked the letter back into her pocket. Bored. She'd like to be bored. Just for five minutes. On any given day. She could write Susanna back. Her address was on the envelope. But then, what could she say? "Count your lucky stars", like mama used to say? Mama was right, people just don't know when they have it good.

A clatter down the hall startled Edna back to activity and she began to rub animatedly at an imaginary smudge, long gone from the window. Jillie stumbled by the doorway alone, carrying a bucket of cleaning equipment. She dipped her head, the tip of her index finger, edging up over her lips in a "shhhh". She grinned at Edna and Edna found herself smiling back. Who could resist smiling with Jillie around?

Dyani was having difficulty settling in. She was constantly being punished for resisting Mrs. Pennyworth's attempts to help her. She refused to cut her hair or to dress 'more appropriately, in spite of repeated admonitions that she'd never find anyone who wanted her as long as she insisted on looking like a squaw. It saddened Edna and all the girls when she lost the battle of the haircut. Her long locks were soon shorn. She cried silently in bed that night. It was the first time she'd cried since coming to Triple Tree.

The girls were kept so busy they hardly had time to think. Or complain. They weren't allowed to talk when they were working, which was most of the time. With school work, cooking and cleaning, and tending chickens, one hardly had time to breathe. For all the eggs they gathered, they rarely got to eat them, as most were sold in town. Edna missed having eggs for breakfast, but she was getting used to everything and making a few friends. She began to feel more comfortable.

Camille seemed to want to be friends, though it was a push-pull relationship. She would push to include herself in what was going on, and then pull back. She did confide to Edna that Camille wasn't her real name. No one else knew that, not even Mrs. Pennyworth. It was a name she had chosen for herself when she ran away from the Kansas family that had chosen her from the orphan train.

Edna knew nothing about the orphan trains. Camille eventually told her that she and her brother were part of the movement to take homeless waifs existing in what amounted to gypsy-like bands roving the east coast, and place them, hopefully, with caring, Christian families in the mid-west who wanted children. Many children found a better life through this effort, but the stories didn't all have happy endings. Camille told Edna she had run away to avoid the abuse, and to find her brother, Travis. A farm family had chosen Camille but not Travis because he was too young to be of any real use and he was deemed to be an incorrigible. He was prone to a nasty habit of biting anyone who showed any interest in taking him or his sister. The last

Camille saw of her brother, he was being herded back onto the train before it pulled out of Salina on a hot and windy Kansas day.

Edna had not grown up with siblings, but she thought she could imagine the loss. She'd had a stepmother who locked her out of the house, but couldn't get used to the idea of people physically abusing children. She couldn't believe people could be so cruel to a child. She began to feel sorry for Camille and to want to be her friend. She even tore the back part of her tablet off and gave it to Camille, so that she too could keep a diary, as most of the girls did. Camille just nodded, took the tablet and laid it on the table by her bed where it remained, unopened, until her last day at Triple Tree. A tablet was of little use to one without the ability to read and write. Camille had not attended school before Triple Tree and she was still struggling with the basics.

Edna didn't understand Camille, but then, Camille didn't tell Edna everything. She didn't tell her about the nights. She didn't tell her about the dream. The nights were the worst for Camille and tonight the dream came again. She hadn't felt well all day and she longed for the oblivion of sleep. She always knew It was a dream. She knew how it would end. Why couldn't she wake herself up? Over and over. The evil presence, the shiny, jagged blade. The terror.

Edna came to, startled by screams that seemed to shatter the cool night air. In the pale moonlight, she saw two figures huddled together on Camille's bed and soon the screams were replaced by Amaretta's cooing. Amaretta held Camille and rocked her like a baby. She smoothed Camille's hair off her brow. They fell asleep like that, like a mother and child. Sharing night terrors, giving and receiving comfort.

By the time Mrs. Pennyworth had donned her respectable robe and padded down the hall, all was quiet. She listened at the dorm door. Nothing. She heard nothing. Maybe she had imagined it. Horrified, for a moment she thought it might have been her own screams. *Oh, my stars in heaven! Could it be? Could I have cried out? What if someone heard? What did I say?* With quivering fingers, she began to nervously tuck wayward copper curls back under her sleeping cap.

She shuffled back to her room, mumbling, thinking only of her own dream. The last thing she remembered was the scene at Harvey House. *I must be losing my mind.* She crawled back into bed, trembling. *Oh Gabriel, where are you?*

But Gabriel, Mrs. Pennyworth reminded herself, never had a lick of sense about timing!

She fell into a fitful sleep, and dreamed of pennies. Giant, copper pennies, light as feathers falling in slow motion onto Gabriel's cold marble headstone until it was covered, finally lost, buried under a mound of shiny copper coins...

Edna however, couldn't get back to sleep. She leaned against the iron bedpost, wide awake, wondering about Camille, until the morning sun invaded their room. She looked over and saw Letha sitting wide awake, as well, her long arms trapping bony knees to her chest, rocking. Letha was humming softly to herself. The tune was vaguely familiar to Edna but she couldn't place it. Their eyes met and neither girl smiled.

Letha untangled her arms and swung her gangly legs over the edge of the bed, her slender feet in search of slippers. She stood and stretched, then shook her head slowly.

"I know 'bout dreams," she whispered. "That girl's in trouble. Might be I ought to fix her up somethin' special to drink. Make those awful dreams just float away an' never come back. Poor girl. She troubled. Mighty troubled."

At breakfast, everyone seemed subdued. Mrs. Pennyworth was obviously lost in a world of her own. With relief she noted that no one mentioned the screams in the night. Thank God for small favors. Maybe no one had heard. She flushed pink recalling her dream, unwittingly. *"Gabriel, Gabriel..."*; *"Penny, my love..."*

Penny. No one called her Penny, only Gabriel. How she missed him. If only things had worked out differently. But he was only a man, and even a good man, a man of the cloth, like her Gabriel could be tempted beyond his ability to resist. It really wasn't his fault. Nor hers, she reflected. God knows, she'd been a good wife to him.

Suddenly a clatter of dishes transported Mrs. Pennyworth back to that day, back to Harvey House. She'd had to force herself to go there that long ago day, to see for herself. She'd been unable, or perhaps unwilling, to believe what she'd heard people saying about her Gabriel. Yet here he was—with *her*. Bold as brass. The woman was almost plain looking now, without her usual 'enhancement' from the devil's paint box.

Maybe he was only counseling her, or checking up on how the job was working out. After all, he was responsible for his convert getting on at Harvey House. But within a heartbeat she knew. It was in their eyes. In Mrs. Pennyworth's vision, the woman transformed into what she knew her to be, a painted hussy, looking like sin personified! She glanced across the room and saw again, two ladies from his congregation, whispering behind gloved hands, taking in what her own eyes couldn't explain or deny. *It will be all over town now. We'll be disgraced...*

Clash! Clatter! Bang! Abruptly she was back in the present, the dining room at Triple Tree, confronted with a horrendous mound of broken china bowls and a splot of thin oatmeal spreading rapidly, behind her chair. Uncharacteristically flustered, she managed to recover quickly and assume her proper role. The clean up was assigned and everyone returned their attention to their plates.

"Gabriel? You were saying..." Mrs. Covington's soft gray eyebrows arched.

Poor Mrs. Covington. She's so easily confused. "Did I say Gabriel?" Mrs. Pennyworth blotted delicately at her lips with a napkin, to buy time. "Yes, well, I guess I was just thinking out loud. Poor, dear Gabriel. God rest his soul."

"Amen", Mrs. Covington echoed. "Please pass the biscuits and gravy."

Timing is everything. It had to be that evening that Edna and three of her dorm mates would be caught doing the unthinkable. Painting their faces. Jillie's older cousin had tagged along on a visit with her aunt the week before, and had smuggled in lipstick, in a deliciously vivid red! Screaming, scarlet harlot red! Of all 365 days that year, Jillie chose that one to share her secret.

Her dream still weighing on her mind, Mrs. Pennyworth came upon the four friends, giggling in the bathroom. She nudged the door open with the toe of her shoe and was aghast at what she saw. Four of her precious charges, clustered around the pedestal sink, jockeying for the best view in the only mirror at the home.

Visions of the scene at Harvey House and that painted hussy gazing at her own dear husband flashed on and off in her brain like a flickering candle flame. For a moment she felt dizzy. When the dizziness subsided, a blind rage surfaced and sprang to life.

The girls had heard the telltale creak of the heavy door and looked up into the mirror to find Mrs. Pennyworth's reflection, eyes aflame, nostrils flaring. Four pairs of garish scarlet lips smiled sheepishly back at her. They whirled in unison, instinctively protecting their backsides by backing up against the cold marble.

"H...h...hello, Mrs. Pennyworth. We were just uh...", Jillie stumbled for words, then falling silent, took shelter behind Edna.

Edna had only colored her upper lip and part of her lower lip. "We're sorry, Mrs. Penny..."

She was cut off as the irate directress strode toward them, hanky at the ready. She took Edna's chin in one hand, tilting her head up and to one side. With her other hand she began to scrub at the offending color with such force that Edna thought she'd rub her lips right off. Her face was bruising, under the death grip.

"Lip paint! What can you be thinking, Edna? Your mouth looks like an old red hen's ass!"

She moved on to assault Camille next. The girls were shocked at Mrs. Pennyworth's language. Mrs. Pennyworth was shocked at her language. She couldn't help it. It just fell out.

The bewildered directress said nothing more but her mind was reeling as she gripped each girl's face in turn and wiped at their tinted lips with a vengeance. Where had she gone wrong? What was this world coming to? Whatever would become of these girls? She felt the hot tears coming, threatening to spill over. Not yet, she prayed and willed them back.

Finally, her mission accomplished, she turned on her heel and left her charges wide-eyed and open-mouthed, their raw lips reddened now, from all the rubbing. They stared after her, then looked back and forth between themselves.

"An old red hen's ass?" Amaretta mouthed without sound. "Ye gawds 'n little fishes!"

The four conspirators broke into stifled giggles.

Inexplicably, no one suffered the ruler at the hands of "Mrs. P", as she was referred to. No further punishment was forthcoming. The incident was never mentioned again. Not by Mrs. Pennyworth, or the girls involved. It would live on, however in the memories of the four orphan girls and one very frustrated Mrs. Pennyworth

When the laughter died down, Amaretta shoved everyone outside the bathroom telling them, "Get on out now. I got the curse. I need some privacy."

The girls allowed themselves to be shuffled out the door where they waited for Amaretta.

Camille had never really had anyone to explain all the mysteries of womanhood to her. Her mother had told her long ago that when she reached a "certain age", she would experience bleeding, so it hadn't come as a total shock to her. She was surprised though, that Amaretta had "the curse", again. She was glad she didn't get it again. She'd only had it once, back on the farm in Kansas, before she ran away to look for Travis. *Poor Amaretta.* Camille hoped she wouldn't have to deal with it again. She felt curiously betrayed that her mother had left out that important piece of information, that it could happen more than once. *If you can't trust your own mother, who can you trust? What else did she leave out?*

Amaretta finally emerged and joined the group. They fell into a jumbled line, headed to their room. It was almost time for lights out. Jillie was busily scrubbing away at a drawing. Another sketch lay unfinished on the floor beside her. Another cat. With no eyes. Again.

Cats were a natural subject for Jillie as there were so many strays lurking around the home. All the strays however, had eyes. It never occurred to Jillie that Mrs. Pennyworth and others would try and hang fancy psychological reasons on her failure to add eyes to her drawings. Speculation ran from the fact that Jillie herself was afflicted with severe nearsightedness, forever holding her work impossibly close, to the possibility of some deep psychological disturbance, no doubt reflecting unfavorably on her very soul.

The simple truth was that the budding artist just couldn't get them right. She preferred to omit them and claim artistic license. It worked pretty well, with cats. Later, when she graduated to sketching her dormitory mates, it became a bit of an issue. More than one of her subjects objected to being depicted without the windows to her soul.

Edna was Jillie's first human subject. Edna sat across the room, writing in her diary, and Jillie found herself sketching her dormitory mate's features. Edna was focused on the tablet in her lap, her newly bobbed hair just covering her ears and edging forward to frame her face, hugging her jaw line. Jillie adjusted Edna's image so that her head tilted even further forward and let her pencil lengthen Edna's hair in quick strokes, allowing it to appear to fall forward, obscuring her upper face. She laced Edna's fingers through her hair, giving her subject a rather despondent look, which at first pleased the artist in her. She assessed the overall effect critically and decided her masterpiece conveyed a certain "feeling". She couldn't have put a name to the feeling—sad, pensive, desperate maybe. The depth of it caught her by surprise. Suddenly she hated it. She crumpled the picture and threw it under her bed, where it kept company with a dozen other, imperfect sketches.

That same night as Camille lay in her bed awaiting sleep, she got to wondering if Edna could be trusted. She really didn't know her very well, but she longed for someone to talk to. Somewhere between thoughts of trust and unasked questions, she fell asleep and dreamed of biscuits floating in the sky, on silver wings, in formation like migrating geese in the fall. Across fluffy white clouds. Then the clouds roiled gray and menacing. A pale silver moon sailed through the ink-black sky, leaving a trail of fiery stars in its wake. The stars snuffed out, one by one like candle flames, leaving only darkness. Her insides screamed, *not again…*

Evil. Terror. Searing pain from the jagged blade. Again and again. *Please God, let me wake up.* She began to moan, in the real world. By the time she sat up, half in—half out of consciousness, Edna was reaching out to her, whispering, "It's all right. I'm here."

Camille suddenly was fully awake, glad for Edna's presence clutching at her in desperation.

"I'm so sick, Edna." I can't breathe and my insides feel all twisted up!"

Edna wanted to soothe Camille to comfort her, but she had no idea what to do. She tried to imagine what mama would have done. She figured maybe mama would fix her a cup of hot chocolate or tea, but of course that was impossible, under the circumstances.

"You're okay, Camille. I'll stay with you." She stroked Camille's clammy hands, hoping it would somehow help.

Camille finally drifted off to the dreamless sleep of pure exhaustion. A sleep so invasive that she missed the first soft flutters, deep within her, like the beating of natal butterfly wings, against the confines of its cocoon. They would come again and initially, they would puzzle the naïve, young girl. In time, recognition dawned. Camille stifled her shame and confided her fears to Edna.

"Feel this!" Camille put Edna's hand on her belly.

Edna was startled but she recognized the faint thump. Once, a few weeks before the last tea party with Lily, Edna had rested her head in Lily's lap and felt a rolling sensation in Lily's tummy, and then a definite thump!

"Say hello to your baby brother or sister." Lily had smiled, and Edna had known that this was a good thing. A wondrous thing. But that was then.

Now she looked at the tears welling in Camille's eyes, and felt bewildered. How could this be? She thought you had to be married to have a baby. And you had to have a big tummy. Camille's tummy was barely rounded. And she was just a little girl. Like Edna. If it could happen to Camille, maybe it could happen to her.

"Mrs. Pennyworth's gonna be awful mad. What are you gonna to do?"

"I don't know, but don't you dare tell anybody. I have to think on it. I can't have a baby. We don't have any baby beds here." An oversimplification, if Edna ever heard one.

Edna wouldn't tell a soul. She didn't want to. She didn't want to think about it. Still, she could think of little else. She couldn't imagine having a baby. She had always longed for a baby brother or sister, but one of her own? And here? How would Camille ever get her chores done?

The following Thursday, Edna woke early to find Camille's bed empty and unmade. A painfully scrawled note with Edna's name on it, lay on the pillow.

Edna,

Sory. I hafta find Trav. hope I see you agin.

Thanx

Edna couldn't bring herself to give the note to Mrs. Pennyworth, and she never showed it to another living soul. It was her secret. A secret that condemned her for her own failure. She had handled it all wrong. Camille had trusted her, looked to her for answers and she had let her down. But what could she have done? What should she have said? Had she had a week or month to think about it, or even a year, she couldn't have come up with an answer. *Some friend.*

For some time Camille's disappearance was the main topic of conversation. Mrs. Pennyworth finally put an end to the speculation by stating in no uncertain terms that Triple Tree was there to help children who needed and *wanted* care and guidance.

"There is precious little we can do for someone who doesn't want our help. Camille was never really with us."

Eventually discussion of Camille and her disappearing act, died down and life went on at Triple Tree. Four months to the day of Camille's disappearance, Edna was on egg gathering duty and made an amazing discovery. She heard a tiny, muffled mewling in the straw and at first she thought that one of the stray cats had foolishly birthed her kittens in the abandoned hen's nest. On further investigation, she discovered a wrinkled, pink newborn but it was without one iota of fur. Or hair. A mirror image of Camille's cool green eyes stared up at her.

Mrs. Pennyworth's gonna have a cow!

Gingerly Edna lifted the precious bundle from the straw and cradled the newborn in her arms, reluctant to go inside and give her up. She marveled at the perfection of each tiny finger and niblet toe. Fleetingly, she wished this baby was hers. She wanted to care for her until Camille came for her, believing with all her heart that Camille would be back. *Hope springs eternal, Lily would have said.*

Edna never dreamed that when she turned the baby over to Mrs. P. that it would be the last she would see or hear of her. She thought of the baby as a temporary orphan and after all, Triple Tree was an orphanage, wasn't it? Surely a newborn would find a home quickly. But aside from grilling Edna about how she came to discover the baby and whether she had any idea where she came from, Mrs. Pennyworth seemed to have little interest. If Mrs. P suspected the baby's identity, she didn't let on. The baby simply disappeared and was never mentioned again. The only explanation or comment given was, "We're not equipped to handle newborns.

Edna decided to call the baby Edan, a rearrangement of the letters in her own name, so she could hold onto some part of this baby and so she could write about her in her diary. She assumed there would be entries to make about the baby, over time. But she would never write of her suspicions about Edan's mother. She would keep Camille's secret. Friends do that. She could at least be that much of a friend.

The weeks turned into months. Edna had learned to play the game and rarely got in trouble much after the "lipstick incident". She had now placed herself with the others, in the unenviable category of waif. She had come to realize that even Mrs. Pennyworth didn't want her or the others.

On Edna's 15th birthday, she gave herself a gift. The gift of a promise to herself to do something to effect a change. It might take awhile but she knew she had to work on it in earnest. Most of the girls who were in residence when she came to Triple Tree were still here. Only Sonja had been adopted, separating her from her sister.

Edna had learned a lot at the orphanage and made a few good friends, but she needed something more. Exactly what, she had no idea. She had learned to cook chicken fried steak, black-eyed peas and grits. In large quantities, for whatever that was worth. She made passable *"fried okra"*, sausage and gravy, and pecan pie. Her house-keeping skills were more than adequate.

Edna didn't know what she wanted but she knew it wasn't three more years of baking biscuits, scrubbing floors and polishing cut glass doorknobs, however pretty. The garden was the only work she truly enjoyed. She hoped she'd have her own garden one day, and she'd plant Rosemary by the roses like Mr. Covington said, to keep the aphids away. She'd plant morning glories and sweet peas, dahlias and hollyhocks and she'd teach her own daughter to make hollyhock dolls. She wondered if there would be anyone to teach Edan to make hollyhock dolls.

Whatever the fate of Triple Tree and all her friends there, she wanted desperately to find a way out. Without the courage to run away like Camille, she'd have to have a plan.

Edna and her closest friends shared a fervent desire to leave the orphanage but no one had a clue as to how that could be accomplished before age 18. And what would they do, even then? Was something magical supposed to happen at the stroke of midnight on their eighteenth birthday and suddenly they'd be in a position to survive on their own? Hardly. How were they ever to meet a knight in shining armor to sweep them off their feet and take them away from their castle keep? Though they all dreamed of that.

Amaretta said you couldn't leave it up to someone else, or fate. You had to be daring. But only Camille had been daring enough to run away and what else was there? Time. For Edna, three more long years.

It was unusual for Edna and Letha to have much opportunity to talk, as they didn't room together and they weren't allowed to talk while working. But it turned out to be Letha who provided the real spark that ignited Edna's imagination, fanning it into an actual, living, breathing flame that Edna could shape into a plan.

Edna had been sent to find Letha, as she'd been too long doing laundry and Mrs. P. was not in a mood to put up with Letha's dawdling that day. Edna had caught Letha with the laundry done and ready, and tending to a personal matter she wouldn't want known. The dark-skinned girl was desperately scrubbing bleach onto her arms and hands.

"Letha! What are you doing?" Edna really couldn't imagine.

"Shhhh! Don't you tell no one! I figure if bleach makes the clothes white, maybe it can make me white, too."

"Oh, Letha. Look at your hands! They're blistering. Come wash it off. Bleach won't make dark skin white. I won't tell anyone, but you have to promise not to do this again."

"I won't. It don't work anyway, I guess. Been doin' it fer weeks an' I black as ever. I had to try it. I gotta get outta here, Edna. Don't nobody want me like I am and wishin' don't make anythin' happen. I'm just doin' what my grammy always tol' me—'Quit exercisin' your wishbone girl, an use your God-given backbone!' She always tol me that."

"Well, no more of this, Letha. We'll think of something else. We all want to find a way out."

Edna helped Letha wash up and together they carried the laundry upstairs. Letha's words clung to Edna for weeks, afterward.

In the time she'd been at the orphanage, Edna had corresponded with several aunts and cousins, on her mother's side of the family. They truly cared for Edna and often expressed their sympathy and concern for her.

Harriet's mother, Caira had written, "It's a shame you can't come here to McAllister. We'd love to have you close by. If only you could get on with one of the families here and work your way through school. I could ask around as to who will be needing someone. In September, poor Mrs. Campbell is expecting her fifth baby in as many years and she'll be needing help. But of course, she'll need help long before you turn 18."

The inquiry from aunt Caira, coming so soon on the heels of Edna's conversation with Letha, sparked a ray of hope and gave Edna an idea. She decided to take Letha's grammy's advice and when she replied, she put her own backbone to use and wrote that, yes she'd appreciate Caira asking around and that she only needed to be 16, to leave the orphanage. As an afterthought, she added, "As a matter of fact, I must find another situation by my sixteenth birthday, as I'm required to leave by that age."

Edna had heard from some of the other girls that some orphanages released their charges at 16. At the time she'd been appalled. How was a sixteen-year-old to make her own way. Now, she was dying to find out for herself.

Edna had great difficulty signing the letter, with her fingers crossed. She didn't used to be superstitious, but she'd seen a few too many of Letha's magic tricks in her years at Triple Tree to discount the possibilities altogether. Lying was never her strong suit. Lily had always been able to tell when she was lying. Hopefully Mrs. Pennyworth would be less intuitive.

In less than a month Edna received a reply from aunt Caira and as she slid a trembling finger under the envelope flap, her eyes inadvertently fluttered closed in silent prayer. She opened her eyes and read the words that sent music weaving through her heart.

"…Mrs. Campbell, would be thrilled if you would be available shortly after the arrival of the baby, to help. She is due sometime in early September and we can get you enrolled in Miss Holcomb's class, so you will be ready to start school. Do you think you could possibly get permission to leave Triple Tree a little early, seeing as how you have a position and school all settled? That way, you won't miss any school. Do let us know. We will be able to come and pick you up. Harriet can't wait to show you all around and have you in class with her. She is helping Mrs. Campbell's rather crabby sister-in-law, Rachel, after school and she could use a little laughter."

Edna clutched the letter to her chest while she twirled herself around the room. It was too good to be true.

"...Mrs. Campbell, would be thrilled..."? No more floors! No more nasty oatmeal! No more Mrs. P. looking over her shoulder! No more sharp raps on her knuckles with Mrs. P.'s wooden ruler, on the now rare occasions when she was 'found lacking'.

Whatever Mrs. Campbell's needs were, it would have to be a breeze after what she'd been through here. Things were going to change for the better. She just knew it.

All she needed now was to convince Mrs. Pennyworth that she was needed elsewhere. A few months before, Letha had been allowed to leave Triple Tree to work her way through school. She hoped Mrs. Pennyworth would be agreeable in her case, as well. She had to be. Edna was becoming desperate.

Edna needn't have worried. Mrs. Pennyworth was suffering her own desperation, for different reasons. Money had always been somewhat of a concern at the orphanage. It was almost entirely supported by donations from Gabriel's old church congregation back in Arkansas. The support of Triple Tree was always dependent on whoever was in charge in Arkansas keeping the needs of the orphanage before the members of the church, and the circumstances of those normally generous souls. Unfortunately times were hard everywhere and donations for this particular mission had fallen off. Only a pittance was realized from the sale of eggs in town and that was used in trade at the store.

In the waning heat of late July, Edna rose early on a Sunday morning and said an extra prayer, bracing for a struggle to convince Mrs. Pennyworth that it was necessary for her to leave the orphanage, just before her sixteenth birthday. Armed with her plan and a letter from aunt Caira, she approached Mrs. Pennyworth's study door and took a deep breath.

Sometimes we have to make our own chances… Babe's words echoed in her head and she used them as permission.

Just as she reached her hand to knock, the door was jerked open as Jillie fled into the hall. Jillie's eyes met Edna's only briefly, just long enough for Edna to see they were red-rimmed and wet with tears. Jillie left the door ajar, straightened the bow in her hair, tugged the waist of her pleated skirt down into place and walked away. Edna debated on whether to go in now or come back later. She sighed, resolutely lifted her chin and knocked softly on the open door.

"Come in." Eyebrows raised in question, Mrs. Pennyworth sat at her desk, behind a stack of paperwork and bills. Edna's eyes fell on the dreaded ruler, prominently displayed atop the stack. Edna summoned her courage and lengthened that backbone, as a reminder.

"Good Morning, Mrs. Pennyworth. You remember my aunt Caira? Well, I received a letter from her and she'd like me to come to Mc Allister to live. She's found a position for me as live-in help, with a neighbor's wife, Mrs. Campbell, who is in desperate need. She has spoken with the school and I could begin attending Mc Allister High in September". Edna rushed on, running her words together. "Mrs. Campbell is a Sunday school teacher, and her husband is an active in church too. They're expecting their fifth child and Mrs. Campbell has not been well, so I'd be helping with Sunday school, as well has helping out with the family at home. I am hoping…"

"May I see the letter?" Mrs. Pennyworth extended a milk white hand, her other hand fingering the locket at her throat. Edna's eyes fixed on the locket.

Skimming the letter distractedly, Mrs. Pennyworth picked up the pertinent points. It seemed that Edna would be in good hands. Her spiritual guidance would be assured and it would certainly take a burden off of the orphanage to have one less mouth to feed. It seemed it would be beneficial to all concerned. Perhaps Edna's aunt Caira could finish taking off the rough edges of Edna's character.

Mrs. Pennyworth's eyes dropped to the pile of unpaid bills obscuring her usually neat desk and made a quick decision. She was, if nothing else, a prudent business woman.

"If your aunt Caira is willing to assume your guardianship and responsibility for your care, I see no reason to object. I'll begin the paperwork immediately. You may be excused."

"Yes ma'am". Edna turned and walked sedately from the room. She was out of the room into the hall before she dared let out her breath. She could scarcely believe Mrs. Pennyworth had agreed. And so easily!

She broke into a celebratory Charleston, not caring who might observe her indiscretion. It felt so good to be leaving Triple Tree. It felt sooo good to be taking charge of her own destiny. She couldn't wait to begin the next chapter of her life.

That night, just before lights out, Edna signed her name to the letter to aunt Caira, sharing her good news.

Now that the wheels had been set in motion, Edna began to have doubts. *What if this isn't the right thing? What if it's awful there? What if I can't get by. Where would I go then? Well, there's no use borrowing trouble.* Hadn't her mama told her that a million times? Everything would work out. It had to.

Nearly a month went by. Then one Monday morning, Mrs. Pennyworth summoned Edna to her study to inform her the paperwork had been completed. The court had been efficient and cooperative and everything was in order. Caira's husband, George had only to sign the papers when they came to collect Edna.

"When can your aunt and uncle come for you?" Mrs. Pennyworth inquired.

"I'll write them tonight, after vespers. I'll let you know."

After all this time, it was finally going to happen. Really. If only Amaretta had someone. And the others. What about the others? In her prayers she said a special thank you for Amaretta and for all her friends at Triple Tree. Even Mrs. P. Maybe she needed prayers most of all. She didn't seem any happier than the girls to be here.

Edna wasn't the only one who'd been curious about Mrs. P.'s locket. A chance to see the contents, came unexpectedly a week after that day in the office. Edna and Amaretta were straggling back to the dorm after vespers and Amaretta spotted something gleaming faintly in the grass by the path. She couldn't believe it was the mysterious locket so often fingered by Mrs. P. With only a moment's hesitation and a quick glance around to make sure they were unobserved, the girls satisfied their curiosity. Clumsy fingers finally freed the clasp and the filigree front sprang away from the back.

Edna glanced at Amaretta. Guilt overshadowed a dozen questions plainly visible on her guileless features. "Oh, no. What should we do?"

Amaretta was speechless. They weren't surprised to find the photo of the handsome, mustachioed man they presumed to be Mrs. P.'s beloved Gabriel. He clutched a Bible to his chest. A shiny gold band, his only jewelry, the sparkle in his eye presumably for his bride.

They had no idea what to think of the other portrait. A chubby, round-eyed infant, in a frilly, long gown, smiling sweetly out at them.

"We can't keep it, Amaretta. Let's take it inside and drop it in the hall by her door. She'll never know we've seen it. Wouldn't you just die to ask her, though?"

But both girls kept their guilty secret. In league with Mrs. P., of all people.

Two of the longest weeks of Edna's life went by before her day of freedom arrived. As aunt Caira climbed into the front seat of the old Plymouth, she turned and took Edna's hand awkwardly, over the back of the seat.

"Harriet was terribly disappointed she couldn't come. She can't wait to see you, but she won't be through at Rachel's until five. She'll have dinner ready when we get home. You can stay with us tonight and meet the Campbells in the morning. With luck, Mrs. Campbell won't have the baby for a few more days. She's looking ripe as a summer melon. I'm so glad you'll be close again, Edna."

"Me too! Oh, it's Modene, now, aunt Caira. I'm going by Modene, now."

She'd made the decision that morning as she packed her few belongings. A new name for a new life. Edna sounded so ordinary and Modene was such a pretty name. After all, her daddy used to call her Edna-Modene and she'd always liked it. She'd never known another living soul with that name. Modene sounded ever so glamorous and grown up to Edna, though she'd never found out where it originated. She hoped it was a family name. The name of someone who'd been loved dearly. Loved enough to name a child after. Well, it wasn't any family she knew of. Now it was too late to ask.

Aunt Caira cocked her head to one side and looked at her niece for a long moment, but she understood how it could be. She smiled and corrected herself.

"Modene, then. Your mother would like that."

STEP 5:
Simmer, Stirring The Pot Often

Simmer, stirring the pot often…

Mrs. Campbell's scream pierced the night, jarring Modene from a deep, dreamless sleep. Slipping into her robe as she dashed barefoot down the long hall, she stubbed her toe on a toy tractor in front of Zach and Calvin's door and hobbled on in the dark. Her knock on the bedroom door was immediately answered and she was let in by a frazzled Mr. Campbell as he rushed out, sleep-mussed hair standing on end, shirt tail flying.

"It's her time. Stay with her", he rasped. "I'll fetch Mrs. Smith."

Modene sucked in a deep breath and willed herself to enter the semi-dark, giving her word to do what she could to keep the laboring Mrs. Campbell comfortable. A single lamp on the dresser cast an eerie glow on the ominous shadow huddled beneath the covers. A quick silent prayer for guidance and Modene set to work, as best she could. She'd had only days to get to know this new family, and now she and her new employers would share this intimate experience. God bless the Margaret Smiths of the world.

In less than an hour, a frustrated Mr. Campbell returned. Alone. Unfortunately, this particular night turned out to be an unusually busy one for Mrs. Smith. It could be that way, with midwives.

"Where's Mrs. Smith?" Modene turned her attention momentarily from tending her patient to the hunched silhouette hovering solemnly in the doorway. "I have the water boiling and the clean cloths are ready. I gave her some of the blue cohosh tea, with honey. Like Mrs. Smith said. There's coffee on the range."

The dead silence in the half dark room caused her to glance back at the expectant father, only to see him shrug his narrow shoulders in defeat. "I left word, but…"

The clean cloths might be ready and Mrs. Campbell was more than ready, but Modene was far from it. Thoughts flooded back to her of the night Doc Raines had attended her own mother in her time. The night Lily died and her newborn son with her.

Just then, Abra swept past her father in the doorway, and challenged Modene.

"We don't need you, you know. I delivered my baby brother. All by myself. I can take care of mother, now. You can go back to bed."

"I'm sure you can. It's just...I wanted to help. I thought maybe..."

"Aaagghhh!" Mrs. Campbell moaned and writhed in agony, hopelessly tangling the bed clothes. "Something's wrong. I knew it last night. It's the moon..." Panic glazed her pleading eyes, and sweat-dampened hair clung in dark ringlets about her flushed face.

"Everything's going to be okay", Modene ventured, but she had her doubts. She had no personal experience in being present at a birth and her only association was that her mother had died giving birth. She felt anything but competent to assist and was happy to step aside and allow Abra the dubious honor.

At thirteen, Abra was three years younger than she, but Modene figured maybe there was something to be learned from her, in order to be of more help if she ever found herself in this position again, God forbid.

Abra took her place at her mother's side, effectively easing Modene into the position of observer. "It's okay, mother. I'm here". She turned on the lamp closest to the bedside, removing the fringed shade and tucking the covers back out of the way. Then she captured her mother's swollen hands in her own, and further asserted her position by tossing an almost off-hand statement in Modene's general direction about how normally the labor was progressing.

"Having babies is the most natural thing in the world. I've seen it lotsa times." She rather delighted in the look of shock and dismay on Modene's face at the goriness of what they were witnessing in the glaring pool of light. Feeling useless at teats on a boar, Clay Campbell had removed himself from the bedroom to the relative calm and obscurity of the kitchen to wait.

The infant's head began to crown, and Modene peered over Abra's shoulder, gasping at the appearance of the purplish, slimy form emerging, certain that this was not normal.

"Oh, no..", Modene breathed, her eyes growing large as teacups. *Maybe this is what happened to my baby brother. It's all going wrong. Who's going to tell Mrs. Campbell? Not me...* Terrified, she suddenly couldn't bear to look. It was all she could do to remember to breathe.

Modene glanced over at Abra's face, trying to gauge the seriousness of the situation but the girl was perfectly calm, mopping her mother's brow and cooing reassurances. A delicate balancing act, all the while supporting the baby's head.

"Is he supposed to be that color?" Modene was incredulous.

"Of course silly. Don't you know **any**thing?"

Within moments, Abra's face reflected that something was frightening even the birth-seasoned Abra and she recoiled. She'd never seen anything like this. Not in the hundreds of imagined birthings.

She recognized the umbilical cord, but it was wrapped around the baby's neck, not once, but twice. Abra tried to feel underneath the cord and could only tell that it was dangerously tight and getting tighter with each fraction of an inch the baby gained on its journey into the cold, real world. Vaiva Ruth's eyes rolled back in her head as she slid headlong into oblivion.

"What do you do now, Abra?" Modene whispered.

"I don't know! It's not supposed to be like that. I just know we can't cut it yet."

Abra's small hands flew to her cheeks and she began to back away in terror.

By default, Modene eased forward. *God, Where's Mrs. Smith?* Modene had washed her hands as instructed, when she was in the kitchen after boiling the water and making coffee. Now she reached uncertainly toward the struggling infant.

Suddenly something gave inside Mrs. Campbell's body, and her eyelids fluttered convulsively as the baby was propelled forward into

Modene's waiting hands. She didn't so much deliver the baby, as catch her. Instantly, blood was everywhere.

I hope I never have to do this again! Why would any woman choose to have a second baby? Once should be enough. More than enough. *I'm not ever going to have a baby. Not EVER!*

Everything fell oppressively still. Modene looked at Abra, who came forward and unwound the now slack cord from the baby's neck, and grabbed a clean towel. With trembling hands, Abra flung it over the too quiet baby. It was Modene who wrapped it around the still body, and instinctively began drying the lifeless form.

"Don't pull on the cord!" Abra commanded, for whatever it was worth.

The combination of relieving the pressure around the newborn's neck and the stimulation of the rubbing brought a cry of protest and the small, still bundle came to life. Modene started so abruptly, she almost dropped the baby.

Abra would have breathed a sigh of relief, but she knew she didn't have the luxury of time. The job wasn't finished yet and she had no idea how to stem the tide of blood that was now free-flowing from her mother.

"What now, Modene?" Panic edged Abra's voice. "What did Maggie say to do for the bleeding? Red raspberry tea, or was it black haw…"

If Margaret Smith hadn't come breezing through the door at that moment and taken charge, Mrs. Campbell would surely have bled to death.

Abra gladly relinquished her mother's care and claimed the newest addition to the Campbell clan from Modene's arms. She busied herself showing Modene how to care for the squalling infant, a welcome distraction for both girls. They were hardly aware of the midwife's quiet and efficient performance of her task. Margaret's practiced eyes never revealed the depth of the threat to her patient.

Mrs. Campbell slowly began to come around. Exhausted and pale from loss of blood, the first thing she saw was Margaret Smith's laughing eyes twinkling down at her. The midwife was all long, naturally curly hair and her smile was years younger than the rest of her. Her calm presence reassured her patient.

"Thank God you're here, Maggie. It's time. Time for my baby."

"Oh, it's past time for your baby, Vaiva Ruth. Lucky for you, you had experts on hand. Abra and Modene delivered your beautiful daughter safely while you slept like a baby. I'm just finishing up the details. Here, drink this. Slowly, slowly…" She held the cup of red raspberry leaf tea to the new mother's parched lips, telling her it would not only help to prevent—and she used the term with some poetic license—heavy bleeding, but help to produce nourishing milk for her wee one.

Sipping gingerly, Vaiva Ruth gazed at the girls with open wonder. "What would I have done without you two? And Maggie, of course."

Modene spoke up and credited Abra. "It was Abra, really. I didn't know what to do. Thank God she was here." Modene sidled a glance at Abra.

"My own daughter! Who would think? I'm so proud of you, Abra Gita. Look at my perfectly beautiful baby!"

"Well, it was a little scary this time, but here she is, mother. She is perfect, isn't she?"

Abra and Modene exchanged vaguely conspiratorial smiles as Abra nestled the newborn into her mother's grateful arms, where she immediately began an eager suckling. "I couldn't have done it without Maggie", Abra demurred.

The new mother lost herself in murmuring endearments into the shell-like ears of her precious newborn, in her native tongue. "Si ir mana masa meitenite."

Maggie waved the praise away. "Nonsense, you had things well in hand. A little more coaching Abra and you would make an excellent midwife." The complimentary words from Maggie made Abra blush.

Meanwhile, it was Modene whose thoughts were running in that direction. She had watched the midwife work her magic and envied her easy confidence, her unwavering smile and reassurance. There was something so miraculous, so wondrous and beautiful about what had just happened here, Modene could scarcely contain her elation.

This joy was tempered though, with a sadness. Sadness that she didn't know how to help her mother. If only she'd been older, known more. If only Maggie had been there instead of that old sot, Doc Raines. Modene knew Maggie would have known better than to give Lily a dose of salts to speed up her labor. She'd heard Maggie say it more than once in the last few days before this birth. "Babies come in their own good time. My job is to comfort mothers. Support, not intervene. God has given us a great store of natural herbs to ease discomfort and the wisdom to know how to use them. The rest is up to Him." And Maggie practiced what she preached. This philosophy was part of her. As much a part of her as her able, sturdy hands.

Modene and Abra eventually trailed back to their rooms as the sun floated up over the little knob of a hill, known as Muffin Mountain. Abra slept the sleep of the dead. Modene was too intoxicated with the concept of being a midwife to sleep. She lay awake next to the slumbering Bethany head to toe and toe to head, dreaming wide-awake dreams of becoming first an apprentice to Maggie, if she'd agree of course, and then a midwife in her own right. She envisioned a life of great satisfaction and joy. Power, even. To hold lives in your very hands. To have the power to help mothers, and to bring untold healthy babies safely into the world. She made herself a vow to talk to Maggie about it at the first opportunity.

Somewhere, hovering around the fringes of this grand and joyous dream was, at first the hope and then an almost prayer, for children of her own. Suddenly she wanted a big family, with lots of children to love, and who would love her in return, nourish her heart and soul. Their would-be father, however was faceless.

Well, she probably hadn't met him yet. Certainly not any of the boys she'd met at school. Not that gangly, ferret-faced Broward boy who teased and tortured her on a daily basis. Come to think of it, Modene couldn't put any kind of face on her imaginary soul mate. She couldn't begin to call one up. Dark or fair? Tall or short? Maybe a face like her father's? No, he was long gone and no one would ever love her like he had. When he died, it seemed all the love went out of her life. Only Babe, and maybe uncle Tim, loved her now, and that was probably only because they felt sorry for her.

She began to realize that was all it was, a dream. Just a silly dream, of course. One that would never come true for her. Who would ever love her, again? Who would choose her to love? Above all others. Better yet, why would they? No, she'd be content to care for the children of other families, as she always had. If she could be a midwife or some sort of nurse, maybe she could fill her life, fill her heart with purpose. It would have to be enough.

Too soon it was time to get up and start the day's chores. Modene's tired body and mind were comforted only by the knowledge that miraculously, after the shared experience last night, she and Abra now had a bond. Hopefully the tensions that dominated their relationship from the start would ease, and life would be less stressful now that she and Abra could be real friends. But change doesn't come that easily for some. If only she could keep in mind her father's admonition, she'd have less disappointments; "Old habits die hard".

Vaiva Ruth broke from the couple's naming tradition and bestowed the name of Hope on her newborn daughter, for her own reasons. Deeply religious, the Campbells had begun their family with Abra, a name they chose together from the Bible. Next, came Bethany, and then Calvin. A devout Catholic, Clay Campbell's plan was to work their way through the Bible, alphabetically. A practical Lutheran woman, Vaiva Ruth's plan was to put a stop to that by naming their last son, Zachariah. Best laid plans aside, Mrs. Campbell now chose Hope, for what she *hoped* would be her last child.

All the Campbell children bore Latvian middle names, at their mother's insistence. It was her way of keeping in touch with her own heritage. The Latvian naming customs were ingrained in Vaiva Ruth Campbell, and she had made a promise to herself to preserve the Latvian culture and customs. Besides, how else could she celebrate "Name Day" with her children?

Probably her parents were turning over in their graves. They didn't live to see their only daughter married. Married to a Catholic, no less. She couldn't have chosen a mate whose religious beliefs were more diametrically opposed to her own. Clay Campbell might not have carried his Latvian bride over the bridge, in at Kuldiga Falls as she would have liked, to bless their marriage, but she was as committed and considered her marriage as blessed, as if they had sealed their vows in this way. It was a challenge, at times. It certainly kept life interesting. They had made a pact upon their engagement not to try and change each other.

That the Campbells were both very involved in church was a given, going into their home to help. That it involved two very different churches, came as a surprise to Modene. There were cultural differences, as well. Not that this unexpected complexity involved her personally, except in terms of adjusting to the undercurrents generated within the family. Clay Campbell called his children by their first names only, whereas Vaiva Ruth insisted on using first and middle names when addressing or referring to her children; Abra Gita, Bethany Larisa, Calvin Nikolas, Zachariah Erik, and Hope Ariana.

As It tuned out, friendship between Abra and Modene was not to be. Earlier tensions between Abra and Modene soon resurfaced and Abra's petty jealously, ruled their relationship. Even Abra's younger siblings were excluded when ever possible. If Abra had her way, it would be just herself and her mother. They didn't need the others.

Why did her mother keep having all these babies, anyway? They had each other.

Abra began spending as much time as possible with Maggie, leaving much of the household chores to Modene. She took to giving Modene orders when she thought she could get away with it, as though she were her personal slave. After all, Abra had to concentrate on her career.

Par for the course. Oh well, everyone who'd come into Modene's life since her father died had been temporary. Every home temporary. This home, these people—all temporary. They'd leave her, or she'd leave them. Anyway, best not to get too attached. What's another transition, anyway? Her life had been one long series of transitions. It never stops. Finally one of life's great secrets had found a home in her heart and mind. *Nothing stays the same.*

Church activities and social events were faithfully chronicled in the town newspaper, the McAllister Monitor, by popular columnist, Patricia Judkins. Patricia was a friend of Vaiva Ruth's, but then Patricia was everybody's friend. In any other town her column might qualify as a "gossip column", but Patricia enjoyed her role and refused to indulge in purely gossipy news, prevalent in some towns. She prided herself on reporting accurately. Her obvious talent for creative writing and sense of humor found its way into her column more often than not, and her regular readers came to expect it. Her column was a pleasing mix of local happenings and reminiscence.

In the next issue of the Monitor, Patricia's column started off with the news of the addition to the Campbell family.

MY WORD! Our favorite midwife, Maggie Smith has been busy lately. With her latest delivery she had a little unexpected help. She tells me Abra Campbell delivered her new baby sister, Hope Ariana while awaiting Maggie's arrival, when our favorite midwife was delayed on a false labor call at the home of Fay Cox. Mother and baby are doing fine. Congratulations to the Campbell family, and to Abra, especially. Next week, Vaiva Ruth is planning big extravaganza for Calvin Nik's "Names Day Celebration". Those of you who know Vaiva Ruth know that will certainly involve serving his favorite treat, *'Aleksandra Kukas*, or *Alexander cakes*'! Happy Name Day, Calvin Nik!

❦   ❦   ❦

Weeks after Hope's birth, news of not one, but two babies lost at Maggie's hands dominated conversation in the household. Modene's great aspirations of becoming a midwifebegan to waver like a mirage on the horizon. Modene couldn't imagine what it would be like to feel responsible for that kind of loss. Not that it was Maggie's fault. No one blamed her.

No one except Maggie. In her mind she knew it couldn't have been helped, but in her heart the hurt was so great, so relentless, she nearly gave up her calling. Just to avoid more pain. Avoid the wondering. They weren't the first babies she'd lost, but they were the first in a long time.

Then a successful birth and another, and soon the joys outweighed the losses again and Maggie's passion for her work flamed anew. Now, she offered to work with Modene and teach her as she was doing with Abra, but the moment had passed. Besides, who'd want to compete with Abra?

"How do you do it? It's such a big responsibility." Modene couldn't stop the questions from forming.

"You just do it. There's a need and you try to fill it. You learn all you can. You never learn enough, though. Nothing you ever learn is wasted." Modene thought Maggie must be the wisest person she knew.

Life in the Campbell's 1800's vintage home fell into a routine. Modene juggled the housework and helping with the children with her schoolwork and weekends, leaving her little time to brood. Sundays were busy with church activities at the Campbell's separate churches.

Though the house was large, it had only four bedrooms. Hope, for the time being shared her parents' room, and Modene shared a room with Bethany. Abra was adamant about needing her room to herself. Zach and Calvin shared the remaining bedroom.

The original structure had been built in 1867 by Clay's grandfather, for his new bride. The current residents had started some revamping, dividing the largest bedroom into two small ones to better accommodate their growing family. At the front of the house, a great room served as living room and parlor, with an archway separating it from the huge dining room. The newly exposed high living room ceiling was still painted the original deep teal green, like the eaves of the house, the only color hornets will avoid for nesting. Ornate crown molding divided the ceiling from mustard yellow walls. Clay had intended to repaint the ceiling, like a dozen other projects he'd started and failed to finish, leaving their home looking like a jigsaw puzzle in a constant state of partial assembly. Vaiva Ruth counted herself lucky that he had finished the bedroom division before Hope's arrival. Even so, the new wall remained unpainted. Later they'd have to make some sort of adjustment to put Hope in with Bethany, but probably not while Modene was there.

Modene threw herself into her high school activities and enjoyed the chance to spend time with the other "Gold Dust Twin" of her childhood, Harriet. They no longer were mistaken for twins. They spent as much time as possible together, were in the same class at school, and would graduate together. Modene was soon taken into Harriet's circle of friends, if not with enthusiasm, at least with tacit acceptance. Lately though, Harriet was spending all of her spare time with Ron, her "intended", and had little time for her cousin. Harriet and Ron were planning to marry right after graduation.

On rare occasions now, Modene had the opportunity to enjoy once again a remembered childhood pleasure. That of sitting in front of Harriet's mother, Caira, while she braided her hair for her. As a child, it was one of the few times Modene could be counted on to sit perfectly still, she enjoyed the process so. It was mesmerizing and the result made her feel almost beautiful. When the braiding was done, aunt Caira would coil the braids into circlets behind her niece's ears or bring the ends up over on top, to meet and frame her face, German style.

Modene's sixteenth summer found her with more time to herself. She and Harriet got Saturday jobs at The Sunflower Café. Though they had few hours available to work outside their duties with the families they helped to care for, it provided them with a little extra spending money. If life at the orphanage had seemed hard, waitressing and taking care of the Campbell household was no piece of cake, but at least now she was compensated for it. Modene was glad for the opportunity to work and save some money. Maybe she could save enough to go to nursing school after graduation next year. How much would be enough, she wondered, and where would she go?

The summer flew by and the girls' last year in high school proved to be little more taxing than previous grades. Modene had managed to save some money but still had no idea where she wanted to go to school after graduation. Mc Allister didn't have a school with the courses she'd need.

For her 17th birthday, Modene received a package from aunt Babe. An actual package, addressed to her, Miss Edna Modene Gillen. She and aunt Babe kept in touch and she often got letters, but never in her life had she received any mail as exciting as that brown paper wrapped box, tied securely with ragged twine. She couldn't wait to tear off the wrappings. Inside she found an envelope on top of a rather weighty, wrapped object. She decided to open the card first, which was only proper anyway, but she wanted to savor the excitement and suspense over what might be in the small, newspaper covered bundle, this layer tied on with strips of lace. As she opened the card, a small piece of tissue thin blue paper fluttered out.

∾

Dearest Edna,

Hope all is well with you and your family there. This is just a small graduation present but I had some money as I've started doing some mending for some of the single men teaching here. I thought you'd enjoy this and it would help you save some memories. Memories can be among our most treasured possessions, in difficult times.

We are all fine except for your uncle Tim's sciatica. We treat it as best we can, but he suffers with nagging pain. He's taken to wearing overalls and you should see him. Says no intelligent person would cut his gut in half with a goll-danged belt, anyway.

Gavin's growing like a weed and loves school. He sure misses you.

Guess what? You know I told you Grey Wolf had a heart attack last year and was in the hospital? Well, he up and married his nurse! Ain't that somethin'? You should see her order him around. He's like a lovesick puppy. Well, he's mellowed some but he's still Grey Wolf.

I wish we could be there for your graduation in June. We're so proud of you. What will you do after graduation? Are you still working at the Sunflower?

Did you hear Susanna had her baby? A little boy. Weighed nearly nine pounds. Big baby for such a little girl. 'Course that no good husband of hers wasn't even there. Mrs. Thornbury is beside herself with worry. I've never seen her so torn. But she can't bear the scandal of a divorce so she keeps spoon feedin' her own daughter one Bible verse after another about obedience to that scoundrel and the Holy Word. I'd ride him out of town on a rail! I think he hits her too. Don't know what will become of her or that sweet baby boy.

Well, congratulations, dear. Gavin blows you kisses on the wind. Hope you get 'em okay. See you soon, I hope. Be good.

Love, aunt Babe

Edna propped the card on her dresser and tucked the letter under the dresser scarf. Poor Susannah. *Well, Congratulations to me!*

She turned her attention to the strips of lace holding the mysterious gift from view. They were only loosely tied and fell away easily, allowing the newsprint wrappings to slide off, revealing a small, paper bound booklet. *Autographs* was ornately inscribed on the cover.

Excitedly she fumbled the cover open to reveal mostly blank pastel pages, some with small ivy motifs adorning the pages. Plenty of room for all her myriad of friends to record their love and best wishes. She gave some thought to who all might want to write in her book and try as she might, could only think of a handful of Harriet's friends who had allowed her to become a part of their group. And of course, Harriet. And aunt Caira. Maybe her teacher, even, Miss Holcomb.

Maybe she'd even ask Louise, the new girl if she'd like to write something. Not that she knew her all that well. No one did. Louise was a funny mix of expensive but ill-fitting clothes on a less than meticulously groomed, frumpy mouse of a thing. Well, mouse was too small a word to describe Louise, but she was quiet and nearly invisible like one. Serious, a good student with zero social skills, almost a full year younger than her classmates. But Modene felt sorry for her. Yes, she'd ask her. All she could do was say was no.

It was an oppressively muggy day in early June that inspired an attack of terminal mischief in the small group Modene now considered her friends. In earlier years she would have been too timid to consider participating. But she was beginning to feel a little freer and more at home. With less than a week until graduation, she was as antsy as Harriet and the others.

Of course Harriet and her beau, Ronald, had their own reasons for wanting to get away unsupervised. Who knew but what they could steal a few moments away from the group for a little clandestine hand holding and smooching. Their planned wedding the weekend after graduation seemed an eternity away. Modene had heard enough details of Harriet's romance with the dashing, slightly roguish, impossibly blue-eyed Ronald to almost make her wish she could look forward to finding someone herself. She was thrilled, and a little envious of her cousin.

Modene had already tasted enough loss of Harriet's time with her to know that, whereas Harriet and Ronald would be close by, she didn't expect to see much of them after they married. Well, such is life. The wedding was a whole week away. They had this time, now.

For the first time in her life, Modene skipped school that gloriously sunny day, with a sense of giddiness bordering on wickedness. Ominous visions insisted on recurring, quite beyond her control. Visions of a stern Mrs. Pennyworth, waggling a finger in her direction threatened to overshadow the thrill of this guilty pleasure.

Each of the conspirators set off as usual for school. One by one they were gathered up by Harriet and her betrothed in his daddy's pick-up truck. Most of the riders were oblivious to the bits of hay and other debris so common in the beds of farm vehicles. Modene squeezed in beside Harriet, neatly sandwiching her cousin between herself and Ron.

One participant had more or less included herself in the outing. Louise had overheard some discussion of it the day before and assumed she was included. Louise was new to Mc Allister, having moved in with her wealthy grandmother after her parents' scandalous divorce in neighboring Hillwood. The towns were too close together for word of Louise's father's misdeeds to go unreported. Too many families had ties to both communities. Louise's mother escaped the resulting gossip and ostracism, by moving out of state, but Louise was not so fortunate.

Most of the students at Mc Allister High had been forewarned about Louise, by concerned parents. It was as though Louise somehow was responsible for her parents' sinful divorce.

Only Modene had befriended her, to a degree, because she knew the heartbreak of exclusion. Louise seemed painfully shy and socially awkward. Stringy, unkempt hair, and a slight, almost comical crossing of one eye did little to improve her chances of acceptance. Harriet and her friends allowed her presence on the perimeter of their group, only because it seemed important to Modene, but they did little to encourage her.

No one made any effort to include her on the route for pick up that day, so Louise arranged her own transportation and arrived at the springs alone, on horseback, ahead of the others.

The group of six graduates-to-be, were hungry for a day of fun and frolicking at the hot springs that gurgled in the shadow of Muffin Mountain. Being a school day, they had their favorite hangout mostly to themselves. Someone years before had tied a heavy rope to the center of a now weathered, wooden plank, looping the other end over a sturdy limb of an old ironwood tree that flirted with the edge of the water. The teens took turns sitting or standing astride the rope and swooping out over the pool of water, eventually dropping off into it's soothing depths.

Tangy sand hill plums, gathered nearby provided a tasty snack as a scorching sun rose high in the endless blue sky above them. Before long, Harriet and Ron absented themselves from the group, to go "climbing" in the rocks. Transparent, at best.

Modene found herself shadowed by Trey James. Somehow, every time she turned around, he was there, grinning ear to ear. In the beginning, it was disconcerting, but as the day wore on, she realized his attention felt more comfortable, and more than a little exhilarating.

Trey was not the least attractive boy in her class. She had thought him a little slow, but his grades were good enough. She decided he was kind of cute, in a coltish sort of way. His wide brown eyes and bubbly manner put her to mind of Jilly. Jilly. What ever had become of Jilly and the others at the orphanage?

When Trey slipped his hand around hers, shaking with his own boldness, thoughts of her orphanage friends burst like a visible bubble. She started to pull her hand away but she looked up into his eyes and found herself incapable of reacting in any way. He squeezed her hand, and without conscious thought, she squeezed back. His smile could have lit the whole Campbell home for a month! There was something intoxicating about learning she had the power to generate that kind of response in another.

They might have gone on to enjoy the delicious flirting and tentative intimacy all afternoon if Modene's encouragement had not had the effect of making Trey feel overly bold and confident. Confident enough to steal a kiss while Modene was absorbed in the glistening springs, and enjoying the water play of their friends. He knew immediately it was a mistake.

Modene jumped up as though she'd been bitten by a snake. A snake in the grass, perhaps. Incensed, she angrily swiped at her mouth with the back of a trembling hand, eyes shooting daggers.

So that was it! He was pretending to like her just to get close to her, take advantage of her innocence. She'd heard about boys like that, but still she'd been fooled. Well, *once bitten, twice shy!*

Hot tears stung her eyes and spilled onto flaming cheeks before she broke and ran, silent with shame, hoping no one had seen.

"Tease," he called after her. "You asked for it. What do you think Harriet and Ron are doing right now, huh? Holding hands?"

Full-blown fury was catching up with her. She wanted to tell him he was wrong. Defend her cousin's honor. And anyway, so what? They were engaged, after all, whereas Trey barely knew Modene. Could he really be that stupid? Was she? What had she done wrong? Suddenly she wanted to be home cooking over a hot stove, or scrubbing toilets. Anything was preferable to this!

She found an isolated tumble of rocks and plopped herself down on a large flat boulder before the flood of tears came. She hadn't seen Louise sitting nearby. She kind of blended in with the stones. Hearing Modene's sobs, Louise was suddenly bending toward Modene, one arm awkwardly seeking to encircle her hunched shoulders. Modene couldn't help herself. She fell into the younger girl's embrace and they cried together, each for her own reasons.

"Are they all like that?" Modene wanted to know.

"What?" Louise was truly puzzled, wrenched from her own thoughts.

"Boys! All they want to do is kiss and…and…other stuff. I don't even know what all."

Louise was quick to answer. "No good, none of 'em. Can't trust a one. It's just how God made 'em. They can't help it, mama says. Original sin and all that. I'm not having any of that. Don't need it."

The girls sat on the rocks in the shade of a lone cottonwood tree, while a cooling breeze soothed their ruffled feathers. The more they talked, the more they found they had in common.

"I can't wait till school's out and summer's over. Mama got a job in Kansas and a place. Pretty soon I'm gonna go stay with her and go to nursing school."

"You're kidding! That's what I want to do, go into nursing, but I don't know where to go." Modene couldn't believe she and this obscure newcomer shared the same dream. Only Louise had a plan. Modene was still casting about for how to make her own dream come true.

"You could come with me. Mama won't care. Trust me, she won't even notice. She's got a new boyfriend. She hardly ever writes except to send money."

"I couldn't do that. I couldn't impose. Besides, what about the Campbell's? How could I leave?"

"They got along before you, didn't they?"

"Yes, but that was before Hope came along and…"

"One tiny baby? You got a lot to learn. Well, think about it." Louise smiled hopefully, into her new friend's eyes.

Modene smiled back, her mind racing a mile a minute. *Could I? Could I really?*

"Well, maybe. I'll have to think about it. I have some money saved, but I don't know. I mean, how much would I need? How much is enough?"

"I don't know. Only you know when you have enough. Can't anybody else tell you that. Figure out what you absolutely need, and make your plans. How bad do you want this?"

"It's everything, but I just don't know. My daddy always says to look before you leap."

"Yeah, well my daddy always told me 'He who hesitates is lost'. Guess he didn't hesitate about leavin' us. You gotta get a plan. Life is movin' on. You won't have a better chance. I'll write and ask mama, but I know she'll say yes. We can get jobs. There's plenty of jobs there. We'll get by."

"Well, maybe, but I don't see how I could…"

"Seems to me most folks pretty much manage to do what they really wanna do. What do you wanna do?"

There it was. Boiled down to bare bones. *What do I want to do?*

Modene and Louise spent the rest of the time chatting about their hopes and plans, exchanging stories of their health related experiences. The time fled way too fast now, and the lengthening shadows told them it was time to return home, as if it were any ordinary school day. Modene found it hard to say goodbye to Louise and watch her ride off, alone. It was like losing touch with her dream.

Everyone piled back into Ron's truck in high spirits, and headed toward home. Harriet held hands with both Ron and Modene, and started singing "I've Got The World On A String", begging them to join in, which they did. Modene only glanced back once at the group in the back of the truck. She saw Trey sitting very close to Ellie. He had a muscled arm draped carelessly around her giraffe-like neck, his hand dangling precariously close to the bodice of her dress, just below the open collar. He looked up and caught Modene observing them through the narrow oval of the back window, and grinned a knowing, "you-missed-your-chance grin".

Modene turned away and raised the volume of her own voice. "...sittin' on a rainbow, got the string around my finger. What a world, what a life, I'm in love..." *Who needs him, anyway. Ellie can have him. I'm going to be a nurse!*

It wasn't that the students' absence went unnoticed. The pure coincidence of those particular students being absent on any given day was not lost on Miss Holcomb. The plain truth of it was that she was as ready for school to be out as her students, and the fact that they all returned the following day, in obvious good spirits, beneath their sunburned flesh was good enough. They were basically good kids. She loved them like she would her own. If she'd had any of her own. The fifty-something teacher had never married, and had gotten caught up in her teaching and her students. She just never seemed to make time in her life for a beau. Still, she felt fulfilled. A few more days and she'd send this batch of seniors out into the world, to test their wings. *Fly, little ones, fly.*

Graduation day was filled with excitement and anticipation. Louise was valedictorian for the class and fairly stunned her audience with an eloquence and insight beyond her years, far above and beyond her normal conversational speech.

Louise hadn't seen her mother before the ceremony and feared her mother would miss her speech. Her mother was to come for graduation and stay a few days before she and Louise were to head back to Kansas. Well, if she didn't show up today, maybe tomorrow. Even Louise never knew what to expect of her mother. It was no surprise to her that she hardly recognized her mother on that warm June day, when the honeysuckle laden air stood stock still. She spotted her mother dashing along to stand behind the last row of chairs, just as Louise was leaving the podium.

Louise introduced her mother to Modene after the ceremony, and while she was friendly to Louise's friend, she gave the impression of being distracted or edgy. She was anxious to get back on the road and she barely heard Louise mention the possibility of Modene coming back with them. "Yes, yes, Louise, that's nice, dear. Who's that nice looking older man in the blue pinstriped suit? He looks so jolly."

"Oh, that's Mr. Kimberling. He teaches math. I was never so glad to get out of a class in my life! So it's okay?"

"Yes, dear, whatever you like."

Modene's thoughts were riddled with fear of the unknown as she pondered this possible change in her life. If she could bring herself to take a chance. This would be a much bigger decision than any she'd ever been faced with and could lead to disaster. Real disaster. Or, the fulfillment of her dream. She decided to listen to her heart. *He who hesitates is lost.* She would cast her lot with Louise and her obviously quirky mother.

Mr. And Mrs. Campbell were milling around after the graduation ceremonies, as their niece had graduated with Louise and Modene. Vaiva Ruth didn't want to intrude on the conversation she overheard, but that night at supper, she broached the subject.

"When were you planning on telling us you were leaving us, Modene?"

At a loss for words, Modene stammered that it wasn't set, for sure. Not yet.

"Well, it's just as well. You know my niece, Ellie. Well, she'll be needing a place to stay. She can stay here and take your place. Some kind of trouble at home. It isn't Ellie's fault, of course. Not her, personally. I don't know what is going on, but her mother is going through some sort of difficult time. Imagines all kinds of problems with Ellie and accuses her of the most awful things. Disgraceful. Ellie's the youngest in the family and I think they just want her out on her own. So you needn't worry about the children. Ellie's quite capable. When are you leaving?"

"Ellie? Well, I think Louise is planning on leaving in a couple of days. Of course, if you need…"

"Nonsense. You're free to go. We wouldn't want to hold you against your will. I think it will work out for the best for all concerned. Calvin Nik! Quit kicking your sister under the table!"

"Well then, I guess that's settled. Thank you. May I please be excused? I want to start packing a few things. I'm not very hungry, anyway."

She wasn't accustomed to leaving food on her plate, but Modene knew if she tried to eat one more bite, it would stick in her craw.

Without waiting for an answer Modene fled to the shelter of the small room she shared with Bethany and threw herself on the bed. What was the matter with her, anyway? It's what she wanted, wasn't it? What did it matter if the Campbells didn't care if she left? They weren't even family. What would happen now? She hadn't even told Louse she'd go for sure. What if the offer wasn't still open? She prayed to God it was the right thing. She didn't pack a thing that night. She fell asleep on top of the covers and Bethany had to slide in under taut blankets, later that night.

The following morning a coolness pervaded the kitchen and conversation was kept to a polite minimum. Clay, oblivious to the icy distance between the females of his household, sipped his coffee and scanned the obituaries, as was his custom.

"I'll be danged! Did you know Scotty passed on? Him so young, and all. Don't make sense. He's even younger 'n me."

"Clay, if you don't quit buryin' yourself in those obits every day, we'll be buryin' you before your time. Finish up and give me the society section. 'Fore the younguns get up."

"All right, all right. I just can't believe that about Scotty. Who are we gonna get for pool on Saturday?"

"Makes no never mind to me. Now let me see if that newspaper got the facts right on the potluck after church on Sunday." Vaiva more or less grabbed the paper from her shocked husband and turned to the article by her friend, Patricia Judkins.

"I knew I could count on her. Right there. First paragraph." She punctuated her statement noisily with a satisfied, one-fingered poking at the open newspaper.

After breakfast, Modene half-heartedly threw a few things in her bag, just in case. She placed her autograph book next to her rag doll, so she wouldn't forget it. It had all of 13 autographs! But first things first. She needed to talk to Louise.

Mrs. Campbell was outside taking clothes off the line when Modene found her. "I'm going over to Louise's for a few minutes, if that's okay."

"That's fine, but I hope you can help fold this laundry when you get back. We have to run to the market." This garbled message was mouthed around a mouthful of clothes pins.

"Sure. I won't be long." Modene set off at a rapid pace, her mind wound around the thought that this might actually happen. She might really be leaving here in a few days, headed for an unfamiliar state with virtual strangers. All she knew about Louise's mother was that she seemed a little strange. Well, they probably would all be so busy, they might not even see much of each other. After all, she and Louise would be working and going to school and studying. Butterflies danced in her belly as she strode along.

Across town, a taxicab was pulling up in front of Louise's grandmother's house. Louise was at the piano and she saw the cab through the front window. Her heart felt heavy and her fingers hung above the keys. *We're not supposed to leave till tomorrow! Am I ready for this?*

Louise hoped with all her heart that Modene had made up her mind to go with them and that she was packed and ready. Ready to go. She had no illusions about anyone being ready to deal with her mother.

Black and white spectator pumps emerged from the cab, and Louise's eyes followed long shapely legs as they unfolded. A raven-tressed beauty emerged regally from the back seat. Gloved hands pressed the taxi driver's knobby fists and he nodded his agreement to wait. The woman bore little resemblance to the blonde who had showed up late for graduation. Louise shuddered. *I don't even know her.*

Fluid knife pleats swirled about her mother's knees, a flutter of vivid plaid in geranium pink and black. A matching plaid scarf topped off the long, black dropped-waist torso. Her bright pink cloche hat, set off her now dark hair, and heightened the color of her rosy cheeks. She glided up the walk like quicksilver, blending in with the riot of color lining the path. Glistening lips formed the words Louise dreaded as she opened the door. "Hey, how's my baby? You ready to go?"

"Almost, mother. We didn't expect you till tomorrow."

"Well, grab your bag, Baby. Time's a wastin'. Joe's waiting at the hotel and he's anxious to get on the road. Is your little friend coming?"

"Yes, mother." She called to her grandmother to say goodbye. "Grams, mother's here, already." Then, to her mother, "My friend's name is Modene. She should be home."

"Well, I hope so. Joe doesn't like to be kept waiting, you know."

"Of course, mother." *No, I don't know. I don't know Joe. I don't know him from Adam. How **would** I know!* She wanted to scream. An obligatory smile briefly touched her lips and she headed down the hall just as Grandma Shirl came in.

"Are you sure you want to do this, Gloria? Louise is fine here with me."

"Don't be ridiculous mother. Look at you! You look just awful. Are you sleeping well? You have dark circles under your eyes and...'

"I'm just fine. Right as rain. You look wonderful, Gloria. Kansas must agree with you."

"Well, it's Joe, really. Mother, he's absolutely wonderful! He plays the sax, you know. Knows just everyone in the business. He has a little café and on Saturday nights he plays for the customers. Has all the women absolutely drooling. We might go to California next year. Or New York. New York's the place to be if you're serious about…"

"I'm ready, mother." Louise had come back into the room, with her bag in one hand, and she cut her mother off short. Did she have even a nodding acquaintance with reality? *More grand dreams. More elaborate plans.* Louise knew better than to take her mother's new plans seriously. They changed with the wind. She'd heard there's a lot of wind in Kansas. *God help us all.*

Gloria and her mother shared a quick, distant embrace and air kisses. Louise reluctantly stepped into the open circle of her grandmother's arms, not wanting to say goodbye. If it weren't for the opportunity of going to nursing school, she wouldn't be planning on leaving her grandmother's in favor of going to stay with her mother. But the lure was too strong. It might be her last chance at independence.

Knowing full well she was exchanging the comfort and security she'd longed for, for a questionable future at best, Louise took comfort in knowing she'd be sharing the adventure with Modene. She hadn't met Joe and had no idea how long her mother had even known him. All this was so strange to Louise, but then she'd never understood her mother.

Louise crossed her fingers behind her back as they got into the cab, praying Modene would be home. She knew her mother would be in no mood to wait. On the short drive to the Campbells, Louise said nothing, while her mother chattered incessantly about anything and everything. Mundane blathering, effectively blocking any meaningful conversation. No, "Sorry I missed your speech." No, "Congratulations" or, "How are you?" No inquiries or comments on Louise. Some things never change.

Then out of the blue, her mother asked her to call her Gloria. "It will be like we're friends. **Best** friends." She squeezed Louise's knee with her gloved hand.

"Sure, mother. I mean, Sure, Gloria."

"This is it. On the right. Stop here." Louise flung the door open before the taxi came to a complete stop, and bolted for the Campbell's front door. "Be right back."

Her knock went unanswered. Louise skipped down the steps and hurried around the west end of the wraparound porch, calling Modene's name. No answer.

The taxi horn honked out front and Louise muttered under her breath. "Hold your horses!" She ventured to the edge of a stand of purple locust trees that butted up against Sugar Creek. "Modene! Where are you? We've got to go!"

Mrs. Campbell poked her head out from behind a sheet on the clothesline. Plucking a clothespin from her mouth, and pinning it to her apron pocket, she dragged the flapping sheet off the line.

"I thought she was with you. She left for your house a while ago. Tell her I need her to get back here."

Rats! "Sure, Mrs. Campbell. Thanks." She was off and running. She barely heard Mrs. Campbell's plea for information on if, and when they'd be leaving. *No time. Joe's waiting. Joe doesn't like to be kept waiting.*

Honk. Honk

"I'm coming, I'm coming!"

Hope was diminishing for Louise and she drug her feet all the way back to the cab, desperately searching for a solution. *Mother won't be willing to drive all the way back to Gram's. Not in a cab.*

"She's not coming, Baby? That's too bad. Well, you can write her a nice letter." That settled, Gloria smiled sweetly.

Louise climbed into the backseat, crossing her arms over her chest. She turned her head to look out her window, not wanting her mother to see her tears. *Yeah, Gloria, a nice letter. That's perfect. Why didn't I think of that?*

Louise was so caught up in her misery and her mother's total lack of understanding, that she almost didn't see Modene walking alone, head down, back toward the Campbells. Modene was returning from Louise's and indulging in her own pity party. *Now what? I missed Louise and I'm out, at the Campbells.*

Louise beat frantically and excitedly on her car window. "It's her! That's Modene! Stop here!"

The taxi rolled to a stop just ahead of it's potential third passenger. Louise flew out the door and took Modene's hands, a pleading look in her eyes. "I thought we'd missed you! You're coming, aren't you? Mother's here early. Come on."

"Now? I'm not packed. I don't know if the Campbells are even home. They were going out. I was supposed to fold clothes…"

"Come on. Mrs. Campbell was hanging out clothes a few minutes ago, but you can leave a note if they've left. Mother won't wait. If you don't come, I'm not going either! We have to do this together."

Honk.

Gloria leaned across the seat and rolled down the window. "Is she coming, or not? We have to go, Baby."

"We're coming." She edged toward the cab, pulling Modene behind her. "We have to run back by the Campbell's to get her things."

"And maybe leave a note…" Modene was terrified and exhilarated at the same time.

"Oh, I don't know, Baby. It's getting late. Joe's waiting…"

"Please, mother. If Modene doesn't come, I'm staying with Grams."

"Don't be so dramatic, Louise Paulette! I don't know where you get that. Oh, all right, but make it snappy." She nodded to the driver and the girls piled into the cab.

Back at the Campbell home Louise scrambled out of the cab behind Modene and into the house. It was empty. Modene scribbled a note, feeling guilty about the unfolded pile of laundry. *Well, let the 'very capable Ellie' do it.* Louise gathered up a few loose belongings and tucked them into the bag on the bed.

"Wait." Modene said. "The rag doll. She's mine. I can't forget Baby."

Besides, Modene had all her savings stashed in the drawstring body, with the dwindling potpourri. And she might need the lucky Indian head penny mama had tucked into Baby's flower embroidered pocket after stitching the little crocheted purse handle to the doll, as the finishing touch. A lucky penny, dated 1922.

Louise picked up the rag doll and glanced at Modene. *Baby? She's serious?* Oh well, she knew how to deal with quirky.

In less than five minutes, they were ready to go. The two excited future nurses, as they considered themselves, answered the insistent honking horn.

"Baby, let Nadine sit by the window, so we can talk."

"Modene, mother. It's Modene."

"Yes, well whatever. And I'm Gloria, remember?"

"Yes, right. I forgot."

"Well try and remember. And from now on, I'll call you Louise. No one would believe I'm old enough to have a daughter in nursing school, now would they?"

"No, I guess not."

"Maureen, roll down your window, dear. It's hotter than blazes in here. Not a whiff of a breeze stirring." Gloria's gloved hand fanned her flushed face delicately with a lace edged hanky.

"It's **Modene**, Gloria." Louise rolled her eyes and stiffened her fingers.

"That's what I meant. Just wait till you meet Joe. He's such a love!"

The three rode in silence back to the hotel. Modene flashed an ingenuous grin at her soon-to-be roommate What am I getting into?

STEP 6:
Fold In A Generous Portion of Love

Fold in a generous portion of love...

The foreboding old Victorian rose two stories above those on either side of it. It must have been grand in its day. Most of the other homes from its era had been torn down and replaced with smaller, brick or stone houses.

It was apparent that Gloria viewed the ramshackle relic with rose colored glasses. When they arrived, she'd slid out of the car with a sweeping gesture using both hands, and gushed in her best deep south accent, "Isn't it just magnificent?" Her eyes glistened with pride. As though they owned it.

"Just the upper floor and attic, Babe", Joe reminded her.

"Of course. I know. Well, Louise baby, you and Maxine will share the attic. There's a kitchenette on our level, but we hardly ever eat at home, do we, darlin'?" She winked at Joe and turned slowly toward the house, continuing to look back at him, as her shoulders swiveled to follow her hips. "Well, come on in girls, you're home!" Louise gave up correcting her mother on Modene's name.

The attic. How quaint. Louise rolled her eyes at Modene and followed her mother and Joe up the walk.

I wonder if it's haunted. Modene kept these thoughts to herself, just as Louise had done.

The odd little family made their way up a rickety outside staircase, and into the dark interior of their apartment. It was too late in the day to get much benefit from raising the shades, so Gloria began turning on all the lights.

"I just can't abide all this darkness. It's like a cave. Just not enough windows, but it'll do for now. Till we decide where we want to settle, right, darlin'?"

Joe didn't answer, but Gloria didn't seem to expect a reply.

"Bathroom's over there and the stairs to the attic are at the end of hall. You girls can go on up and get comfy." Gloria had pulled off her gloves and waved a hand in the general direction of the darkened hallway, never taking her eyes off of Joe.

Louise and Modene excitedly rushed upstairs to survey their private space. A flickering hall light allowed them to find the pull chain for the overhead light in the dingy attic, and Louise tugged it on.

"Oh, my G…" Louise's response hung on the air like the cobwebs that covered everything in the room. "I guess they weren't expecting us." *Right. Typical.*

Modene was speechless. She couldn't say what she was thinking. She could hardly say "This is impossible!"

Both girls dropped their bags where they stood in the dim circle of light.

"Okay, okay. It's not so bad. We can move that table over here under the light. In the middle of the room. It's wide enough we can put a chair on either side, so we can both study. Chunky hands framed the space and Louise's eyebrows lifted, exploring what else they could use. All Modene could see was a dusty old attic, filled with old junk—trunks, hall trees, musty clothes and tattered quilts, an old, cobweb-draped dress form near the east dormer window. Other mysterious, less identifiable objects filled the dimly lit space. *Hopeless.*

Louise's hand fell on the handle of what turned out to be the door to a large closet, tucked away under the eaves. It was nearly empty. "Eureka! Give me a hand with that old bentwood rocker."

"The seat's all busted out."

"I know. Let's stash all this useless stuff in here. Then we can see what space is left. Louise began tugging on one arm and Modene came to her aid. To what end, she couldn't imagine.

"No, we need the floor lamp over here, ugly or no. It works. I tried it."

"What about this old chest?" Modene pushed at it with the toe of her shoe.

"We can use it for a table. Or a nightstand!"

The time flew by once they bent themselves to the task at hand. They quickly sorted through most everything, and once they'd stashed the unusable and unlovable pieces, they found they had rather a lot of space. Dirty space. Louise's spirits were so high, she drug her roommate along by sheer momentum.

Louise spied an old maple four poster bed. "We can share it," Louise proclaimed delightedly, "It's big enough." Later they'd lucked out and uncovered an old wicker chaise lounge. "This is mine! I'm sleeping here", Louise shrieked. "You can have the bed."

My own bed, Modene marveled. How long had it been since she'd had a bed to herself? And never had she had the luxury of so much room, all to herself.

Louise dictated that they should arrange their "beds" on either side of the east dormer, under the eaves of the long narrow room. That suited Modene just fine. They dragged the trunk over under the window and if fit perfectly between their beds. The girls began emptying the contents into an empty wicker basket. They found only one usable item in the depths of the trunk. A nearly translucent alabaster statue of a woman in a gossamer gown, her gaze following one outstretched slender arm, to the tips of her fingers. Calla lilies clustered around the hem of her gown. It intrigued Modene. She set the goddess-like form on the trunk, in the moonlight.

The table they had selected for their "desk" turned out to be an old game table with a checkerboard inlaid in light and dark woods. They found chess and checker pieces in a wooden crate, along with dominoes that appeared to be made of real ivory, and Mah jhongg pieces which were interesting but unrecognizable to the young girls. A shallow drawer in the center front of the table had plenty of room for all the game pieces, as well as pens and pencils, Perfect for study or leisure time.

"Do you play chess, Modene?"

"No, I never learned. The pieces are beautiful."

"I'll teach you. It's easy, once you learn how the pieces move."

"Sounds more complicated than checkers."

"It is. It's much more fun. More challenging."

Challenging wasn't the most appealing word to Modene. She'd had enough challenges to last her a lifetime. She had yet to discover that challenge could be good.

Modene found an old broken handled broom and was able to make some progress on the dusty floor before exhaustion overcame her. They'd left the windows open at either end of the room and they remained that way, as the girls collapsed on their beds and chatted into the night. Before they fell asleep out of pure exhaustion from the drive, and then the work of trying to make their cozy niche in one end of the room livable, they shared an optimism that had been absent when they first viewed their new quarters.

The next day the girls again spent most of their time in their own miniature apartment, and Modene was amazed at the transformation. She began to feel very optimistic indeed about her decision. Two lace draped windows sparkled with new life and opened out onto a whole new world.

If Louise had one good feature, it was her flawless complexion, inherited no doubt from Gloria, Modene assumed. She never seemed to go through that awkward, pimply stage. Modene learned that Louise and her mother had a beauty routine that included use of a mysterious paste they used religiously. Part of the concoction labeled, "Ancient European Beauty Potion", was kept on the bathroom sink. Modene's curiosity got the better of her and she finally asked Louise about it one night, as they were getting ready for bed.

"Oh, it's simple. Hold out your hand."

Modene did as she was told and found her palm held a small amount of table salt that Louise took from under the sink. A few drops of some sort of oily substance from the mysterious jar were added, and then Louise duplicated the process in her own palm.

Modene was staring at the mess in her hand. "Are you sure about this, Louise? It looks…blicky!"

"I'm sure. Just mix it into a paste with your finger. Like this."

"How do you know how much to use?"

"Doesn't matter. Just so the special oil and salt make a paste. Kinda like applesauce. Now use your fingers to rub it all over your face."

"Ooh! This is too greasy! It'll never rinse off."

"Sure it will. Try it." Louise began lightly scrubbing her face with the mixture. Modene followed suit and tasted the salt on her lips. She didn't recognize the smell of the olive oil, the only ingredient in the Ancient European Beauty Potion.

"Now, before you rinse it off, rub what's left on your hands. Just like it was soap. Easy, huh?"

Modene was amazed at how easily the oil and salt washed off. Running her tongue over her lips, she loved the smooth, velvety feel. "Wow! It's so soft."

"Gloria says that's why she doesn't have any wrinkles. Her mother died at eighty-three with barely a ripple or crease anywhere. Except for a few laugh lines, which she claimed she cherished."

The two new roommates brushed their teeth and fell into bed, trading other secrets and experiences late into the night. Modene found Louise too easy to talk to. Later she wondered if she'd shared too much. It had been so easy and it was nice to have someone to confide in. Well, they were going to be best friends and she felt so comfortable with Louise, she decided to trust her instincts.

Modene had been right about one thing. She and Louise saw very little of Gloria and Joe, which seemed to suit everyone. At mealtimes, everyone sort of fended for themselves. Modene and Louise usually ate in their room. They existed on cold cereal, peanut butter sandwiches, fresh fruit, and their dreams. It was like they were on their own. Modene had never tasted such freedom and it was delicious!

Summer was a settling in time for everyone. The girls excitedly registered for school in the fall and Louise was able to work at Joe's café. He claimed he had only room to hire on one new waitress, but

Modene found a job at Woolworth's Five and Dime. It wasn't as many hours as she'd have liked, but she was able to meet her school expenses with enough left over to buy a few new clothes for work and school. She shopped carefully and managed to squeeze out enough for a plain, dark skirt, a simple tailored white blouse with a Peter Pan collar, and a beige cardigan sweater. She hoped they were all nondescript enough that no one would notice how often she'd have to repeat the simple pieces in any given week. These pieces would augment what she'd brought with her and she'd add to her wardrobe as her budget allowed.

When school started, Modene and Louise shared many of the same classes and were able to ride to school together in the second hand car Joe had bought for Louise. For the rest of Modene's classes, and for work, she had to rely on public transportation or bumming rides from other students or dime store employees.

Life fell into a predictable routine at home, and Modene and Louise made their living quarters comfortable and clean for studying and relaxing, when they had time. Louise taught Modene to play chess but they found they had little time for frivolous endeavors. Classes were more demanding than they'd experienced in the past. Louise was a whiz at math, Modene excelled at language and spelling. They studied together, sharing their individual strengths with each other. They quizzed each other on medical terminology and anatomy. Modene had never worked so hard in her life, but it felt good. She'd never wanted anything in her life as much as she wanted this. Nothing that was attainable, anyway. You can't wish someone back from the dead, no matter how hard you work at it.

At first the nursing students practiced injection techniques on oranges, and then on each other. Modene and Louise thrived on every aspect of their studies and hungered equally for knowledge. This shared passion reinforced a growing closeness. Modene had never known this depth of friendship, and it was great to have someone to do girl stuff with; to play at painting fingernails and try different hairstyles. Louise took a new interest in her appearance and blossomed with her friend's encouragement. With the proper makeup, it was possible to draw attention away from Louise's slightly crossed eye and she became almost pretty. Hard work and meager eating habits took a few pounds off of both girls.

Lawrence had the largest, most fabulous library Modene had ever seen. It smelled of old leather and furniture polish, and sunshine streamed in through the diamond shaped, beveled window glass. It felt homey and welcoming. She often went there to study and just to read. She got her first library card there and became well acquainted with the facility and the staff. It became one of her great joys in this new life she'd chosen for herself. *She'd chosen*. She couldn't get over the awe of it.

The highlight of her off hours came when she and Louise had enough money and spare time off, at the same time, to enjoy a movie together. This was a new delight for Modene, and she enjoyed everything about the experience, but mostly the freedom and the power to provide this for herself. She had always been an avid reader and movies enchanted her, and brought stories to life. She'd never gone alone to the movies, but this particular Saturday, Spencer Tracy was playing in "Guess Who's Coming to Dinner", and she couldn't wait to see it. In her newfound emancipation, she decided to brave one more adventure.

Engrossed as she was in the opening credits of the film, Modene didn't notice the well-dressed young man slide into the seat next to hers. The credits always fascinated her, and Spencer Tracy was currently her favorite leading man. Her preoccupation with the silver screen would be the direct cause of the popcorn incident, which would change her life forever.

As she shifted in her seat to counter the move of a tall man in the seat in front of her, her purse knocked against the young man's arm, causing him to spill his bag of popcorn in her direction. Embarrassed at her clumsiness and fearing his outrage, she wasn't prepared for his calm reaction. Humor even, in the face of this disaster.

She knew her face had colored and said a silent prayer of thanks for the darkness. She launched into a splutter of apologies. He began to apologize at the same time, and then he broke out into laughter, which provoked an immediate and fervent "Shhhh!", from the couple in front of him. Modene was dumbfounded. A moment later, she succumbed to the giggle that bubbled to the surface and would not be suppressed.

It was a small spill, from a rather large bag of popcorn, and on impulse the young man offered to share it with Modene. She hesitated briefly, but seduced by the heavenly aroma, and deciding it could do no harm—they were, after all in a packed movie house and she knew how to scream—she plucked a few kernels from the bag and savored them. A nursing student could barely afford the luxury of a movie ticket. Adding popcorn to the tab would definitely strain her meager budget.

A new distraction occupied her mind for the duration of the movie. Who was this easy going stranger? What did he look like? Was he as young as his voice sounded? More importantly, was he a threat? Mrs. Pennyworth, at the orphanage, would purse her lips and sternly warn her that he was. Modene wanted to talk to him, to hear his voice again, but could think of no acceptable ruse to engage him in conversation. She might be a no-account orphan, but she was no hussy.

When the movie ended, they exited to the same aisle and the handsome stranger stepped back, offering her a clear path to melt into the stream of chattering movie-goers. *Hmmm, a gentlemen, and good looking as well.* Deep in thought and afraid the last moment for exchange was looming, she was startled to hear him address her as they entered the lobby. "My name is Harrison", he said simply. She knew she should ignore him, pretend she didn't know he was speaking to her, but she responded almost as though she weren't in control of her own mind and voice. Indeed, strange forces were at work.

"Modene", she muttered and lowered her head, reluctant to meet his eyes. "Modene's my name." Probably, when he saw her plainness in the light of day, heard her speak her silly name, he would turn and leave without another word.

"Modene." he said, "What a pretty name. It's so unusual." Humor flickered, warming his steady gaze with sparks of gold.

Unusual. Yes, that might be a kind way of putting it. Or was he making fun of her? She wanted nothing so much as to fade into the crowd and disappear. Why, in the name of heaven, had she ever thought Modene a more suitable or attractive name than Edna! *Dumb, dumb, dumb!*

"Mine's unusual too, I guess. It's a family surname. We're supposed to be related to President Harrison, way back." His easy smile was casual, nonthreatening.

Unbelievable. He was a sly one, all right. Mrs. Pennyworth's admonitions assaulted her conscience. If he were as nice as he seemed, why in the world would he be interested in the likes of her? No, Mrs. Pennyworth would **not** be pleased. The thought somehow amused Modene.

"What?" she said. "I'm sorry I didn't hear…"

"Would you join me for a cup of coffee?" His voice had raised a bit and he leaned in toward her to be heard over the noisy crowd.

She hesitated slightly but before she knew it, she had committed. "Well…I shouldn't, but…maybe just a cup of coffee…"

"Just a cup of coffee", he reassured her, and confidently took her arm as though it had been decided. He began steering her through the crowd as it spilled out onto the sidewalk.

How very wicked she felt. Walking along, arm in arm, with this tall stranger with the pleasant face and charming voice, to who knows where. To who knows what. Somehow it didn't feel threatening, or ominous. It felt exciting and more than a little delicious. He liked her. Or at least maybe he found her somewhat attractive.

What was he saying? She really must try and pay attention. In time her nervousness faded and she enjoyed the easy conversation about the movie and how riveting Spencer Tracy's performance had been. Definitely an award winning portrayal, but then who would expect less from the magnetic star that all America seemed to love.

Other movies and music of the day provided safe subject matter as they lingered over one more cup of coffee, and then one more. Neither of them seemed willing to call an end to so enjoyable an evening. But they must. "Just a cup of coffee", he had promised. And Harrison Arthur Woods was a man of his word.

And so they parted company, each silently regretting the conventions of the day. No self respecting girl would be so careless or bold as to allow a strange man to 'pick her up', at a movie house. So that was it.

"Good bye, and thank you."

"Yes, goodbye. I enjoyed it..."

What were the chances their paths would ever cross again in a college town the size of Lawrence, Kansas? Slim to none, she conceded grudgingly. He was obviously older than Modene. More of her own brand of luck, she mused as she watched his retreating back. How foolish she was. Allowing herself to dream of fairy tales and happy endings. Who did she think she was, Cinderella?

As the weeks passed, Modene was disconcerted to find herself watching for him everywhere. What was the matter with her? *Is that him at the produce counter, buying apples? No. What a relief.* She didn't have to duck out of the store. One Tuesday morning she thought she saw him walking down Lawrence Avenue, but then the man turned to greet a friend and when they embraced, she saw it wasn't him after all.

It was like with her father. She often thought she saw him, too. But that couldn't be, could it? He'd been gone a long time. It was just her heart playing tricks on her. What she wouldn't give for five minutes to talk with her father again. To tell him how much she loved him, and all the other things little girls don't know they need to say to someone who could be lost in an instant.

Early one fall day she was hurrying to anatomy class when she caught her first glimpse of him on campus. Or was it him? Was that possible? What would he be doing here? It couldn't be him. She could only see his back, but that familiar tilt of his shoulders, propelled her to keep moving, keep watching. Maybe from a different angle...But as he came into 3/4 view, she knew, and her heart lurched. *Oh no. How embarrassing!* One part of her wanted to see him again, talk to him, but she couldn't get past the old pain, the knowledge of who and what she was. And what must he think of her, if indeed he remembered their encounter the previous month at all? *A loose woman, no doubt. Woman.* The word sounded strange to her.

Who was that he was talking to? Of all people! It was Chloe! That stuck up little bird brain from her medical terminology class. *She doesn't know her trachea from her tibia!* Well, if Harrison was interested in that kind of girl, he certainly wasn't Modene's type. It figured. What did she care, anyway?

She hurried on to class and promptly and efficiently flunked the day's quiz. Her first "F". Her eyes stinging from tears, she bolted from the room and ran smack dab into—who else, but HIM! He caught her elbows and prevented her from spilling her armload of books all over the hall. She looked up into his mirth filled eyes and died a thousand deaths. She pulled away and hurried on before he could speak.

It was a big campus. With luck, maybe she'd never run into him again. But then, she was always short on luck.

Two days later, she sat Indian style on the lawn with her homemade checkered skirt billowing about her, studying. She looked up from her peanut butter sandwich when she saw a pair of handsomely clad legs, just above the top of her biology book. It was him. Staring down at her, no doubt observing her flaming cheeks and totally mis-interpreting the reason. He caught her off guard with a friendly greeting, and she found herself willing to be drawn into a mundane conversation. What was the harm in that? It wasn't as if she cared what he thought. It was harmless enough.

Soon she forgot about Chloe and her too tight pink angora sweater. She was lost in Harrison's charm. And that was the beginning.

Modene couldn't have anticipated the events that would unfold, or the treacherousness of the path that lay ahead of her. She was too naïve, too inexperienced. And too enthralled with this marvelous turn her life seemed to be taking. She was totally captivated with this dashing, "older man", a med student who made her heart skip beats, and who was so funny and wise. He was certainly different than the boys she had known, and even played with dating. Before she knew it, she had lost her heart.

As the weeks went by, they saw each other often, and grew comfortable with each other. She could scarcely believe her luck. It was too good to be true. Why her, of all the girls in Lawrence? He could surely have his choice.

She often saw Harrison chatting with one or another pretty girl or in a knot of students embroiled in deep discussion, but she was the one he chose to spend his time with. Even so, she couldn't seem to overcome her feelings of jealousy. It wasn't in her. She wanted this man and she wanted him to care for her, and only for her. From now on. Was that too much to ask? She dared hope not. She almost dared to believe that he felt as she did.

Louise lost her study partner, as Harrison and Modene now studied together. They ate together. They spent every waking moment together when they weren't in class. It was never enough time. She learned so much about him and everything she learned only made her love him more. A doctor. He would be a doctor. And, in her mind, she would love him forever and bear his children. And he would bring her roses and write poetry just for her.

But she became aware of gulf between them. Maybe not so much a gulf, as a yawning chasm. How could she tell him of her childhood? She was carefully stingy with her own information, lest she scare him away. The more she learned about Harrison, the more the gulf grew. She didn't notice the big hole in his life that was left unexplained. And he wasn't ready to share that part of his life. He didn't want to scare her off. She was so innocent. How could he expect her to understand?

Modene couldn't help but compare their backgrounds, and doubts began to creep in. She learned he had graduated from high school at the age of 14. He had been forced to wait until he was 16 before starting college. They had said he was prepared academically, and more than up to the task, but that he wasn't ready for the social aspects of college. He already had acquired a degree in business and was now in pre-med.

She saw that he had come from a loving home, with God-fearing parents who had raised him and his much younger sister, Rachel to be self sufficient and confident.

Harrison's family believed fervently in higher education and had made certain their only two children would follow that path. He had grown up with pets, on a farm in Kansas, and had worked in the fields with his father. He had aspirations, dreams. Hers were paltry, by comparison. His dream was for his life to count for something, to help people. To earn a good living and be able to provide for a family. Her goal was to survive. And she had little confidence she could even do that. Beyond tomorrow, or next week. She hoped she could help someone along the way.

Once, when Harrison had complimented Modene, she rejected it, out of habit.

"That looks lovely on you." he'd said.

"What? This color?"

"Well, that too, but I meant your smile."

What a flatterer. She knew better. Her teeth were too prominent and she always tried to smile closed-lipped, but she'd forgotten for a moment, and a genuine smile had escaped. All expression immediately closed up, at Harrison's words.

"Right. And pigs fly."

Harrison tipped his head to the side and paused, evaluating her response. She was serious. Then he scolded her, ever so gently.

"Compliments were made for strangers, not for friends. This is not idle flattery, it's just how I feel. You need to learn to be willing to believe good things about yourself. Don't you know how special you are? Why do you always put yourself down?"

Modene thought it should be obvious. She was embarrassed and humbled, and made no reply, other than a furious blush.

By the time Modene learned of the chinks in Harrison's armor, it was too late. He could not keep them from her. Didn't want to, considering their feelings for each other, and the question he wanted to ask her. He had delayed much too long and now it was more difficult. It was not like him to be anything but direct. The time had come lay his cards on the table. Time to tell her that he had been married before.

Harrison gave considerable thought to the time and place to share this part of his life with the one he hoped to marry. He prayed it wouldn't make a difference to her. He didn't want to lose her, but it was part of his life and if they were to be together as he wanted to be, they would have to face it. If she was the woman he thought she was, she would be able to handle it. She would love him in spite of it, and be willing to make the effort to work on her feelings about it.

He was well aware however, that she hadn't told him much about her own life. He wondered what kind of childhood she'd had. She never talked much about her family. She seemed loving and kind, but distant in a way he couldn't put his finger on. She would be a good mother, of that much he felt confident. A good stepmother to his daughter, and maybe, if things worked out the way he hoped, to other children of their own.

He planned the evening carefully. They always enjoyed attending the movies, and he had found a nice quiet restaurant for an after movie meal. An out of the way place where they could talk without being disturbed, or observed.

Harrison showered and dressed in the tan slacks and V-necked, heather-toned sweater vest he knew she liked. As always, he wore the small round pin on his sweater. If Modene recognized what it was, or read it, it might work in his favor. She had never asked about it yet, though, so he'd never had a chance to tell her it was a perfect attendance pin from Sunday School. He still treasured it. A dash of bay rum and he was ready. He hoped he was ready. He was ready for Modene to be open to him. He was not prepared for rejection.

Harrison arrived a few minutes early and quietly exited his car, carrying a small paper bag. He moved silently to the bottom of the outside stairway, where he began to pound a small stake into the ground, near the hand rail, using a piece of cloth to cushion the sound of the blows. One end of a string of twine was tied firmly around the top of the stake, and he now tied the other end loosely to the railing, before proceeding upstairs to claim his date. He checked his watch. Right on the button. Harrison Arthur Woods, forthright, creative—and—punctual!

He took the stairs two at a time and knocked on the door. Gloria answered, took his hand, and welcomed him inside. If he didn't know better, he might have thought she was actually flirting with him. He gave her the benefit of the doubt. *Maybe she's just an extremely gracious hostess.*

Gloria continued to hold onto Harrison's hand until Joe appeared over her shoulder, glaring at Harrison. She called upstairs, "Madeline dear, your date is here."

When Modene came downstairs and saw him, her face fairly glowed. Harrison took her hand and drew her to the front door, anxious to be on their way. He couldn't bring himself to make small talk when all he wanted to do was be alone with Modene and show her his surprise. He was like a kid on Christmas morning.

Near the bottom of the stairs, he told her to stop and close her eyes. He squeezed past her, turned, and untied the end of the string from the handrail.

"No peeking." he ordered.

"I'm not peeking! Hurry up, I'm getting dizzy standing her with my eyes closed!

Harrison took Modene's hand from the railing, slipped the loop at the end of the string over one finger, and folded his hand over hers, partly to steady her, and partly because he just didn't want to let go. "Okay. You can open your eyes, now."

"Harrison, what are you up to?"

He tugged her hand open to reveal the knotted string around her finger.

Modene looked down at the unfathomable "gift" and remarked, "It's very...impressive, Harrison, but really, you shouldn't have." *Surely he's gone over the edge. What could this possibly be about?*

"Look at the other end." Harrison was about to bubble over, waiting for her to get it.

Modene peered over the railing and her eyes followed the string to the stake, where it was firmly planted in the earth.

"Okay, Harrison. I give up. What am I supposed to do with it?"

"Accept it," he said, "I'm offering you the world on a string."

The world on a string? Unwelcome thoughts of another day. A lazy summer afternoon, on the way home from a disastrous romantic encounter at Muffin Mountain were borne on the familiar melody as it wove its way through her brain. Then realization struck her. Modene didn't know whether to laugh or cry. This man had to be crazy. A wonderful kind of crazy. She looked down into his hopeful face, filled with warmth and laughter. She reached out to him with both hands.

"Harrison, you've lost your mind. Some doctor you'll make. You'll have your patients bursting their stitches."

Harrison bypassed her hands, taking her firmly at the waist and lifting her off the stair. She grabbed onto his shoulders to steady herself as he spun her around, and she couldn't help but be caught up in the fun. When he set her down, her arms lingered around his neck. This was more heart pounding excitement, than she'd ever experienced in any Hollywood film she'd ever seen. When their eyes met, their laugher turned into something else, something totally earnest and unfamiliar. He lifted her chin gently and captured her lips for the first time.

Modene didn't bolt and run. It didn't occur to her. Did she have a right to be this happy, to feel this wonderful?

It was Harrison who pulled away, leaving Modene, face upturned, her eyes closed dreamily, lost to reality. "We'd better get going, or we'll miss the show."

"Show?" Modene asked, her eyes fluttering open.

"Yes, we just have time. We're going out for a special dinner afterward."

"We are?"

"We certainly are."

Harrison led her to the car and helped her in. Modene sat like a statue, a little afraid of what else he had up his sleeve. As they drove into the night, practicality took hold of Modene and shook her to the core. *Oh, my gosh. What have I done? What now?*

A curtain in the window of the living room upstairs fell back into place. "Well it looks like our little Miss Goody Two Shoes isn't as innocent as she'd have us believe." A self-satisfied look crept into Gloria's knowing eyes. "Louise would be a much better match for you. Your loss, Doctor Woods."

When the movie ended, neither Modene nor Harrison could have told anyone what it had been about. They were each lost in their own thoughts of what was to come, tonight, and in the future. Modene worried that she'd given the wrong impression again. *God knows what he thinks of me now. What's the matter with me?*

As promised, Harrison took Modene to a quiet little Italian restaurant for a dinner of spaghetti and Chianti wine, lingered over in the company of a solitary candle. They made small talk until they ran out. For a while, silence reigned. Harrison was reluctant to bring up the subject that was the whole point of the evening. Modene didn't know what to expect next, but it wasn't a confession. Not from the perfect Harrison Arthur Woods.

Dinner was over. There was no more wine left in the bottle, only a little in each of their glasses. It was as good a time as any. Harrison reached across the table and took Modene's hands in his. Somehow, Harrison felt he had to be touching her, connected to her, to have the courage to get through this. She couldn't bring herself to pull away, though she knew this wasn't proper.

"Modene, there's something I have to tell you. I hope it won't affect your feelings for me."

"Harrison, you sound so somber." *Don't spoil this lovely evening. Please don't say it's over and you don't want to see me anymore. Is there someone else? Why did you have to kiss me? Please love me. Don't throw me away.*

Harrison squeezed her hands, took a deep breath and plunged ahead before he could weaken. "I have to tell you something about my life."

"Your life?" Modene was relieved but incredulous. She laughed. What could he possibly confess to her that would change anything? She loved him with all her heart. She knew him. Knew him well, she thought. He was kind and loving and honest. What could there be to tell? She should be the one confessing.

"I know," she said, "you forgot to tell me about your prison record. It's all right. I've always admired villains." A hollow laugh betrayed her.

"Modene, don't make light of this. It's hard enough to tell." With that he stumbled through the whole ugly mess. He managed to get the facts out about his first marriage and how it had ended in divorce. He said nothing negative about his ex-wife. After all, it really wasn't her fault. It wasn't anybody's fault. Could Modene understand that?

She felt betrayed by him, and jealous of the woman who had been his before he'd known her. But the worst was yet to come. They had a child, a daughter, not quite four years old.

Modene thought her heart would break. She had known there must be something wrong. Something would come along to spoil it. But in her wildest dreams, she would not have suspected this. She knew married folks had quarrels. But you don't just walk away. You don't desert a 4-year-old child and leave her brokenhearted. Not if you can help it. It hit too close to home, and the sadness of it threatened to tip her world, precariously. How could he do this? She felt ill.

She rose from the table and without so much as a backward glance, made straight for the restroom, where she promptly lost her dinner.

After a good cry, she doused her face with cold water and rinsed the bitterness from her mouth. if only she could she rinse it from her heart. She reminded herself that she was a foolish young girl wishing grown up dreams, far beyond her grasp. She returned to the table and made her excuses.

"Gosh, just look at the time! I have to get home and study."

"Of course." Harrison had gambled and lost. She was too young, of course. He'd wanted the evening to go so much differently. He'd wanted to have an open talk with her, learn more about each other and see if they really could have a future together.

Harrison's car rolled to a stop in front of a darkened house. "Don't get out. It's late. I can find my way. The porch light's on. See ya'"

"Sure. See you soon." Harrison held his breath. "Modene, I'll call you tomorrow…"

"I'm pretty busy tomorrow, studying for finals."

"Well, maybe after finals."

"Sure. Maybe." *Maybe not.*

She couldn't bring herself to say "Never darken my door again."

It was an impossible nightmare of conflict. Who was she to throw stones? Look at her own life. Modene hurled herself out of the car into the night, wearing her confusion and rage like a cloak, flowing behind her on a dark wind.

Harrison felt the jarring of the slammed car door to his very marrow. *It's over. I should have known she couldn't accept it.* He sat in silence watching her retreat into the darkness. He breathed a heavy sigh and slowly pulled away from the curb and out of sight.

Modene crumpled on the bottom step and burst into fresh tears. Before going upstairs, she pulled up the stupid string and stake, and threw them in the incinerator out back. *The world on a string? For me? Sure.*

It was two weeks before she saw Harrison again. She'd been miserable, but would not have imagined the depth of his misery, as well. They both got through finals and on the last day of official school for the semester he saw her sitting at a table in the cafeteria and decided he had nothing to lose, he may as well approach her and find out which way the wind was blowing. Maybe she'd had a change of heart.

"Mind if I sit down?"

Modene couldn't bring herself to speak. It amazed her how Harrison's presence could just fill up a room. Fill it up with his charm and warmth, so that it must be tangible to everyone present. Her heart was filled up with Harrison and all the she felt. She could only stare into Harrison's warm hazel eyes. How she'd missed them looking back into her own.

Harrison broke the awkward silence. "When I saw you…well, I just want to tell you how sorry I am about our last talk. I shouldn't have sprung that on you, like that."

"Oh well, what's done is done." She couldn't tear her eyes from his.

"You seemed so hurt. I never meant to hurt you. I never want to do that."

"I know. Look, I'm not judging you. You're a good man. I know that. Certainly better than I deserve. I just don't believe in divorce."

"Would you believe I don't either? Well, I didn't. The point is…"

"The point is, you don't need to apologize. If you really knew me, you'd know I'm the one who should be baring my soul."

"You? What could you possibly feel the need to confess to me?" Harrison couldn't think of anyone who seemed less likely to have dark secrets.

"I don't really want to talk about it. Let's just say you'd be better off finding someone else to give the world to."

"Someone else? I don't want anyone else. I want you. Now and forever." He hadn't meant to give so much away, but he felt her pulling away.

Modene decided she might as well get it over with. Let him be the one to call if off and walk away.

"You think so? Do you think you know me?"

Tears sprang into her eyes and try as she might, she couldn't will them away. The truth came tumbling out. Well, not all of it at first. She managed to withhold the part about her Indian blood. No use in pulling out the big guns unless it was absolutely necessary, to make him go away.

"My father never went to college. He was a coal miner. He died when I was very young. I was an orphan and...no one wanted me. I..."

Incredibly, Harrison's eyes revealed no shock, no revulsion or disdain, only love.

"Is that all?" He took her hand to his lips and brushed them with the softest kiss. In the cafeteria, right in front of God and everybody.

"None of that is your fault. You can't blame yourself for what fate has dished out to you." He knew now that he could make her feel loved. All he wanted was to take her in his arms and kiss all the hurt away. But they were in the middle of the cafeteria and they were gathering an audience.

"Let's go outside." Harrison tugged a reluctant Modene out to the lawn where he pulled her down to sit beside him in the shade of an ancient elm. He tucked her into the crook of his arm, and they settled against the tree trunk and each other.

Darn him! Why did he have to be so sweet about it? Was there really a person on the face of this earth who could understand? Who could love her, warts and all? And had she found him? She couldn't come this close only to lose him later when he discovered the worst part. That would be unbearable. No, if it was to be over, better to get it over with now. She pulled away from Harrison, braced herself, and rushed on before allowing herself time to reconsider.

"You don't know the worst part...I'm...part Indian." Modene lifted her chin, daring him to comment. Her cheeks flushed noticeably.

Harrison leaned toward her and raised an eyebrow in feigned seriousness. "Really?"

Her courage faltered. "Well, maybe," she hastened to backpedal. "I mean some of my relatives say that's not true, but that we're "Black Dutch", whatever that is. On my mother's side. Maybe I'd rather I was part Indian."

"Hmmm. Part Indian? Which part?" he inquired in mock earnestness.

Harrison wasn't ready to let her off the hook, yet. And she couldn't read his expression. Shocked? She didn't think so. Just thoughtful? No, he'd have an opinion. Merely surprised? No, amused! That was it.

"I don't see anything wrong with any part." Harrison finally threw his head back and laughed uproariously.

"It's not funny, Harrison! I unburden myself to you and you laugh at me!" She tried to stand up and retreat, but he reclaimed her hand and held her in place.

"I'm not laughing at you, sweetheart. I'm laughing at me. My family's Indian blood is Cherokee. I was kind of hoping that wouldn't make a difference to you." That flicker of humor still glittered in his eyes.

"Cherokee?" she spluttered. "Really?"

"My father's mother was supposed to be half Cherokee. I'll have to show you some of her photos! She looks full-blooded Indian, to me. She's beautiful!"

At this, Modene collapsed back onto the ground, laughing with him, finally seeing the humor in their situation.

Harrison's chiseled face took on a serious expression.

"Modene, stop looking behind you. Can't you see us together, deliriously happy, even when we're old and gray? You know, Lily Langtree once said, 'Anyone who limits her vision to memories of yesterday, is already dead.' Don't be afraid to live Modene. Take a chance with me. With us."

Modene was thoughtful. "Then you don't mind? About all of...this? My past?"

"Mind? Don't you see, 'all of this' is what has made you who you are."

"Really? And who am I?"

"You," Harrison said in earnest, "are the lovely young lady I hope to charm, all the way to the altar."

"The altar? But Harrison, your school..."

"Shhhh. We'll work everything out. We can work and go to school, or take turns going to school, or postpone school. Whatever we do, we'll do it together. More than anything, I want to take care of you. I won't let us starve, I promise. If all else fails, I have an accounting degree. Medicine can come later. We'll be fine."

Was she mistaken, or did the man of her dreams just propose to her? In a flash her future loomed before her framed in question marks. No, she couldn't see any of this happening to her. Was it possible? Finally she found her voice.

"I guess we deserve each other."

"You bet we do." His agreement had a positive ring to it that her statement was lacking.

She hadn't said yes, and Harrison didn't give her a chance to say no. They remained there, under the tree, hands entwined, caught up in thoughts of their future together until the twilight tumbled down around them like gentle rain.

Harrison had to keep winning her over, overpowering her doubts when they crept in. The one thing they couldn't deny was their love for each other. And Modene was willing to be won over. She chose to believe him when he said he would take care of her, and that their love would see them through. After all, when she'd confessed her sins of guilt and unlovableness, hadn't he held her in his arms and told her not to worry? He made it all seem believable, possible even.

Harrison invited Modene to come home with him for Thanksgiving, to meet his family. His reassurance did little to calm her fears of rejection. If she could have found a reasonable excuse not to go, she would have avoided it like poison. Harrison and his family were so close. What if they didn't like her? Secretly Modene wondered if he'd told them the "truth" about her.

Practicing the Power of Positive Thinking, she gave herself permission to take this step with fear in her heart, and feelings of great joy and sadness, all at once. It could be the end. She tried hard to visualize it as a successful encounter.

When Harrison picked Modene up for the trip, he was ecstatic with anticipation. She was sick with fear. Harrison's playful greeting broke the tension. When she answered the door, Harrison bowed deeply, stepped inside and casually inquired, "Remember me?"

Dumbfounded, Modene stood speechless wondering what he was up to now. She never knew what to expect.

Harrison took her in his arms and waltzed her around the small entryway, singing softly in her ear. "Remember me, I'm the one who loves you…" The lyrics became standard fare, whenever she was anxious or unsure of herself. It never failed to lighten her mood.

She found his family warm and loving and they embraced her, figuratively and physically. Though she cherished the thought that they had provided a nurturing environment for the man she loved to grow up in, she could not help the pangs of jealousy that again plagued her. It seemed he'd led a charmed life.

Old doubts nudged their way into her thinking. What could have gone so terribly wrong that it would cause him to break his vows and choose divorce from a woman he couldn't bring himself to say an unkind word about? He would never, in their life together, say any more than that they had married young and it didn't work out. She could see it tore at his heart to be away from his daughter, Jessie. It was one more thing that endeared him to her. After all, would she want him if he didn't love his own child and take responsibility for her?

She knew he would be a good father, should she find the courage to follow her heart and marry him, and maybe have his children. It frightened her, this past life of his.

That familiar green monster raised its ugly head. No matter that it was unreasonable. Jessie was after all a child, and Harrison's love for his daughter was very different from the love that he shared with her. But she was a very real reminder that there had been someone before her that he had at least thought he loved.

Modene felt so welcome in his family, so safe in this world, just possibly within her grasp. If she could just let go of her past. So, once again, she was lulled into believing that it could work out. That she could find happiness at last. Balm for her soul.

Harrison was like no one she'd ever known. He surprised her with a gift of a book, for no special reason. He was like that. Just something he enjoyed and wanted to share with her. The book was a collection of poems and he read her all is favorites. She'd never cared much for poetry but hearing Harrison's voice reading them with such passion and expression, made her want more. He read "Barefoot Boy", "The Highwayman" and "Sea Fever". In time, she found her own favorites. "Trees", by Sergeant Joyce Kilmer, "Little Boy Blue" by Eugene Field and most of all, Henry Wadsworth Longfellow's "Hiawatha's Childhood".

When Harrison surprised Modene with a simple ring to seal their engagement, she was overwhelmed. Diamonds? For her? Never in her wildest dream would she have ever thought she'd possess anything to precious. Her heart filled with love for this man who seemed to love her so.

"Diamonds? Harrison you can't be giving me diamonds! Tuition is due and…"

"Very tiny diamonds, I'm afraid. I read somewhere that a diamond is just a chunk of coal that made good under pressure."

Modene was learning to understand Harrison and his dry sense of humor. Not long ago, she'd have questioned whether this remark was a dig about her father being a coal miner. But now, she knew better. He was merely trying to make her feel at ease, accepting this treasure. She couldn't recall ever feeling happier or more special.

And so it was that January 3, 1937 found them before Judge Bert Rogers in Olathe, Kansas, repeating their vows in the heartfelt belief that they had a future. Modene had tucked her lucky 1922 Indian head penny from the pocket of her rag doll into her shoe. It was her way of creating a sense of her mother's presence on this very special day. Their only witnesses were the wife of the judge and a gardener who'd been trimming the hedges along the walkway.

Harrison's family hosted a scrumptious celebration supper for the returning newlyweds. The homemade meal consisted of a simple pot roast, fresh, homegrown green beans, mashed potatoes with gravy, and aunt Helena's 'Christmas White Salad', now adapted as 'Wedding Salad'. Dessert of aunt Helena's prize winning 'Pineapple Drop Cookies' topped off the perfect meal. Modene immediately fell in love with Harrison's merry aunt.

During grace, Modene said her own fervent prayer that she had done the right thing, for once in her life.

"Please, God, let this turn out right."

Amen.

STEP 7:
Hand Down Recipe and Pray

"Hand down recipe and pray…"

"You be a good girl, Coral," Harrison's mock scolding of his and Modene's not quite two-year-old daughter. "You too." he said, patting Modene's overripe belly. "Call me if anything happens. Today's the day, I think." It *has* to be. *Before midnight.* No self-respecting accountant would stand for a new deduction arriving on New Year's Day—a day late for Uncle Sam."

Modene smiled weakly. "Uh-hmmm", she murmured against his sweet smelling neck as he leaned over to give her a peck on the cheek.

"I don't think this baby's ever coming. I'll die of old age with this big belly. No New Year's party for us this year."

"Now, honey." Harrison glanced out the window and pronounced it a bad night to go out for New Year's revelry, anyway. "We'll celebrate with dinner tomorrow at Laurie Jean and Erik's. Concentrate on looking forward to her *'New Year's Good Luck Hoppin' John's'*. It's going to be a good year. A lucky year for us. Remember, short day today. We'll knock off at noon for the office party, and I'll come right home."

He ruffled Coral's hair on the way out and Modene took up her post at the window, coaxing Coral up onto the couch beside her. Dragging behind Coral, as though it were attached by magnet, was the faded, circle motif afghan her mother had crocheted years ago.

"Wave bye-bye, Coral. Wave bye-bye to daddy."

Dark clouds scudded overhead as Harrison dashed to the curb and climbed into the old De Soto. He entered on the passenger side waving to his family, before sliding over behind the wheel and grinding the engine into reluctant submission.

The expectant mother glanced up at the threatening sky and patted her swollen belly. "Please don't come today, little one. Nothing good has ever happened to me on a day like today."

Her mind wandered back to the night Coral was born. She was crazy to be doing this again. She'd been lucky with Coral. She wanted nothing more than to get past this delivery, but not today! "Sorry Harrison. Hang Uncle Sam!"

She was rudely jarred from her distracted state of worry over her impending delivery, by a sudden swoosh of water, and the immediate onset of labor pains, five minutes apart from the outset.

Not now! She watched in a panic as Harrison's De Soto disappeared into a mist of low-lying clouds in their sleepy Kansas City suburb. She calculated it would take him at least a half hour to reach the office! Picking up the phone, she quickly dialed her closest neighbor and good friend, Laurie Jean. "Can you come and get Coral? My water broke and I have to try and reach Harrison...he's already left for work and..."

Modene's voice trailed off and Laurie Jean hooted into the phone, "No kidding! Well, I guess you're on your way. Better you than me. I'll be right over. Larry's still asleep in his crib."

Modene counted herself lucky to have Laurie Jean for a friend, and now a neighbor. The two had met in the maternity ward of the hospital when Modene had Coral and Laurie Jean had given birth to her firstborn, Larry. They immediately felt comfortable and attached, and discovered they had a lot in common besides their new motherhood. When Laurie Jean and her husband moved in next door to Modene and Harrison, it made it easy to continue their friendship. Coral and Larry were play buddies and Laurie Jean and Modene sewed together, exchanged recipes and thoroughly enjoyed their close friendship.

Before Modene could dial Harrison's office a cloudburst opened up. Damn! Doesn't anything ever go right! She had the phone in her hand, mid-contraction when the door burst open. Expecting Laurie Jean, she was startled to see Harrison standing there in the doorway, dripping wet and looking sheepish.

"Forgot my galoshes honey, will you...Modene, honey, what's wrong? Is it the baby?" He couldn't conceal his delight, on several counts.

At that moment, Laurie Jean stumbled up the steps, head down and plowed right into Harrison, knocking him stem-winding. In her un-pregnant state, she was hardly threatening. Eight months pregnant she was a wall of hurtling steel. Modene laughed in spite of herself until she was gripped by the next contraction.

Laurie Jean scooped up Coral, balancing her precariously on one hip, the toddler's right leg riding up over her bulging midsection. Harrison grabbed the small bag from the coat closet and helped Modene down the steps. The car was still idling at the curb. He tossed the bag onto the back seat and settled his wife as comfortably as possible in the passenger seat. He dashed around the rear of the car and dived in on the driver's side. "Ready?" He tried to paste a hopeful look on his face.

There was no answer and Modene appeared absent from him and the situation, far away in some sort of secret world. Probably the pain, he figured. "It'll be over soon. It'll be all right."

Harrison eased the sedan back out into the light flow of traffic and fought the urge to push the hunk of steel to its limits. He knew this baby was likely to come faster than Coral had, and with Modene's pains five minutes apart, it could be very soon. Medical training or no, he wasn't prepared to deliver their own baby. His hands gripped the steering wheel tighter with each contraction he monitored by his wife's stifled sobs. *Why didn't we call the doctor first,* he admonished himself silently, *so he'd be there?*

As luck would have it, Dr. Reitz was already at the hospital, tending another patient, and her pains were still ten minutes apart. It appeared that Modene would deliver first. Until her labor stopped. Harrison checked his wristwatch. Still plenty of time. The hands on his watch seemed sluggish, as though they were moving underwater.

Dr. Reitz predicted a long wait and suggested Harrison go get a bite to eat. But the anxious father to be couldn't tear himself away. Modene clutched his hand so tightly that he lost all sense of feeling in it. Then the pins and needles started and he had to transfer her grip to his other hand.

Dr. Reitz's other patient had a long and difficult labor, lasting into the early evening. Still Modene's baby seemed to be reluctant to join the family. And Modene worried, in spite of Harrison's reassurances.

When Dr. Reitz checked on Modene around 10:00 p.m., he looked as haggard as his patient. Seeing Modene sleeping, he told Harrison he was going to the doctor's lounge to catch a few winks. "They'll call me if anything happens." He stripped down to his shorts and promptly fell into exhausted sleep.

Hope of a New Year's Eve baby was fading for Harrison and he too dozed off, in the middle of a prayer for the safe arrival of his baby, and an easy delivery for his wife. He was awakened abruptly within an hour, when Modene cried out.

Before he could orient himself and check his watch, she was racked with another contraction. He called for the nurse and murmured soft words of love and encouragement into Modene's ear. Always a joker, he found even light humor was not well received, at this particular time. He'd modified his approach and was trying to keep to positive reassurances.

Modene was rushed into the delivery room, and sedated. Harrison was barred. The stern, Swedish nurse was unmoved by his claims that he'd been a medical student and was perfectly well prepared to witness the birth of his child.

His last glimpse of his wife, as she was whisked away down the hall, she was unable to acknowledge his presence. She was obviously frightened. Even Harrison felt uneasy. He'd been so confident all along, but now his confidence faltered. What if she was really in trouble?

Always ready with a joke, he failed to even recognize the opportunity for humor when he saw Dr. Reitz dash out of the doctor's lounge and sprint down the hall—in his shorts! But he'd remember it.

Harrison stole a peek at his watch, then self-consciously looked around to see if anyone had observed him. It was only natural he'd wonder how long it would take. It was after 11:30. He lit a cigarette and paced the hall.

Inside the delivery room, Dr Reitz was calm and efficient, barely conscious of the nurses giggling at his lack of professional attire.

Modene was in a dark world, somewhere just the other side of oblivion. She was reliving the night she gave birth to her firstborn. She'd been afraid then, too. And where was Harrison? She thought she heard him calling to her, but she couldn't see him, couldn't see anything. Then it was over and he was beside her, kissing her hand telling her how much he loved her. How perfect their firstborn was. A girl. A perfect little baby girl.

"She is perfect, isn't she? What shall we call her, Harrison?"

Even in her current state of half consciousness, she could sense his agitation, all over again.

"What do you mean, what shall we name her?" He had tried hard to keep the edge out of his voice, but after all, it was their first baby. He certainly had a right to be consulted on the name.

"You already named her," he'd said, dryly.

"Harrison, I'm serious. We don't have a girl's name picked out. You were so sure it was going to be a boy. Well, what names do you like?" The words echoed in her head, like they were far away.

"No, **I am** serious. You already named her."

"That's ridiculous! I only just woke up…" It had come back to her then. "Oh, no. What did I name her?"

Harrison suddenly felt guilty for being so sharp with his wife after she'd been through so much and his tone softened.

"Amaretta. Really honey, don't you think that's an awfully long name for such a little baby?

Even now in her dream, she was embarrassed at her own stupidity. But then they never should have asked her while she was still under the effects of the anesthetic. It wasn't fair. And what could they do then? Only add another name in front. So they had discussed it and squeezed Coral into the small space in front of Amaretta. Now visions of their first baby and Modene's friend, Amaretta, danced in and out of the blackness.

"Is that you, Amaretta? I'm having a baby. Come and see us sometime. My husband's going to be a doctor, you know…"

Lily's face appeared to Modene and she was smiling sweetly, looking like some sort of angel and reading aloud from a worn book. Modene was so comforted that her mother was here and somehow the odd words brought comfort, too. "Hush! The naked bears will hear thee." the vision of Lily and the real Modene each put a finger to their lips and made a "Shhh". Then Lily and her soft voice faded away.

Suddenly bright rings of light invaded the darkness and Modene was aware of voices around her. "Put her over there…";…there, there little one, what's";…"what was the exact time of birth?"; "birth weight again, please…"

Her? A girl? I hope Harrison's isn't disappointed. We don't have a girl's name picked out…

Modene was thrilled to have another daughter, but she dreaded seeing her husband. She knew he wanted a son. And she was NOT going through this again! He'd just have to be content with two girls. She drifted off to sleep with visions of Harrison drifting out of her life. She should have known she'd mess it up… Where am I? she wondered.

Harrison's beaming face was swimming within a circle of hazy light.

"Harrison?"

"I'm right here honey. She's perfect. She's just perfect. And you did just great!"

"Oh, Harrison," she began. "I'm so sorry. It's a another girl".

"I know and she's just beautiful! Looks just like her handsome father!"

"Harrison, did you hear me? It's a girl…"

"Yes ma'am, just what I wanted!"

"Have you lost your mind?"

"We have to think of a name. Together, this time. I was thinking of Marisa."

"It's really okay? That it's a girl, I mean? I know you had your heart set on a boy…What are you going to do with the baseball mitt?"

"Hey, no reason girls can't play baseball. So what do think? Marisa?"

They settled on Marisa Kate, and once Modene was satisfied that Harrison was really happy with his new daughter, she broached another touchy subject.

"About the time, Harrison. I tried, I really did."

"What do you mean?"

"I mean her birth date. I know you were hoping it would be before midnight."

"Honey, didn't Dr. Reitz tell you? Marisa Kate was born at 11: 52! Among other things, that kid has a perfect sense of timing. Happy New Year!" He kissed a beaming Modene tenderly on the cheek.

Whatever had she done to deserve this? Without warning, old questions came back to taunt her.

How do you know? How do you know if you're really loved? And in that moment, the answer came to her. Like it had been waiting there all along. When you're really loved, you know, because you don't hunger for it anymore.

not the end…

Epilogue

EPILOGUE
BY MARIS KATE

Edna Modene Gillen Woods~

So, did Modene and Harrison live happily ever after? I can't say every waking moment together was pure, unadulterated bliss. Modene had a lot of what we would call today, "baggage". Was Harrison her perfect mate? If Modene's early experiences did nothing else, they prepared her to choose the perfect mate for herself. My father was a wonderful compliment to her and they balanced each other. Together they were stronger than either one alone, and they raised my sister and me to be responsible, caring adults. They had their ups and downs, as all couples do. I think some of their happiest years were their last years together. My father was devastated when my mother lost her battle with cancer in 1962.

What kind of mother was Edna Modene Gillen Woods? She was the kind of mother who told her daughters they were "pretty little girls" and taught them early to smile without showing their less than perfect teeth. She made sure we took dance lessons as children, and as preteens, modeling and "charm class", not with an eye to a career but more to develop poise and grace. Qualities she perhaps felt she lacked for too long.

As children, mother often read to us. She read us Grimm's Fairy Tales and later, poetry. She often recited her favorite poems. Poems such as "Abou Ben Adhem", "Trees" and especially "Hiawatha's Childhood". Tucking us into bed at night, she would quote from Hiawatha; "Hush the naked bears will hear thee!" I can remember trying to envision naked bears.

Mother was ahead of her time, in many ways. In the early 1950's, long before the relationship of sun exposure and skin cancer was a proven fact, she warned her daughters constantly of the dangers. Long before it was fashionable, she insisted on time for herself, to renew her spirit. It was an unspoken law that she was not to be disturbed when after her shower, she took time for herself to rest on her bed "to let her antiperspirant dry". She would close her eyes and meditate. She became a student of Mary Baker Eddy and Norman Vincent Peale and practiced "The Power of Positive Thinking" every day of her life, and tried to instill its principles in her daughters. When Coral and I would 'play act' she would always caution us not to play that we were ill or unhappy, because she felt that could open a door that would draw those negative things to us.

Mother never finished her degree and became an RN, but she did graduate as a "Practical Nurse", an equivalent to today's Licensed Vocational Nurse. Though she never really worked in the profession, she did volunteer at Harbor General Hospital in Southern California's South Bay. She worked in the pediatric ward and Coral and Marisa Kate volunteered there, as well, as "candystripers". When discussing career planning, mother always told us that nursing and waitress work were the two hardest professions for women. Better we should consider a career in banking. The hours, she said, were great.

Mother never could resist a stray. When we brought home stray kittens, she always said, "No. Tomorrow you take it back." Then if we got up after going to bed, we would find her holding and petting it, cooing to it as though it were her own baby. They never "went back".

Mostly, mother was a "stay at home mom". She worked occasionally, if she wanted to. But she preferred to be at home when her children came home, and to have the freedom to read. I can't recall that she ever had any actual hobbies, other than her family and reading.

Probably mother's most compelling leftover baggage from her childhood was a restlessness and insecurity about staying in one place too long. It was a long time before I understood who it was in the family that was so fiddle-footed. Coral and I attended some 23 schools by my freshman year in high school.

There is never a good time to lose one's mother. Mother was with us long enough to see her youngest daughter married, and to have her first blood grandchild to dote on, Lori Anne. And dote she did. She often cared for Lori when I worked. Lori was two years old when we found out mother had ovarian cancer. She was operated on, which did not result in prolonging her life or giving her any relief. She died three weeks later, shortly after Thanksgiving.

In November of 1962 dark clouds hovered over Torrance Memorial Hospital and a soft, warm rain was falling. Coral and Marisa Kate were just outside her door. Jessie, Harrison's oldest daughter had been called to the hospital as well, and she had come, waiting with Coral and Marisa Kate. Harrison's sister, Rachel was there, having come from Tusla, Oklahoma. Daddy told mother that Rachel "happened to be in town for a convention". Mother accepted that without question. Daddy was with her when she slipped away at the age of 48. For days after mother died, he kept mumbling, "It's so…final."

I miss her every day, and this book is in tribute to her and all that she overcame. I love you, mother.

Harrison Arthur Woods~

My father was loving, intelligent, witty, patient and charming. Anyone who knew him would tell you that. His favorite poems, "The Barefoot Boy" and "Crossing the Bar" can be found in any good poetry book, and reveal much about the man my father was. He loved music and was an excellent dancer. He was a lifelong golfer and loved baseball. He taught Coral and I to pitch and catch, respectively. On Sunday drives, if there was ball game on the radio, we all listened to it. Otherwise, he tuned in "The Shadow", the "Green Hornet", or "Inner Sanctum" (the squeaking door…).

No children we knew had a father who was more fun or more involved in his children's lives. When we were very young, he taught us to read using the funny papers. He always had a joke or a magic trick up his sleeve. You never knew what to expect. He taught us games and songs, riddles and proverbs, and seemed to be the self appointed tour guide on trips, while mother relaxed. We would go for a ride and she would put noxious Noxema Cream on her face, lean back and close her eyes, and daddy would keep us entertained.

Daddy made sure we attended Sunday School and participated in extracurricular activities at local parks, scouts, and various clubs, including Rainbow Girls when were teenagers. He helped us name our pets and saw to it that we learned to take responsibility for caring for them. He made Mother's Day a special day for our mother, and to remember the grandmothers Coral and I never knew. The whole family always wore appropriate colored carnations to church on Mother's Day, to indicate if our mother was living or deceased. I don't see anyone do that anymore and I miss it.

Harrison was the type of husband and father any family would cherish. He was always a romantic as well as a comedian. I remember waking up one night when I was five or six years old, and while tip-toeing to the bathroom for water, I saw him and mother dancing in the living room to dreamy music on the radio. Even as a small child, I recognized that moment as special.

If our mother taught us about spirituality, our father taught us about integrity and honesty in dealing with people. What was "fair" was less important than what was "right". I learned you didn't cheat, or worm little boys out of their money (or their marbles—not all of them, anyway) just because you could. If mother ran out of patience, mostly with me, daddy had a seemingly unending supply. He taught us to love nature and especially the ocean. To this day, when I am near the ocean, I feel near him.

In all our moves, we rarely moved to a neighboring city. We moved from California to Charlotte North Carolina. We would move from Denver, Colorado to Salt Lake City, Utah, or from Kansas City, Missouri to Long Beach, California. Yes, daddy was in the Navy, as a naval officer for a time, but that didn't dictate all the moves. When we were little, daddy thought it was educational to see the country and live in different environments, but when we were older, like in high school, Daddy took pity on us girls. We had bought a house in Manhattan Beach, California and I started and finished that first year in high school, all at the same school. A rare occurrence, because though we moved pretty much every year, it was rarely at the beginning or end of a school year. At the end of that school year, when mother was restless to sell the house and move, my father put his foot down. He said we could sell the house and move—as long as it was in the same school district. He didn't want to move us again to a new school where we would have to start over with new friends. Bless him. I completed all four years at Mira Costa High School in Manhattan Beach and delighted in the rare treat of sharing and keeping friendships over such a long period of time.

Perhaps it is a tribute to a happy marriage that he eventually found love again.

My father passed away of heart problems and stroke just after his 65 th birthday. His memorial folder included the words to "The Crossing of the Bar" and his ashes were scattered at sea. I'm so glad that Lori and my sons, Will and Wes had a chance to know him, and vice versa. Not a day goes by that I don't think fondly of him and miss his presence in my life. What I wouldn't give for five minutes just to talk with him, now. I love you Daddy.

Coral Amaretta Woods~

Harrison and Modene's oldest daughter was the "good child". Coral was always bright, pretty, and perfectly behaved. Her teachers all loved her and used her as an example. She graduated from Long Beach State College and became a social worker. Marrying later in life, she waited till after she had all her "ducks in a row", as daddy would have said. Coral has one son, a delightful young man, now beginning a teaching career.

From the time we were children, Coral was the best at being a big sister. She spent untold hours mentoring her bratty baby sister. She taught me about the constellations and how to make doll clothes.

When we engaged in the popular past time of the late 40's, 'trading cards', she patiently tried to impress upon me the value of quality over quantity. *She's a fool,* I thought. *Just look at the size of my thick pack of trading cards!* If we weren't as close as children as we might have been, it was because I was too jealous, too out of control. I tormented her mercilessly, and she further frustrated me by being incredibly, perfectly tolerant. That she survived me as a sister and is sane today, is a tribute to her own character.

Coral was forced to retire early for medical reasons, after a massive stroke in 1985, and she now lives in California's high desert, near my husband and me. We are closer than ever.

Marisa Kate Woods~

If Coral was *the good child*, that left me the role of...*the difficult child*. That I survived my own childhood is a tribute to something. A loving and forgiving God, perhaps. And patient, loving parents. I was what would today be called, a hyperactive child, and I was a challenge to my parents, my sister, and every teacher who ever had the misfortune to have me in a class. I was a daredevil and was not blessed with my parents common sense. I might easily have drowned (on more than one occasion) or fallen to my death from a rocking ferris wheel basket, or met with one of a dozen other less than ideal fates.

Fortunately, I did survive my childhood and an early, ill-fated marriage, to find the love of my life, Dave. Together we raised three beautiful children, of whom we are appropriately proud. I survived the early loss of my mother and eventually developed an interest in family history and genealogy, which led me to write to this story of my mother's early life.

Today, I live in Lucerne Valley, California working part time in the library there, and I do medical transcription at home. Typically, I pursue more hobbies than I have time for. I enjoy quilting, gardening, bear making, graphic arts, photography and writing. I belong to the Friends of the Library and our local writing group, L.V. Writers' Ink.

Ruby Gillen~

Ruby eventually remarried but never had children of her own. In later years, she and Modene renewed their relationship, and it seemed to be important to both. Coral and I were never able call her "grandmother", though Modene never revealed to us any of her early, unpleasant experiences with her step-mother. It was only later, through a Townsley cousin that I learned of Ruby's misguided treatment of my mother.

Gavin—The irrepressible son of aunt Babe, and his lovely wife Ginny were not blessed with children. He became a newspaper editor and writer. His sense of humor reminds me very much of my father. We met in the 1980's and maintained an enjoyable and enlightening correspondence. He eventually turned over the *"family hairlooms"* to me for safekeeping. Aunt Babe's collection of locks of hair contained a number of small, clear envelopes with labels like "Babies' hair", some with names.

Gavin told me a wonderful story of a visit he and his parents made to Kansas City, Missouri on the occasion of Coral's birth. He adored my father, and on this visit, when Gavin was about 15 years old, my father took him out and taught him to drive a car. A rather selfless endeavor, I thought, in an atmosphere of excitement of a visit to share a new baby.

I hold Gavin very dear to my heart, and always will.

Harriet Townsley~

Harriet and Ron were married until Ron's death. They had three children, one daughter and two sons. Harriet never remarried and is living with her daughter in the Pacific Northwest. Harriet and Modene remained lifelong friends and Modene and Harrison visited

Harriet and Ron as often as possible on their sheep ranch in the San Francisco Bay area of California. These visits were especially treasured by me, because I adored the open spaces and all the animals. The highlight of any given day there, was if "Uncle Ron" would wake me early and let me accompany him to feed the sheep. He carried an oversized baby bottle of milk in the old pickup truck and sometimes let me offer it to the baby sheep.

Experiences on the ranch were not all so happy. I quickly made favorite pets of the luxuriously soft white bunnies in the cages out back. Sharing a large, tasty family-style meal one evening, I commented on the delicious "fried chicken". My cousin, Burl delighted somewhat in informing me it wasn't chicken but fried rabbit. "Here, have another leg."

Harriet and her family were fortunate to all live near each other, on the same rural road. Her parents Flora and Gabe lived within easy biking distance, and Harriet's sister, Anise was not much further down the road. I loved nothing better than to go to "Aunt Flora's" and "Uncle Gabe's" and let Harriet's grandmother braid my hair "German style". I still bear a scar on my lower lip from one of these visits. It seems my cousin Burl was to take me somewhere on his bike. I perched on the handlebars and my older cousin pedaled us down the road. When we came to Flora and Gabe's, I decided I wanted to have my hair braided and tried to steer the bike into the drive. Burl was trying to stay on the road to our intended destination, and this fight over control led to a nasty spill. I cut my lip on a spoke and DID get my way, as we had to then make a stop at Flora's for some tender loving care and bandaging.

Anise's house was another favorite visiting place for both Coral and me because Anise was so interesting and had led such an incredible life. She'd been in the service and traveled the world over gathering souvenirs and decorator items. She often sheathed her slender body in authentic, colorful silk kimonos and wore "chopsticks" in the ebony bun she coiled on top of her head. There was no end to the intriguing objects that adorned her eclectic abode. Lacquered boxes with gold dragon motifs, incense holders, and tea service of oriental design. Carvings and jewelry like nothing we had ever seen before. We could listen to her for hours. Being older than Harriet, Anise's only son was grown and out on his own. She was long divorced and lived in this fantasy world that Coral and I couldn't get enough of. Like everyone in the family, we were devastated to learn of her death from brain cancer at a relatively early age.

Edan~

Mother never knew what became of Edan, or her mother. So she invented a story that suited her fancy. She liked to pretend that Edan was adopted by a wealthy, loving couple who lavished every luxury upon her, but most importantly, treasured and adored her. Just as mother felt every child deserved, regardless of circumstances. In mother's perfect world, Edan and Camille found each other in later life and enjoyed a close relationship. Edan married well and lived a dream life with her successful, adoring husband and two beautiful, intelligent children. Always treasured, always loved. Or so mother chose to believe.

Adamsville, Oklahoma~

The small mining town of mother's early childhood grew up around the coal mining industry, its history punctuated with mine tragedies. In 1925 when my grandfather, Edd Gillen was killed, Adamsville was on the decline. It is virtually a ghost town, now. Some say it is watched over by the ghosts of the many miners who lost their lives over the years. Deep pits pockmark what's left of the town where the slope mines have collapsed. The idle mines continue to rumble and settle, and polluted ponds have formed. The water that flows from them is highly mineralized and has contaminated the nearby streams into which it flows, killing untold numbers of fish. The Rock Island and Katy railroad trains no longer stop in Adamsville for coal. Only a dozen or so buildings and homes remain standing, peopled with a handful of diehard citizens, mostly retired or semi-retired. A small mom and pop store with one gas pump is the only thriving business on Main St. It survives on trade from visitors in need of convenience foods, film and bait for camping or picnics at nearby Carson Lake.

Recipes By Chapter

From Step One~*Dredge In Flowers*
FUNERAL PIE (or Rosina Pie)
Pennsylvania Dutch Raisin Pie often taken to funerals as it kept well
with no refrigeration.

You need 1 nine-inch pie shell. Place ½ cup chopped black walnut
meats in the bottom of the pie shell.

Combine:
1 1/4 Cup seeded raisins
½ Cup sugar
½ Cup molasses
½ Cup water
1/8 Tsp salt
Stir well and cook for 15 minutes in the top of a double boiler, stirring occasionally.

Stir in:
4 TB flour
3 TB water
Cook filling for 15 minutes longer, stirring occasionally. Cool
slightly.
Add:
½ tsp cinnamon

Fill the pie shell, covering walnuts and bake at 450° for 10 minutes.
Reduce heat and bake at 350° for an additional ½ hour.

From Step Two~*Stew in own Juices*

Aunt Fanny's Scrumptious, Blue Ribbon "Crystal Pickles"

7 pounds green tomatoes
2 gallons of water
11 1/2 gram bottle of lime
4 1/2 cups of sugar
2 qts. of vinegar
2 TB salt
1 tsp. grated nutmeg
1 tsp. ground ginger
6 or 7—2 inch cinnamon sticks
4 cloves, without heads (secret ingredient)

Wash tomatoes thoroughly and drain. Slice into 1/4 inch slices and place in a large container. Dissolve lime in water and pour over tomato slices. Let stand 24 hours, stirring occasionally. Remove and rinse well several times in cold water to remove all lime sediment. Soak in cold water for 4 hours, changing water every hour. Drain. Dissolve sugar in vinegar, add spices tied loosely in cheesecloth. Bring to a boil. Add green tomato slices and boil rapidly until slices are glazed and sirup clings to spoon in drops. Remove from heat and allow to set in sirup overnight. Drain off sirup and bring to a boil. Pack tomato slices loosely in preheated jars, leaving 1/2 inch head space. Cover with boiling sirup. Fill and close jars. Process for 10 minutes, cool and store.

Makes 7 pints.

From Step Two-*Simmer in own juices*

Vanilla Milk Tea or Cambric Tea
"Suitable for very young ladies"

Ingredients:

1 cup milk
4 tsp. black tea (or 4 tea bags)
2 tsp. vanilla extract
1 quart boiling water
Sugar to taste, added individually to each cup

Pour milk into a saucepan, add vanilla, and bring to a simmer, stirring often. Remove the pan from the heat and let it stand until the milk is cool. Place the tea leaves in the teapot and add the boiling water. Cover with a towel and steep 5 minutes. Pour about 1/4 cup of the cooled milk into each teacup. Stir and strain the tea into the cups.

Makes 4–5 servings.

From Step Two-*Simmer in own juices*

Aunt Corrine's Mint Soother Bath Salts

1 Cup Table Salt (sea salt can be substituted)
1 Cup Epsom Salt
½ cup Baking Soda
Small amount of Mrs. Stewart's Concentrated Liquid Bluing, just enough to tint soft blue.*
1 tsp Oil of Wintergreen (from the pharmacy)*
(for an invigorating "scrub", omit bluing and add 1 Cup Cornmeal)

Mix all ingredients together. Without cornmeal, a small handful or about 1/3 cup makes a soothing, minty bath balm. Made with cornmeal, it makes a refreshing body scrub. Use on elbows, knees and heels to soften dry, rough skin. Avoid area around eyes.

Store in a small, tightly covered jar. This makes a wonderful, personal gift tied with a coordinating sheer ribbon.

*Today you can use other coloring agents and fragrant or essential oils. My preference is for a pale lavender bath salt scented with 1/4 tsp. of lavender oil, or almond oil.

From Step Three~*Season with bitter roots*
Aunt Babe's 'Irelandish Potatoes'

6 medium sized potatoes, skins on
1 tsp salt
1/2 small head of cabbage, shredded
3 TB butter
1/3 cup hot milk or cream

Wash potatoes thoroughly and boil in water to cover, until tender. Mash potatoes with a potato masher or fork, while steaming shredded cabbage. Add salt, butter and hot milk or cream. Beat potatoes with a fork until creamy. When cabbage is just tender and bright green, drain steamed cabbage and stir into potatoes. Serve with butter, salt, pepper and paprika.

Serves 6 to 8.

In regard to French Fried Potatoes, a 1938 Reader's Digest quoted:

a French fried potato is *"in your mouth a few seconds, in your stomach a few hours and on you hips the rest of your life."*

Better stick to these yummy potatoes…

This recipe included in remembrance of Nick Thornton.

Birthday Charlotte Russe

3/4 TB gelatin
1/4 cup cold water
1/3 cup scalded milk
1/3 cup powdered sugar
1 cup heavy cream
1/2 tsp. Maple flavoring
2 TB strong coffee
Lady Fingers (enough to line a mold—18–20)

Soak gelatin in cold water. Dissolve this in the scalded milk.

Beat in powdered sugar and cool. Stir in maple flavoring and coffee.

Whip cream until stiff and fold lightly into chilled ingredients. Line a mold with Lady fingers and poor in pudding. Chill thoroughly. Unmold and serve.

Serves 6 to 8.

Fried Corn Meal Mush

Corn Meal Mush or Grits
1 Cup corn meal or grits
1 cup cold water
1—½ tsp salt
Combine and stir.

Place in top of a double boiler:
4 cups boiling water

Stir in corn meal mixture gradually. Cook and stir over a quick flame for 10 minutes. Steam it, covered, over boiling water for 1 hour or longer, stirring frequently. Serve with butter and salt as a side dish, or with milk and sugar as a cereal. May be molded in a small loaf pan, for slicing and frying, later. *Or be like me and buy prepared corn meal mush in clear plastic tubular packages at the supermarket...*

To serve fried

Cut corn meal mush into 1/4 inch thick slices and flour both sides. Slip floured slices into hot drippings or butter and fry until crispy, golden brown. Remove and drain on brown paper bag or paper towel. Butter and serve with eggs in place of potatoes, or add maple syrup, honey or jelly.
A favorite of Marisa Kate's to this day.

From Step Four~*Stuff with sour grapes*
Tomatoes & Okra

Melt:
2 TB butter or bacon drippings (mother always kept a can of bacon drippings on the stove)
Add and saute until brown:
½ cup chopped onion
Add and saute for 5 minutes:
1 quart of okra (1 pound)
Add:
2 ½ cups (No. 2 can) canned tomatoes, or fresh skinned tomatoes
1—1/4 tsp salt
½ tsp paprika
1/4 tsp curry powder
2 tsp brown sugar

Simmer these ingredients covered until the okra is tender. Add garlic and green peppers if you like. Even better served with melted cheese on top (What isn't?)

From Step 5~*Simmer, stirring the pot often*
Aleksandra Kukas (Alexander Cakes)

Aleksandra Kukas are the nicest creations you can make for a party, or to take along as a guest. Everybody is very glad to see Aleksandra Kukas, because they are very delicious. You may double the recipe so you may have more.

Cake:

2 C flour
1 ½ tsp double-acting baking powder
½ tsp cinnamon
¾ C sugar
½ C sweet butter
½ C salted butter
1 egg
½ to 1/3 C jam (berry is best)

Bake at 375–400 degrees for 20 minutes, until it is slightly brown.

Glaze:

Iingredients:

Butter, powdered sugar, lemon juice

Instructions:

In a bowl, sift together flour, baking powder, cinnamon, and sugar. Crumble in the butter, working it in well with your fingers. Add lightly beaten egg and add it to the butter and flourmixture. Refrigerate for at least ½ hour, until it is easy to roll out. Place the dough on agreased cookie sheet and roll the dough. Puncture dough with fork tines, and bake. Right way, slip the cake out of the pan, and cut the cake into 2 equal pieces to cool. Before it completely cools, spread the jam onto the bottom cake, and place the top cake over the jam. Drizzle glaze over the top. When the cake is cool, and the glaze is stiff, with a sharp knife cut into decorative shapes, i.e., diamond or "chevron" shapes. The best result is: after you make the cake, the cake should stand for at least 8 hours before serving. This allows the cake to soften, and the crumbs will not drip into the laps of your guests.

From Step Six~*Fold in a generous portion of love*

Ancient European Beauty Secret... Shhhh!

Olive oil—mix into a paste with table salt for an exfoliating, softening scrub.

From Step Six-*Fold in a generous portion of love*

Christmas White Salad
Adopted as 'Wedding Salad'

Made by Aunt Helena Woods Maples every Christmas for sixty years, and never after her husband's death. She prepared it for Harrison and Modene's wedding supper, beginning a new tradition—"Wedding Salad".

1 Cup mayonnaise
1 Cup whipped cream
1 Tb lemon juice

Combine mayonnaise and lemon juice and fold in whipped cream. Chill.

1—15 oz. can Queen Anne (white) cherries
1 8 oz can pineapple chunks
2 Cups halved green grapes
2 Cups banana slices
½ Cup flaked coconut
1/4 Cup slivered almonds

Gently stir fruits, coconut and almonds into prepared dressing in a large bowl and serve immediaely.

From Step Six-*Fold in a generous portion of love*

Aunt Helena's Pineapple Drop Cookies

Cream:

1 cup brown sugar
1 cup white sugar
1 cup shortening

Add 2 eggs, 1 tsp. Vanilla, 4 cups flour, 1 tsp baking powder, 1/2 tsp soda, 1 tsp salt, 1 cup nut meats, and a 10 cent can crushed pineapple (15 ½ oz can, undrained).

Drop by teaspoonfuls on greased cookie sheet and bake 12—15 minutes at 350–400 degrees. Makes 5—6 dozen

From Step Seven~*Hand down recipe and pray*
New Years Good Luck Hoppin' Johns
Traditional New Year's meal to bring good luck.

Heat 2 TB olive oil in a large Dutch oven or other large pot over medium heat. Saute until onion is translucent:

1 large onion
1 medium green pepper, seeded and diced
1 clove of garlic, minced
1/4 Cup chopped, fresh parsley

Add:

1 lb. Kielbasa or smoked saugage, sliced and previously browned
1—15 oz can black-eyed peas
3 Cups chicken broth
1 tsp salt
½ tsp freshly ground black pepper
Bring to a boil.

Add:

1 Cup uncooked rice (I prefer Basmati rice)
Return to a boil. Cover tightly and simmer for about 45 miutes. No peeking under the lid! Season with additional salt and peeper if desired and add 3 or 4 chopped green onions, tops and all, mixing well. Let stand 5—10 minutes and serve!

Serves 6—8

Edna Modene's Recipes and Additional Family Recipes

EDNA MODENE'S RECIPES AND
ADDITIONAL FAMILY RECIPES

Forward by Marisa Kate

Whatever the reason, mother was funny about food. She never cared much for elaborate cooking. It could have been due to having to do so much cooking and cleaning for other people from such an early age, and she was simply was tired of it. In any event, mother's approach to cooking was unusual. In the early years, before I was too young to remember, she may have prepared more conventional meals. Meat and potatoes and vegetables. She was always conscientious about providing balanced meals with all the necessary nutrients for her family.

My earliest memories of mealtimes was during the war years. The years of rationing when scarcity of foods was always an issue. At our table, we were never to waste food. "Better finish up, if you want to belong to the 'Clean Plate Club'!"

I really wasn't interested in being in any club, and I sure as heck wasn't interested in those peas! I might have acquired a taste peas as an adult if I hadn't been forced to eat them as a child. "If I eat those peas, I'm gonna throw up."

"Children are starving in China." (You know the drill, if you grew up in that time period.)

Silently, *Then send 'em these dang peas, 'cause if I eat 'em, I'm gonna throw up.* I lost the battle. I ate the peas. I threw up. Presumably, most everyone was satisfied. I never learned to like peas. Not cooked peas, anyway.

Mother had two essentials in her kitchen for as long as I could remember. One was her iron skillet. She swore by it and I have it still. The other indispensable item was soup. All kinds of soups. Tomato soup. Cream soups—Cream of Celery, Cream of Mushroom, Cream of Chicken. And Chicken Gumbo. Always Campbell's soup. You'll see them in some of the recipes that follow.

Over the years, her utensil of choice changed, though the iron skillet was always there. As artists had their 'blue period' and later their 'red period', mother had her 'pressure cooker period', her 'juicer period' and later, her 'electric skillet period'. I have no doubt if she'd lived long enough, she would have enjoyed her 'microwave period' most of all.

I have no recipes from her pressure cooker period, but her routine on Sunday mornings was to start the pressure cooker with either split pea soup, lentil bean soup or chili beans and leave it to cook all day while we went for a ride after church. When we got home, dinner was essentially ready and it was a fairly easy evening for her. After a fairly easy day. It was understood that these rides were family time, but also time for mother to relax. Especially mother. Daddy entertained us in the car, teaching us games we could play as we drove along, and he initiating singalongs. As long as we didn't get too rowdy and disturb mother. Sometimes she joined in, especially on her favorites like "Ol' Buttermilk Sky", "Don't Fence Me In" and "The Three Little Fishes". Daddy was inclined to teach us songs like "Roll Out The Barrel", to mother's great displeasure.

I hope you enjoy this collection of old recipes, some handed down for generations. I've added a few newer recipes that have become favorites of my family and my daughter's family.

Bon apetite
Marisa Kate

BREAKFAST

Pineapple Rice Breakfast Cereal
Strawberry Frostie (from mother's "Blender Period")
Orange Toast or Cinnamon Toast
French Pancakes

SNACKS AND LUNCHES

Frosted Graham Crackers
Carrot Juice Pick-me-up (from Mother's "Juicer Period")
Olive Cream Cheese Sandwiches
Celery or dates stuffed with peanut butter or cream cheese
Date Shake

DINNERS

Tuna 'n Rice Skillet Dinner (from Mother's one dish meal, "Electric Skillet Period")
Gumbo Burgers (Mother's version of today's "Sloppy Joes")
Baked Ribs with Sauerkraut
Baked Beans and Brown Bread
Tamale Pie

SIDE DISHES

Frozen Pea Salad
Cucumbers and Onion

DESERTS

Cherry Kool Aid Ice Cream
Pineapple Buttermilk Ice Cream
Date Torte
(As a rule, mother was not a cookie, cake or pie baker)

Breakfast

We did eat standard fare for breakfast most of the time. Daddy after all, grew up on a farm and was a meat and potatoes kind of guy. He was used a breakfast of ham, bacon or sausage, **and** pork chops, three or four eggs, biscuits and gravy, plus pancakes.

Mother had no special recipes for oatmeal, scrambled eggs, or eggs over easy, which were Daddy's favorite and the bane of Coral's existence. They would not excuse her from the table while daddy ate them. Just the thought of them made her physically ill. Coral was not an egg eater.

So the only recipes included here are the unusual ones, the ones that 'us girls' would have on occasion. Cinnamon toast was a favorite, but one that everyone knows, and which we, probably like all children, loved. Just hot toast, heavily buttered, with a sprinkling of sugar and cinnamon. Mother considered honey butter with cinnamon (1 cup of room temperature butter creamed with ½ cup honey, and cinnamon to taste) on toast healthier because she believed that honey was healing and soothing. Below is another variation on it that mother did like to fix and, again, felt was a healthier choice.

ORANGE TOAST

Six slices of lightly toasted wheat bread
1 can of frozen orange juice
sugar to 'taste'

Open the can of frozen orange juice and dump about half of it into a small bowl. The rest can be diluted, as directed to drink. Break up thawing juice in the bowl with a spoon and stir in enough sugar to make it spreading consistency. Spread onto warm, buttered toast and place on a cookie sheet. Toast under broiler until orange juice topping is bubbly and glazed. Remove from oven and let cool slightly. Enjoy.

Process can be repeated of course, for desired number of additional slices.

Orange Pineapple Breakfast Cereal

1 15 ½ oz. Can crushed pineapple (juice pack)
1 1/3 cups orange juice
4 tsp brown sugar
dash ground allspice
1 1/3 cups quick cooking rice
additional allspice or cinnamon, etc. as desired

In a sauce pan, stir together the undrained pineapple, orange juice, sugar and the dash allspice. Bring to boiling. Remove from heat; stir in rice. Cover and let stand for 5 mins. Transfer to serving bowls and sprinkle with additional allspice or cinnamon, nutmeg, etc., as desired.

Makes 4 servings.

SNACKS AND LUNCHES

Graham Crackers with "7-Minute Frosting"

Not a recipe really—Just frost a few graham crackers with 7-Minute or your favorite frosting (or canned frosting). I'm sure mother felt graham crackers were better for us than cookies. She always worried about our sugar consumption, issuing dire warnings about concerns of excess sugar intake resulting in diabetes. Neither Coral nor I ever developed diabetes.

Carrot Juice Pick-me-up (from Mother's "Juicer Period")

If mother had a specific recipe for this I never found a copy. But carrot juice was her favorite, mixed with celery (several stalks, leaves and all), garlic and clam juice, if she had it. She would slip a slice of celery, leaves attached into the glass when serving it.

Black Olive Cream Cheese Sandwiches

Here again, mother's "recipes" were usually very simple. She liked to mix equal parts of mayonnaise and cream cheese, just enough to hold together a small can of chopped black olives and spread on plain white bread for sandwiches. If it was to take to a pot luck or luncheon, she would trim the bread crusts off and cut into quarters, diagonally. These were always well received!

Stuffed Celery or Dates

Those dates again. They weren't our favorite but we loved them stuffed with either peanut butter of cream cheese. Stuffed celery is still a staple at Thanksgiving, filled with either peanut butter or cream cheese. No fuss, no muss. Just stuff, and stuff.

Date Shake

Mother loved dates. She loved ice cream and malts. She also loved attending the Date Festival in Indio, California and Winter weekend trips to Palm Springs and other California desert destinations in the late 40's and early 50's. It's no surprise she developed a taste for "Date Shakes", combining two of her favorite food types. Here is mother's version, which she often made as a special treat. Like after a visit to the dentist, when Coral and I couldn't chew anything for the novocaine numbness.

Chill tall glasses
½ cup dates (pitted and coarsely chopped)
1 cup nonfat milk (save a calorie wherever you can…)
2 ½ to 3 cups vanilla ice cream (nonfat frozen yogurt works well and is lower in calories)

In a blender, blend dates with milk until smooth. Add vanilla ice cream and mix until smooth. A healthy snack, if I ever saw one. None better!

Makes 3 to 4 Servings…

Strawberry Frostie
(from mother's "Blender Period")

1 Cup buttermilk
few drops of pure vanilla extract
6—8 large frozen strawberries
3 or 4 ice cubes

Pour buttermilk and vanilla extract in blender; add frozen strawberries, ice cubes and blend. No added sugar.

French Pancakes

3/4 Cup bread flour, sifted

Resift with:
½ tsp salt
1 tsp baking powder
2 TB powdered sugar

Beat:
2 eggs
½ tsp pure vanilla extract or grated lemon rind
2/3 Cup milk
1/3 Cup water

Make a well in the sifted ingredients. Pour in liquid ingredients and combine with a few quick strokes. Ignore lumps. They will be taken care of in the cooking.

Heat a small skillet and grease with a few drops of oil. Add a small amount of batter and tip skillet so batter spreads over the bottom of skillet. Cook over moderate heat until the thin pancake is lightly browned on the bottom. Flip pancake and lightly brown reverse side. Add a few drops of oil for each pancake.

Spread each pancake with orange marmalade or your favorite preserves, roll up and sprinkle with powdered sugar.

SIDE DISHES

Frozen Pea Salad
1 10 oz. pkg frozen peas—thawed
1/4 cup diced red onion
1/4 cup diced celery
6 strips of bacon, fried crisp and crumbled
½ cup sour cream (I use low fat sour cream or IMO)
½ cup mayonnaise or salad dressing

Mix all ingredients except bacon and chill in refrigerator for 2 hours. Garnish with crumbled bacon, stir and serve.

The following have been added by later generations:
½ cup nuts (cashews, peanuts or smoked almonds)
cauliflower flowerets
1 small can water chestnuts, slivered.

Cucumbers and Onion
(Great with fish)

3 cucumbers, sliced thin
1 medium onion, sliced thin
1 TB salt
½ cup white vinegar
3 TB thick, sweet cream

Add salt to sliced cucumbers and let stand for ½ hour. Squeeze salt from cucumbers and combine with sliced onions. Add vinegar and mix well. Add cream and garnish with pepper or paprika.

DINNERS

You could say mother had a soup fetish. Whether it was ease of preparation or economy, Mother loved to cook with soups. It could also have been partly due to her preference for "one-dish meals". In any event, she was very creative with soups as a base for meals.

Mother's Tuna/Celery Soup/Rice Recipe (from mother's electric skillet period)

1 cup uncooked, white rice

1—6 oz. (Or larger) can white meat tuna

1 small can of peas (or use thawed, frozen peas)

1—10 ½ oz. can cream of celery soup

Prepare rice according to package directions in electric skillet. Add tuna, peas and undiluted cream of celery soup. Stir and heat through. Serve over toast.

Serves 6.

Hamburger Stroganoff

1 lb. Ground round, crumbled and browned
1 Cup sliced mushrooms, sauteed
1/4 Cup chopped onion, sauteed with mushrooms
1 small clove of garlic, sauteed with mushrooms and onions
1 can undiluted cream of mushroom soup
1 can undiluted cream of chicken soup
1 TB sour cream

Add sauteed mushrooms, onions and garlic to browned meat in a large skillet. Add cream soups and stir. Heat through. In the meantime, prepare rice or noodles to serve Stroganoff over. Just before spooning Stroganoff over rice or noodles, stir in 1 TB sour cream. Heat briefly and voila! You won't find this one in any Weight Watchers literature or cook books...

Serves 4.

Gumbo Burgers

1 lb. ground round, crumbled and browned
1/4 Cup chopped onion
1 small clove of garlic
2 TB catsup
1 TB Worcestershire sauce

Add onion and garlic to browned beef in a skillet. Cook till onion is transparent. Pour off fat and stir in undiluted Chicken Gumbo Soup, catsup and Worcestershire Sauce. Heat through and serve over toasted English muffins.

Serves 4.

Baked Spareribs with Sauerkraut

Place in a mound in the center of a small roasting pan:
2 quarts sauerkraut
Wipe with a damp cloth:
3 or 4 pounds of spareribs and season lightly with salt and paprika.
Fold ribs into halves. Place between the folds, slices of onion.

Cover the sauerkraut with folded spareribs and bake at 400 degrees until they are nicely browned. Baste them frequently with the kraut juice. Turn ribs and brown on other side. Add water, if necessary. Cover the pan. Reduce the temperature to 350 degrees.
Parboil 6 medium potatoes till nearly tender and add to roasting pan with meat and kraut. Turn potatoes frequently permitting them to brown. Serve ribs and vegetables when meat is tender.

Baked Beans and Brown Bread
This is really easy. Are you ready?

1 large can baked beans
6—8 strips of bacon, fried crisp and crumbled
½ cup fresh, chopped onion
Heat beans. Add crumbled bacon and sauteed onion.

Open 1 can Brown Bread with raisins. Spread slices with cream cheese.

On occasion, mother served a hamburger patty on the side, but this was not considered required.

Tamale Pie

2 slices bacon, cut in half crosswise
1 medium onion, chopped
1 clove garlic, chopped
1 lb. ground round, or 2 cups cooked chicken, cut up
1 10 ½ oz can condensed tomato soup (Campbell's, of course)
2 tsp chili powder
1 ½ tsp salt
1/4 tsp paprika
1 large sweet green pepper (cut into 5 "rings")
8 large ripe or stuffed olives, cut in half lengthwise
1 15 1/4 oz. can whole kernel corn (drained)
1 cup all purpose flour
1 cup yellow cornmeal
1 TB sugar
3 tsp baking powder
1 egg (slightly beaten)
1 cup milk
2 TB butter, melted
1 8 oz. Can tomato sauce
4 black olives

Heat oven to 375°

Cook bacon in large, cast iron skillet, over medium heat till crisp. Remove from skillet and drain on brown paper bag or paper towel. In skillet with bacon drippings, cook onion and garlic till slightly softened—3–5 minutes. Add beef and cook breaking up with wooden spoon till no longer pink—about 5 minutes. Stir in condensed soup, chili powder, ½ tsp salt and paprika. Transfer to a bowl.

Move skillet off of heat and place green pepper rings, bacon, and halved olives. Top with corn and then meat mixture.

Sift flour, cornmeal, sugar, baking powder and remaining 1 tsp. salt together into a bowl. Mix egg, milk and butter in a small bowl. Pour into flour mixture and mix with a fork just until combined. Spread batter evenly over mixture and bake in 350° oven for about 25 minutes or until top is golden brown and set. Remove from oven and cover tightly. Let stand 10 minutes

Heat tomato sauce, and small can of sliced olives in a small sauce pan, 5–7 minutes

Invert tamale pie onto serving platter and cut into wedges. Sprinkle top with Parmesan cheese and serve with tomato sauce with olives.

Serves 6

Desserts

Edna Modene's Cherry Kool-Aid Ice Cream

1 2/3 Cup evaporated milk—Tall can (NOT sweetened condensed milk)
1 Package Cherry Kool-Aid (or preferred flavor)
1 TBS sugar

Place can of evaporated milk in pan of cold water and bring to a boil. Remove can. When cooled, place in refrigerator until well chilled. Open and pour into a chilled aluminum bowl and whip with whisk or electric mixer (on medium speed) until frothy. Pour into aluminum ice cube trays with dividers removed. Place in freezer until ice crystals begin to form. Replace in chilled bowl add package of Kool-Aid and sugar. Beat or whisk again, and return to freezer in ice cube tray until fully frozen. Ice cream will remain semi-soft. Mmmmmm! Incredibly delicious!

4 Servings

Buttermilk Sherbet

2 Cups buttermilk (the ever-present buttermilk)
1 Cup crushed pineapple (canned is fine)
½ Cup sugar

Combine first three ingredients and freeze to consistency of mush. Place in a chilled bowl and add:

1 egg white
1 ½ tsp. Vanilla

Beat mixture until light and fluffy and replace in refrigerator (ice cube) tray. Freeze until firm, stirring frequently.

5—6 Servings

Quick And Easy Date Torte

2 eggs
1 cup sugar
2 TB butter, melted

~

1 cup sifted flour
1 tsp baking powder
1 tsp Cinnamon
1/4 tsp salt
1 cup chopped dates (packed)
½ cup chopped pecans

Beat eggs and sugar well. Stir in melted butter. Stir dry ingredients together and add to egg mixture, with dates and nuts. Pour into greased round glass pie pan or 9" square cake pan. Bake at 350° for 25 to 30 mins, til "set". Cut into wedges or bars while warm. Can be sprinkled with powdered sugar when cooled.

Additional Family Recipes

ADDITIONAL FAMILY RECIPES

Harrison's Heavenly Hash Browns
1 Bachelor's serving—

1 baked potato (bake the night before or use leftovers)
1/4 cup chopped red onion*
garlic powder (not garlic salt) to taste
salt and pepper to taste
1 TB butter
grated cheese for topping
1 TB sour cream or imitation sour cream

Dice potato(es) with skins on. Brown and heat trough in butter, adding onion. Salt and pepper to taste. When potatoes are browned and onions are done, sprinkle with grated cheese (he preferred cheddar, but Jack is fine, or any other). Add a dollop of sour cream and serve with poached or over easy eggs.

This is the one and only recipe I can credit my father with. He swore using the baked potato made superior hash browns.*As for the onion, he loved onions and always told us that if an apple a day keeps the doctor away, an onion a day will keep everyone away.

White Chili
(Six main ingredients—Count 'em)
from Lori Anne Sirs of Idaho—**Family Favorite!**

2 Cans navy beans (or dry equivalent, cooked)
1 can Ortega chopped green chiles
1 medium onion, chopped
Chicken or turkey (as much as desired…a great way to use left-overs)
1 can chicken broth (or bouillon)
salt, pepper and garlic to taste

Top individual servings with:
grated cheese, sour cream and your favorite salsa—try chile verde salsa—Mmmm!

Add first 7 ingredients to saucepan. Heat through and simmer for about an hour—or it's great cooked in a crock pot.

Serve with biscuits or cornbread. This is a boon to working wives. Couldn't be easier or more appreciated. If I fix chicken earlier in the week, I try to fix extra for use in this quick and easy dish.

Clam Chowder
Lori Sirs

In a big pan:

Saute':
several strips of bacon, cut up.
½ Cup chopped onions
½ Cup chopped celery, including leaf

Cube 3 small potatoes, and saute' briefly in pan with bacon, onions and celery, to coat with bacon drippings.

Add:
Clam juice (drained from can of canned clams), water to cover the vegetable and bacon mixture. Cook until tender.

15 minutes before serving, add 1 pint half and half (may be part cream if you like), salt and pepper to taste, ½ tsp basil, 1/4 tsp oregano. Add thickening if desired (flour and milk mixture).

Just before serving, add clams. The clams should be added just long enough to warm through—if they cook too long, they become tough.

This is a favorite of ours from time spent in the Pacific Northwest on Vashon Island in Pugeot Sound. If available, you may substitute fresh clams or Geoduck ('horse clam') meat.

Fumi Salad
From Linda Olsen of Maui, HI, as shared by her mother-in-law, Vi Olsen
Now a family favorite

1 head chopped cabbage
8 Tbsp Slivered almonds
8 Tbsp Sesame seeds
8 green onions, chopped (green tops also)
2 packages Top Ramen noodles (any flavor)*

Brown almonds and sesame seeds under broiler; watch carefully. You can use less than 8 tablespoons. Mix cabbage and onions in large bowl. At last minute add sesame seeds, almonds and crushed Ramen noodles (uncooked). Pour dressing over all, toss and serve.

*You do not use the flavoring in the package. You can use less than 2 full packages of Ramen noodles.

Dressing:

4 Tbsp sugar or honey
1 tsp pepper
1 cup salad oil
6 Tbsp rice vinegar
2 tsp 'Accent'
2 tsp salt

Mix well and pour over salad just before serving. (You may heat dressing in microwave or other to dissolve sugar or honey, then cool.)
Shredded chicken breast may be added for variety.

Marcia's Favorite Corned Beef and Cabbage

3 TB olive oil

2 cups frozen O'Brien potatoes (loose hash browns)

1 ½ Cup shredded cabbage (I use packaged cole slaw, with carrots)

1—12 oz Can corned beef (or equivalent deli corned beef, in chunks)

4 oz shredded jack cheese (I am my mother's daughter)

4 eggs

1/4 cup low-fat (1%) milk

1 TB catsup

½ tsp salt

1/8 tsp pepper

Heat oil in large, nonstick skillet over medium heat. Add potatoes and cabbage: spread into an even layer. Cook 5 minutes. Stir well. Spread evenly again and cook 2 minutes longer. Remove from heat. With pancake turner, gently scrape loose from bottom of skillet. Stir in corned beef (chunked), and cheese.

In a small bowl, beat eggs, catsup, salt and pepper. Pour over potato mixture. Cover and cook over medium-low heat 7 minutes or until eggs are set. Loosen around bottom and sides with pancake turner and invert onto serving plate.

Makes 4 generous servings.

Strawberry Dessert
Ariana Sirs

2 small packages of Strawberry-Banana Jell-O
2 small cartons of frozen strawberries
½ pint sour cream

Prepare the first layer as follows:

Make 1 package of Jell-O as directed, and stir in one carton of strawberries. Pour into an 8 X 8 pan and chill. After it is set, spread one half of the sour cream on top. Prepare the second package of Jell-O as directed, and stir in the other carton of frozen strawberries, pour over first two layers in pan and chill. After it is set, spread the remaining sour cream on top and chill another hour.

This is Ari's favorite and she prepares it every Thanksgiving for her family in Idaho.

Modene's Afghan of Many Colors

Using size J Crochet hook and scraps of 4-ply yarn, create yarn 'yo-yo's, leaving five inch tails on each circular motif. To start chain 5 and join to first chain with a slip stitch, closing into a circle. Work 15 double crochet stitches into the center of the circle and join with a slip stitch in top of first dc. Leave 5 inch tail for joining to other rounds, or for fringe.

Join round motifs into a "chain" as long as you wish the afghan to be. Then join the chains together, side by side, nesting the top motif of the chain to be joined between the first and second motifs of the previous chain. Alternate by offsetting the starting motifs so that you have a scalloped border top and bottom. Use matching yarn for each beginning and ending motif, top and bottom, to fringe with a 5-inch, or preferred length fringe so the color appears to flow down into the fringe. This is a great take-along project.

Afterword

The story of Famished Heart grew out of my genealogy research. Having lost my mother before beginning this project, and given that mother was an only child and orphaned young, there were few close relatives to help. Stories mother had told us and those shared by cousins were my inspiration. Original documents, newspaper articles, family photos and recipes, letters and gravestones were utilized for information and documentation. Many other resources were helpful in compiling this book, including books and the Internet.

In researching the various elements of my mother's family, I realized there was a fascinating story here. Wanting to know more about my mother's early life in order to understand her better, I delved deeper. I soon knew I had to write it as a story. Names of people and places have been changed in some cases, and great thought was given to the use of names that would be meaningful to the family or honor friends and family members.

By placing myself in her position at various times and situations in her life, I found I not only gained a new perspective of my mother, but of myself as well. There is much of Edna Modene Gillen Woods in the author of Famished Heart.

Lest it go unnoticed, there is a food theme to this book. There is a reason for that. Mother battled her weight off and on for most of her adult life. If reading it made you hungry, I apologize for that. I challenge readers to count the number of times Edna Modene was given bad information on when and how to eat. Most of my friends in T.O.P.S. (Take Off Pounds Sensibly) will recognize them easily. You're sad? Eat. You're happy? Eat. You're angry? Eat. Nervous? Eat. In pain? Eat. Celebrating? Eat. Eat whether you are hungry or not. Eat "comfort food". And more. Unfortunately, mother passed on some of these messages. She saved the 'weight battle genes' for me. To this day, though we ate much the same all our lives, Coral remains slim. You can guess the reason for my association with the terrific self-help group T.O.P.S.

Certainly I was guided during the process of chronicling my mother's story. I often almost felt she was leading me, painting scenes in my head. My goal was to paint them in words.

Thank you for the opportunity to share with you this personal journey.

About the Author

Marcia Feese is a proud mother and grandmother, living in Lucerne Valley, California. Her interest in preserving family history for her children and grandchildren prompted her to set this record down in print, but her writing interests are many and varied. They range from poetry, Haiku and short stories, to newsletters and articles revolving around the library and community interests.

Marcia is a former Chamber of Commerce office manager and now a library assistant, who cherishes the opportunity to share the joy of reading with a new generation of readers through poetry and story times at Lucerne Valley Library.

An art major in school, Marcia's other interests run to all sorts of crafts, photography, quilting, graphic arts, and more recently a passion for creating unique Teddy Bears.

You can reach the author of Famished Heart at her email address:

madfeese@lucernevalley.net (it's not as 'mad' as it sounds—the 'm' is for marcia, the 'a' for and, and the 'd' for dave feese).

You're welcome to stop in and share some nifty 50's memories with Marcia and Dave at 'Dave and Marcia's Rockin' 50's Drive-In web site: **www.lucernevalley.net/~madfeese**

Bibliography

BOOKS:

"We Rode the Orphan Trains" by Andrea Warren—Houghton Mifflin Co., Boston:
An excellent account of the Orphan Train phenomena, and the plight of orphan train riders as they told their own stories. Includes photos and background of this incredible movement.
"Ghost Towns of Oklahoma" by John W. Morris (Norman: University of OK Press, 1977)

INTERNET SITES:

On the American Indian Boarding Schools **http://www. charleslummis.com/indianrights.htm http://www.twofrog.com/rezsch.html**

On the Orphan Trains **http://www.pbs.org/wgbh/amex/orphan/**

On Harvey House **http://www.angelfire.com/ks/cwpcarousel/1harveygirls.html**

On Midwifery **http://www.midwifeinfo.com/history.php http://pregnancy.about. com/library/stories/blmidwifestory.htm**

On Latvian Culture
http://www.daily-tangents.com/Kalendars/
http://www.angelfire.com/al2/LatvianStuff/Cuisine.html

History of the Cherokee
http://cherokeehistory.com/index.html

State of Oklahoma
http://www.state.ok.us/

0-595-26822-6

Made in the USA
Middletown, DE
19 December 2016